H.H. Laura

Heartseed

sensate nine moon saga

Heartseed

Sensate Nine Moon Saga
by H. H. Laura

1ˢᵗ Edition

Published by RNL Associates
July 2016

Cover art copyright by Cora Graphics, Inc.
July 2016

ISBN No.: 978-0-9846678-7-1

Sensates.com

License Notes

This Book is licensed for your personal enjoyment only. If this book has no cover, please return to the seller and purchase a legitimate version. Thank you for respecting the hard work of the author.

Dedication

To my most wonderful husband, who journeyed with me throughout the creation of my beloved Sensates. His thoughtful comments and continued support served as inspiration and encouragement to see the Prophecy through to the end.

Preface

Heartseed is the third book in the Sensate Nine Moon Saga series and although it can be read as a stand-alone book, I believe you will derive much more pleasure if you read the series in order beginning with *Larkspur,* followed by *Ryeth*, and ending with *Heartseed*

In all three books you will find that I adhere to certain principles: true love is pure, it harbors no guile or pretense, and endures an eternity. I believe in what lurks between the lines and the process of 'fade to black,' and finally, that good shall always prevail over evil.

Please enjoy my Sensates and have as much fun reading about them as I did creating them.

Table of Contents

Chapter One

Early Spring, 1938 – Waynesburg, PA

Two men stood on the crest of a hill facing each other in a heated debate.

"Teater, don't do it," said Jediah. "You don't know what might happen."

"I'm afraid you can't stop me, boy," said Teater. "Listen, I'm as certain of this as I am about the Prophecy. I know in the very essence of my being that I am supposed to do this."

He rubbed the back of his neck in exasperation. Jediah made some valid points, and it would seem that his best retort, as feeble as it was, fell on deaf ears.

He placed his hand on Jediah's shoulder, and forced his gaze to his. "My whole life has been what I needed to do for others. *This* I have to do for me. Can't you understand how important this is to me?"

Teater shoved his hands in his pants pockets to stop from waving them around. It would do no good for Nancy Jane, who stood at the bottom of the hill, to see them arguing.

Jediah dropped his shoulders. "I just want you to fully consider the ramifications. We are Sensates; we have powers we must use cautiously; we live our lives quietly without drawing attention to our group; we live by a strong moral code and if no one kills us, we live for a very long time."

Teater turned away from him. "Don't you think I know that? I've given my share. I've devoted my life to others since I was a young lad."

Jediah grabbed his arm and forced Teater to face him. "What I'm saying is: we are not gods," he said. "We are merely humans with special gifts. We're not meant to go traipsing among the stars, and if we were, we would do so with much more forethought and consideration to the consequences of our actions."

"How do you know for certain that we aren't meant to be the ones who make first contact with others?" asked Teater. "If we sat on our hands and did nothing different from the guy sitting next to us, nothing would ever change. We'd stagnate and get old, nothing more."

"But this is so far-fetched," said Jediah, shaking his head. "There's no telling what might happen."

Teater's face hardened. "To Hades with your consequences. With or without your blessing, I'm going."

Jediah threw his hands up in exasperation, and then dropped them to his side. "You will never get my approval."

"Then I'll leave without it," said Teater.

Jediah pressed his lips together in a firm line. "I can see you've made up your mind," he said.

"I have," said Teater. "I made my mind up years ago and held off doing this as long as the compulsion would let me. I am out of will power to fight the urge, so I've given myself to it wholeheartedly. It may be foolhardy and a grievous folly on my part, but the decision rests with me. I wanted your support, but you apparently don't comprehend my need."

Resigned to his mission, Teater gave a half-smile to Jediah. "I ask you one thing…" He hesitated a split second before continuing. "Promise me you won't tell Nancy what I'm up to," said Teater. "I don't want to scare her. I promise, if this fails, I'll stop wandering and never do it again."

Even as he said the words, if he failed, he wasn't sure he could keep his word to Jediah. If the compulsion persisted, he would end up in the same dilemma again.

Jediah sighed, "This one time, I'll agree, and I do so against my better judgement, but never again. After this, your escapades are on your own shoulders. I'll not be part of your schemes any longer. Either you tell Mom what you're up to, or I will."

Jediah turned away from him and headed down the hill to meet James Dawson and his mother.

Teater couldn't stop the spread of a slow smile. Partial acceptance from Jediah, no matter how miniscule, was better than none. Excitement filled him until he thought he'd burst.

He'd fulfilled one of their cardinal rules: don't attempt an unknown ability without telling another Sensate. When he told Jediah, he hadn't planned on Jediah's lack of vision. If they were given an ability, weren't they meant to use it? As far as he could ascertain, the action would do no harm to anyone other than himself, and if he was willing to risk his life, wasn't that his choice to make?

He looked to the base of the hill. His darling wife, Nancy Jane, motioned for him to get a move on and join them.

He ran down the hill with euphoria speeding him onward, passed Jediah like he was standing still, scooped Nancy Jane up in his arms and flung her around in a circle.

Her cries of delight filled the mountain air as the sunlight sparkled in her hair and her skirts wrapped them in a cocoon of pure love. She was the light of his world since he was sixteen and first laid eyes on her.

His family had 'given' him to some distant relatives who had fallen on hard times. The sharing of workhands allowed two families the opportunity to make good instead of one - his family in Wheeling didn't have to feed the extra mouth, and the Madison's family in Waynesburg received a strong male worker for their farm.

As he worked in the field, a clear voice entered his mind. She introduced herself as Nancy Jane and she told him he was special and that he had a part to play in the grand scheme of things. He came into his powers with Nancy Jane acting as his guide and learned all there was to know about being a Sensate – a powerful person with abilities linked to his senses.

Years later, he'd followed her instructions to return to Wheeling and marry. The years away from Nancy Jane and the Sensates were not without love and happiness, but internally, he yearned to return to Waynesburg and his beloved Nancy Jane.

He stayed in Wheeling and provided for them until they were grown. Only then was he free of his obligation to the Sensates. Teater had fulfilled Nancy Jane's instructions.

After his wife died, he was free to marry Nancy Jane. Nancy's fire and Teater's quest for the unknown were the root of many disagreements. However, nothing ever came between the two or diminished their love.

"Teater, you're crazy," said Nancy Jane. "Put me down before I get sick."

He set her down with care. As she straightened her skirt, his palm caressed her stomach.

She pushed his hand away and looked around to see if anyone noticed his loving touch. Nancy glared at him, then linked her arm in his as they all headed down the mountain.

On the way, they stopped to glance at the cistern Teater created. The walls were intricately formed of stones laid one by one.

"That's quite a bit of talent you've got there, Teater," said James. "Those stones look like they were cut with precision instead of carefully planned."

"Thanks, James," said Teater. "Now, if it just happens like it's supposed to."

Jediah leaned over and moved the cover off. He glanced up at Teater and said, "I just want to see that hole one more time."

"There it is," said Nancy Jane as she pointed to a small opening in the otherwise solid walls. "Let's just hope she finds it."

Jediah slid the cover back over the opening. "She has to; if not, we'll be left with a Prophecy and only a partial resolution."

He could feel the solemn air around him. They all knew the importance the mountain and cistern played in their future.

"Remember," Teater said, "no matter what, no one touches this cistern. It's important that it be left alone."

They heard a click and turned to see James, who stepped away from them and snapped a picture with his new camera.

"Gotcha," said James. "You've now been caught as a moment in time. You can never go back again, but I can."

"We'll see about that one," said Teater as he squeezed Nancy Jane. "We'll see."

Chapter Two

Present Day

Teater didn't know exactly how long he'd been gone, for time didn't adhere to the same principles as on Earth. Nancy Jane would be furious with him, as she always was when he went off on one of his adventures, but in this instance, he was certain his discovery was worth her wrath.

Unobserved in the pre-dawn light, he positioned himself on a hill overlooking a small village to watch the unfolding of a new day. He stood perched atop an outcropping of crystal shards and viewed the valley below with its mishmash of white homes built on white sand.

As the rays from twin suns rose on opposing horizons, they caressed mammoth natural prisms that poked randomly through the valley floor and covered the surrounding hills. One by one, the prisms caught the suns' rays and bathed the valley in wondrous rainbow hues. The view took his breath away.

Teater marveled at the engineering feat required to create such a village. The inhabitants positioned their lodgings to reflect individual prism rays so that no two buildings were exactly the same color at the same time. Without the twin suns, an observer might think the inhabitants lacked a sense of order, due to the house placements, but the scene before him proved otherwise.

When the suns' rays beamed on the white sand-like material, it became a deep shade of purple, almost black. The foliage on the flora was unlike anything he'd ever seen. Leaves, if that's what they could be called, appeared like feathers and tufts, with their stems and veins black. Each tuft captured the light and glowed, which was more prominent at dusk and in the early morning light. The majority of the plants and shrubbery were neon turquoise in color, the others, varying shades of lavender, pink, yellow and blue. It appeared they had eliminated all the harsh colors of the spectrum using their technology to create a visually stunning city of pastels.

The village inhabitants started to move about as he watched the tiny town awaken. They wore long hooded cloaks that hid their body structure and appeared to float instead of walk, for he determined no gait, nor saw anything resembling a foot touching the ground.

The hoods were so large they completely hid the inhabitants' faces from his view. They looked of normal height as compared to an earth human. Their houses, which seemed modest in size, had doors with handles and windows, so he surmised they had eyes and hands. He could make no further observations regarding the life forms, but could add that he noted no roads coming or going from the village, and no shops where supplies could be garnered, so how they made a living and what they survived on remained a mystery.

He sensed no emotions. As they passed each other, some paused as if conveying thoughts, but, even with his heightened hearing and his mind reaching out to touch theirs, he heard nothing.

Although he made no attempt to hide himself, either they were unaware of his presence or he was of little consequence to them, for they gave no indication they noticed him at all.

Sitting on the prism, he retrieved a notebook and pen from his knapsack and sketched the scene below, along with the placement of the two suns. Although he was no artist, the rendition seemed to take on a life of its own. When he was done, Teater couldn't believe the final product. It was one of the finest pen and ink drawings he'd ever seen. The view before him could not have been captured more precisely had he used a camera.

Teater carefully rolled the drawing and placed it in his knapsack. After three days on the planet, it was time to go home.

He smiled at his discovery, took one last look around, and then transported himself back to his home, and to Nancy Jane.

He had so much to share. A new planet, people or inhabitants, technology to color a world, and space travel. Would they believe him? It would take some convincing, for even though he had traveled far and witnessed the other-world creatures himself, he knew the ability to grasp the concept would be difficult.

In the blink of an eye, Teater arrived at Larkspur, the lovely Victorian house that was part of Nancy Jane's estate. He didn't sense his wife on arrival, but looking around, she'd apparently been busy. New furniture and paint greeted his observant eyes. Teater shook his head. Nancy Jane could get more done in a few days than most could get done in a month. He liked the changes, they reflected his wife's sense of order and flair for color.

Teater quickly showered, trimmed the three-day growth from his short beard and mustache, combed through his long unruly dark blonde hair and fastened it with a thin strip of brown leather into a pony tail that hung between his shoulder blades.

As he stepped into the bedroom, he sent a quick message by telepathy to Jediah to let him know he had returned.

Before he could fasten his pants, Jediah appeared at his side. Caught off guard by his quick appearance, Teater jumped backward.

"What? You don't allow a man to dress in private anymore?" he asked, his humor displayed in a smile.

Jediah glared at him.

Teater's smile left when he sensed the extent of Jediah's wrath.

"You fool," yelled Jediah. "Where have you been? Do you have any idea what you've done?"

Teater grasped Jediah's fury in an instant. His chest fell. "Is it Nancy Jane? Is the baby all right?" He reached out mentally to locate Nancy Jane, but could not sense her mind. Short gasps caught in his throat as the worst possible scenario filled his thoughts. "Tell me! Are Nancy and the baby okay?"

Jediah slowly shook his head. "I am sorry for you." Disgust showed on his face.

"I was only gone three days." Teater's words were almost a whisper.

Jediah grasped him hard by the shoulders and shook him. "Three days? You think your stint lasted three days? Try *seventy-eight years*!"

The words echoed in his ears. It couldn't be. A physical shock went through his system. Time on

Earth couldn't have moved so quickly. The blood left his face, the strength drained from his legs, and Teater dropped to the floor.

The images came slowly at first, then played quicker as Jediah imprinted the missing years in his mind.

Teater squeezed his eyes shut against the pain and shuddered. "No! Nancy Jane and the baby are *both* gone? My God, what have I done?"

His body convulsed into sobs as he learned the baby died in childbirth, and that Nancy Jane had suffered the loss without him. She had lived her remaining years alone awaiting his return. Since he had sworn Jediah to secrecy, Teater felt the angst he'd put Jediah through because his promise didn't allow Jediah to tell his mother where Teater had gone.

The pain in his chest was so great he thought he might implode. The joy, the dainty life that was his wife was gone. The baby they had planned for and loved in her womb, gone. His life, his dreams, his world, gone.

He looked up to see Jediah viewing him with distaste, his thoughts filled with scorn. He deserved all the anger and disappointment and any other punishment Jediah could muster.

"Jediah, my actions caused you and your mother great anguish." Teater dropped his head to his knees. "I had no way of knowing. Oh, the heartache I've caused. All because I dreamed of the stars." He choked out the words. "What have I done?

In a voice nearly inaudible he added, "Please forgive me."

Teater sensed Jediah's pain, anger, and resentment as Jediah spat, "Who am I to withhold forgiveness? You've already received the worst punishment imaginable. You'll have a hard enough time forgiving yourself. I am sorry for you." Without another word, Jediah left.

Teater inched close to the wall and leaned against it, defeated. Emptiness began in his core and spread throughout his body, swallowing him from the inside out. His hollow heart left him chilled to the bone. Alone with his sorrow, he drew his knees up to his chest and wrapped his arms around them to stop the shuddering that wracked his body. His head fell to his knees as he closed his eyes to re-live every memory Jediah had shared.

Seventy-eight years of his humanity was condensed into a memory transfer. The thought alone sickened him. No warm touches, no yearning for his bride, and no child in his arms. He learned that Nancy Jane had forgiven him even though she didn't know where he'd gone or what he'd done. As every day of his missing years found a place in his memory, he knew he'd never forgive himself for the wrong he'd done.

Chapter Three

Alexandra heard his arrival before she saw him. Jediah rarely exhibited intense emotions, but this time something had him in an uproar. She not only sensed anger, the man was livid. When she heard the kitchen door slam, she turned to face her mate.

Their eyes met first; he attempted to control the rage burning inside.

"Maybe you should just spit it out," she said.

"I can't," he said. "It's not my place to tell you." His jaw clenched tight. Violet eyes darted around the room, edgy, seething, as his breaths escaped his nostrils like that of a raging bull.

"Your face is so red it looks like you're going to pop." She walked over to him and put her arms around him. His chest rose and fell, deep and forceful. "You're my husband, you should be able to tell me anything."

She felt his muscles tense and release as he tried maintain composure. Jediah was tied in a knot so tight that Alexandra was at a loss to aid him.

He stood stalwart and unmoving in her arms and said, "Hah, one would think so. But it doesn't apply if I've given my word of secrecy."

As she pulled away from his embrace to watch the emotions play across his face, she said, "Secrecy? Again? How many secrets are we to have in this marriage?"

"One, there's only one. I gave my word long before we met, so it doesn't really count, does it?" said Jediah

"Certainly it counts," she said, then it dawned on her. "Hey, your only secret has to do with Teater. What could my great-great grandfather who has been dead for umpteen years possibly have done to make you so angry?"

Jediah hung his head and sighed. "I can't tell you."

Perplexed as to how Teater could have produced such anger from the grave, she shrugged and shook her head. "Will you ever be able to tell me?" Alexandra reached up to push the unruly lock of hair from his brow as she sensed Jediah coming to terms with his anger.

Slowly, he raised his face to meet hers; his eyes held a slightly wicked glint. With one eyebrow cocked, he said. "Soon, very soon, we will have no more secrets."

She melted into him and raised her lips to his.

The kiss lasted long enough for her to have twinges of guilt. Would she always be able to keep her promise of no more secrets?

It seemed like every day the weight of being a Sensate burdened her more. She could almost kick Teater's butt for drawing her into this group of gifted people. Almost. Without him, she would've never met Jediah, married him, and sat on the High Counsel that governed their elite group. Never would she have gained a family as wonderful as the Saffles after the loss of her own. A gal could do far worse than marry for love and inherit a whole mountain.

Maybe she shouldn't blame Teater so much. He couldn't possibly have known *all* the ripples he would cause when he placed the stone in the cistern. She mentally corrected herself: the *enchanted* stone; the one that caused her to come into her powers.

She was a Sensate, and not just any Sensate, she was their youngest and most powerful Sensate, a load foisted on her shoulders by the Prophecy and Teater. Being a new wife plus a new Sensate wasn't enough, not by a long shot. It was her responsibility to save them from a great evil.

Life was complicated. Much more than any other twenty-two year-old, she'd bet.

Surely having to say one more time, 'I can't tell you,' regarding his oath to her great-great grandfather wasn't the source of his anger; it was much deeper than that. Though she loved his sense of honor, she questioned Teater's hold on him from so long ago.

She leaned back from his embrace and studied his face: clean-shaven, with piercing violet eyes that smoldered when he kissed her and turned so pale in the sun they sparkled. She reached up and messed his hair.

"Hey," he said.

"I like you with a just-tousled look," she said.

He smiled. "I like you anyway you look."

No longer angry, he became the Jediah she knew and deeply loved. "How's Ari?" he asked.

"She spent the majority of the day in front of the TV. It'll be some time before the novelty wears off."

"I suppose so." He nodded. "The Fringe Science Bureau keeping her captive so long will have a profound impact on her recovery. She's missed out on more than fifty years of life."

"I can't even imagine the thoughts going through her mind," said Alexandra. "How do you go from a girl of sixteen to an adult in captivity? The thought alone boggles my mind... She thanks me for her rescue at least four times a day," said Alexandra.

"Is she joining us for supper?"

"No, she wore herself out with the physical therapist. She's sound asleep."

Jediah sniffed the air. "What's for supper?" he asked.

"It's a surprise."

"Smells good," he said. He walked to the stove and reached for the cover on the sauce pan.

"Don't you dare peek," Alexandra said. "Go somewhere else until I call you."

He removed his hand, kissed his wife, and left the kitchen.

Alone again, Alexandra pondered the possibilities for Jediah's outburst. What could it be? Whatever it was, it was enough to cause her level-headed husband to let his ire show, and that rarely happened.

Right before Jediah came home she'd felt a strong surge in the power that normally surrounded her. Were the two connected?

Ryeth, her rogue Sensate, as she liked to think of him, said he felt a surge of power when Nancy Jane passed away. At the time, she didn't understand what he meant. Now, she did.

She contacted Ryeth by mental telepathy.

Ryeth?

Yes, Alexandra.

Did you feel a power surge a few minutes ago?

I did, he said.

What was it? she asked.

You know more Sensates than I do; did a few of them come into their full powers?

24

I don't think so, they are all older than me, she said. *They reached their peak long ago.* She paused.

She sensed Ryeth's concern grow. *Let me check with Alice Jane and I'll get back to you.*

The connection ended.

The pot on the stove hissed. Alexandra removed the lid, stirred the contents, and lowered the heat.

I'll be back soon, said Jediah from somewhere outside. *Just holler when supper's ready.*

You've got plenty of time; I forgot to preheat the oven for the rolls, she said.

Chapter Four

Jediah regretted the way he'd treated Teater. He acted out of pain for his mother's life and death, and hadn't fully considered the impact on Teater.

After holding his lovely wife in his arms, his chest hurt with just the thought of losing her.

He transported back to Teater and found him as he'd left him, huddled against the wall. Teater made no movement that he acknowledged his presence.

Jediah lowered himself to the floor and sat next to him. "I'm so sorry, Teater. I can't begin to imagine your pain."

"It's my own fault," he said as he raised his head. "I deserve this horrific justice."

Shaking his head, Jediah said, "No one deserves your fate."

"My Nancy Jane had to suffer the loss of our child alone. I'll never forgive myself for letting her go through life not knowing what happened to me," said Teater.

Jediah sighed as he searched for words to comfort his friend. "She never stopped loving you, and she never chided you for your adventures. My mother knew you well, accepted you as you were, and loved you all the more for it."

Jediah stared off into space. "It was as if she knew, deep-down that everything was as it should be. Don't get me wrong, losing you was hard on her, but her love for you was stronger than that loss, and it carried her through until the end."

Teater shifted against the wall. "Yes, she loved with every inch of her body and then some. I knew I was loved, and loved deeply, which ironically, gave me the confidence to go adventuring."

Thoughts of Nancy Jane filled both men's minds as they sat lost in thought.

Jediah was the first to return to the present. "I hate to bring this up, but we need to figure out how to handle your return," he said.

"Oh no, Jediah," Teater pleaded. "I just want to be alone."

"Can you, at least release me from my promise not to tell anyone what happened to you?"

"Yes, yes. Of course. I should have never made you take an oath in the first place. I was wrong, so very wrong," said Teater, his voice merely a whisper.

Teater's eyes were hollow. The vibrant step-father who'd been his best friend no longer exhibited the well-known charismatic spark. Before him now, was an empty shell.

Teater continued. "I don't want to see anyone. I have too much to think through before I can handle seeing people who have missed me for seventy-eight years." Teater toyed with his shoe string. "I just saw them three days ago. I can't even get my mind around that..." He sighed.

"Of course, I didn't mean now, but we do have to decide where you are going to settle. You've hopped into a hornet's nest. The Prophecy is near."

"The Prophecy?" Teater was far away in his thoughts and failed to grasp his words, for his eyes never changed.

"Yes," said Jediah. "The plans you made regarding your great-great granddaughter have taken place."

27

Nothing seemed to affect Teater. His huge loss consumed him. Jediah placed his hand on his shoulder and transported them to the Saffle Family Retreat in the country.

"Listen," he said to Teater. "I need you to stay here and keep away from Larkspur. I'll take care of all the arrangements. Call for me if you need me."

Teater made no indication that he heard Jediah or that he even cared whether or not he was there. Jediah stood, looked hard at Teater, and then walked into the solarium.

Why did everything always hit the fan at once? Ari's release, the FSB, the Prophecy, Ryeth, and to top it off, Teater's return.

Where could Teater possibly have been to make him think he'd only been gone three days? He'd been toiling with the idea of space travel, but had he gone through with it? What had he done this time?

Teater always had cockamamie ideas and he never seemed satisfied with his powers, always pushing the limit one way or the other. More than once Jediah'd rescued Teater from the brink of disaster. Memories of lava tubes, unexplored caves, scouring the bottom of the sea for lost ships, and climbing the highest mountain peaks on Earth raced through his mind. The man thrived on adventure.

Teater's accomplishments were many; he served the Sensates with unconditional love. He was the one responsible for many of the changes in Balisier. It was he who thought to enrich the village so that, if the need arose, Sensates could live there for years without ever needing to leave. Not only had Teater seen to their safety, he had completed his efforts with astounding beauty. The Sensates owed their very comfortable existence to his efforts.

It would take time for Teater to heal. The impact of his extended journey would cause repercussions throughout their Sensate community. Jediah sensed long-range implications, and the shorter ones regarding his new wife.

Jediah peeked in on Teater, who appeared numb, and then heeded Alexandra's call to supper.

Chapter Five

Jonathan rechecked the contents of his suitcase. It wasn't very often that their leader requested services from Sensates, so when Jediah asked him to watch over Teater, he knew it was important.

He arrived at the Saffle's Family Retreat by car and inspected the grounds on entry. The well-kept country place had every modern convenience yet offered it in a comfortable home style way. Green rolling hills outlined by pristine white fences shaped the immediate view against a back drop of deep green forested mountains. It was a landscape that spoke of care and attention.

While Jonathan spent most of his time at Balisier, the Sensates' secret hideout, this venture outside his comfort zone offered a chance to see how the other half lived. Like many Sensates, he considered Balisier his safe haven surrounded by other Sensates.

His greatest fear was to compromise their existence to the outside world. Coming to the country and spending time outside Balisier would be an adventure. Since Jediah had assured him complete autonomy, he knew he'd be safe, even if he slipped up.

He parked his car near the detached garages, grabbed his suitcase, and walked up the stairs to the front door.

He knocked, but no one answered. He tried the knob. The door was open, so he walked in, closed the door and set his suitcase down in the foyer.

The interior of the home complemented the exterior. It was grand, yet cozy. To the right was a sitting room, straight ahead, a large hallway with a curved staircase, to the left, massive mahogany doors he assumed went to the library or den.

As he entered the sitting room he came upon a thirty-something man with sun-streaked dark blonde hair. An expressionless face tilted slightly to greet him.

"Teater, I'm Jonathan," he said. "It's good to have you back home."

Teater gave an almost imperceptible nod.

Jonathan continued. "Jediah asked me to stay with you to answer any questions you might have. Have you eaten?"

"No," said Teater. "I'm not hungry."

"That's fine," he said. "I'll check with the housing staff to make sure rooms are made up for us. I'll be around if you want to talk."

He left the room in search of Maisie, and located her in the maid's quarters behind the kitchen. Jediah assured him she was circumspect. She must have just arrived; she was unpacking her belongings.

"Hello, Maisie," he said. "I'm Jonathan Gellner."

"Yes, Mr. Gellner," she said. "Mr. Saffle told me to expect you."

"When you are settled in, could you make up two rooms, please?" he asked. "One will be for me, and a second for our guest, Mr. Theodore Higgins."

"Certainly, Mr. Gellner," she said. "Will you be needing supper this evening?"

"Yes, nothing much. Maybe some sandwiches and coffee. Just leave it on the counter in the kitchen."

Maisie stored her suitcase under the bed and straightened to face him. The efficient maid was ready to begin her tasks. "I'll take care of everything," she said.

"Thank you for coming on such short notice."

"Don't you think a thing of it, Mr. Gellner," she said with a flip of her hand. "I'm always willing to work for Mr. Saffle. He keeps everything stocked at all times, so it's easy to get up and running."

Jonathan nodded, and walked back to the sitting room. He took a seat across the room from Teater, and reached for a recent copy of *People Magazine.*

Teater looked up, sniffed and said, "What are you? Some sort of baby sitter?"

A small smile crept across his lips. Now *that* sounded like the old Teater he knew. "No, I'm just here for you to use."

Teater frowned.

Jonathan continued. "Think of me as a reference book. A lot has happened since you've been gone. Some things might not be self-explanatory." He reached for the remote control and hit the power button.

A panel above the fireplace slid open to reveal a forty-eight inch, high definition TV. Fox News appeared with the stock market ticker scrolling across the bottom. Jonathan reduced the volume.

Teater was drawn to the screen. "I see," he said.

Jonathan turned the TV off and placed the remote back on the coffee table. He picked up the magazine and continued reading and noted a slight change in Teater.

Jediah said nothing in regards to Teater's return, only that he should pretend that Teater had been asleep for nearly 80 years and he would have no knowledge of modern gadgetry. It was an odd request, but Jonathan figured Jediah would share the story of Teater's return later. Until then, he would reacquaint himself with the fascinating ex-leader of the Sensates.

Pretending to read the magazine, Jonathan stole glances at Teater. His outward appearance looked the same as he remembered, but his spark and vitality seemed shrouded in... in a vacuum of sorts. Did he just hear of his wife's passing? How could he *not* have known?

Stirrings of all sorts of questions and answers instantly invaded his mind. He shut the extraneous thoughts down. Not one to assume or guess, Jonathan preferred to wait for the facts.

After an hour, he stood and stretched. "Maisie, our housekeeper left us some coffee and sandwiches in the kitchen," he said. "I'm going to eat mine."

Jonathan left the sitting room and headed down the hallway. He heard Teater rise from the sofa and smiled.

* * * * *

After supper Jediah grabbed Alexandra's hand and led her outside to the arbor. The wind blew her long hair around in swirls. She caught it up in her hand and held it so she could see. He sat on the stone bench and pulled her onto his lap.

She sensed his turmoil, but said nothing.

Finally, he spoke. "Teater made this arbor. He hand-carved every stone." His finger played in the ivy carving on the pillar.

"I never knew," she said. "I always thought it was made by some famous artisan. It's even more special to me now…"

"He made it as a gift to my mother," said Jediah. "I never saw two people more in love. He completed it early in her pregnancy and planned to give it to her when the baby was born and tell her of his plans for a mountain top home."

"A baby?" she asked.

"The Infant Higgins, 1938 tombstone in the graveyard…" he motioned.

"Oh… I wondered," she said.

"He never knew the baby died in childbirth; he was gone before the baby was born," he said.

Her brow came together as she worked on some mental calculations. "Wait a minute, the dates don't match up," she said.

"What do you mean?" he asked.

"He wrote the letter to me in 1925 and died in 1928. How then could he plan to build a house after he died on the land he willed to me? How do you reconcile his making a home here in 1938, but giving the land to me thirteen years beforehand?"

"I think he planned to change the will," said Jediah, "but never got around to it, which, as you can see, worked out pretty well."

"Oh no!" her mind was moving too quickly. She had to pause a second to make sure her facts were correct. She was correct. Her head spun. What was going on here?

She slipped from Jediah's lap and walked around the arbor. "His tombstone said he died in 1928. How could he have impregnated your mother prior to 1938 if he was dead?" Realizing she wouldn't find the answer in the beautiful stone floor of the arbor, she stared at Jediah.

"He decided to die in 1928 when he was sixty-nine," said Jediah.

"Decided? What could you possibly mean by that?" she asked.

"I have five tombstones," said Jediah. "William has twelve, and he's seriously considering his thirteenth right now."

The realization hit her. Of course they had to die… well, at least pretend to die. How else could they maintain a life outside Balisier if they didn't?

"You must think I'm short on mental capacity," she said. As an afterthought she said, "Then when *did* he die."

Jediah looked at his feet as he rubbed the back of his neck. "That's just it… he didn't."

"He didn't die? Where is he? Did I already meet him as someone else?" she asked.

She paced in circles, following the tracks of her mind. She stopped and turned to face Jediah, her hands on her hips. "The next thing you say had better be one heck of an explanation, and if it isn't you are in *big* trouble, mister."

"First," he said, "it was not my story to tell. Teater did disappear in 1938, and no one, except me, knew where he'd gone. That's the secret I can't reveal; it's Teater's secret and he must tell you. On the other hand, he returned this afternoon."

Excitement filled every pore of her freckled frame. "Take me too him. I want to meet him," she said.

"It's not a good time…" said Jediah.

"What do you mean by *that?* Jediah, for heaven's sake, make some sense." She sighed, and plopped down on the bench beside him.

He wrapped his arm around her, pushed her hair from her flushed cheek and said, "He's been gone for seventy-eight years. He didn't know about the baby dying or my mother's passing."

She felt her shoulders sag in his embrace. He pulled her close. Teater hadn't known? How could that be? Nothing made sense.

The heartbreak he must be suffering. As hard as she tried, she couldn't begin to imagine how he must feel.

"How is he?" she asked.

"Not good," he said.

"You should be with him," she said. "Don't leave him alone."

"Jonathan's with him. Remember him, he's one of the Ultras. You met him at Balisier."

She nodded.

"I'm keeping myself busy running around attempting damage control so I don't go numb," said Jediah. "He came home to Larkspur and, as we agreed, he communicated with me on his return. Luckily, Alice Jane was with Ryeth and not at Larkspur."

"Oh my, you had to tell him…" she said.

"I'm afraid I was rather rough in my wording," he said. He hung his head. "I yelled at him and screamed out their deaths with no compassion whatsoever. I was so angry with what he'd put my mother through all those years without him that I couldn't hold back."

He ran his fingers through his hair. "Teater was inconsolable. I'd hit him with the worst news he would ever hear in his life, and he heard it from a raving lunatic."

She pulled from his embrace, and wrapped her arms around him. Leaning up, she kissed his cheek.

He shook his head. His voice was soft. "He'd never shown me anything but love, and I knocked him down and kicked him. I'm so ashamed."

She whispered to him. "And on top of that, you tried to tell me, and I got huffy and made you answer twenty questions."

She placed her hand on his cheek. "We may be Sensates, but we're still human. We lash out at those we love, especially when we're hurt. Teater didn't just hurt your mother, he hurt you too."

The sun was setting over the top of the mountain before they were ready to leave the arbor. Jediah looked at her with compassion. "I have to tell Alice Jane. Do you want to come with me?"

"Sure," she said as she placed her hand in his, for there was nowhere else she'd rather be.

Chapter Six

Alice Jane took the news well.

"Did he say where he was?" she asked

Jediah shook his head. "No, I really didn't give him a chance," he said. "Teater said something odd. He said he'd only been gone for three days."

"Three days?" said Alice Jane. "He really said that?"

"Yeah," said Jediah. "It has me baffled."

Alice began to sit in a chair, but lost her footing and fell into it instead. Jediah sensed she was deep in thought.

"What are you thinking, Alice?" he said.

Alexandra perched on the arm of the chair and placed her hand on Alice Jane's shoulder.

Alice Jane took a deep breath, let it out, and ran her hands through her long hair. Her eyes focused on nothing in particular. Her voice spoke with a calm that contained awe.

"Have either of you ever heard of Einstein's *Special Relativity* or his *Gravitational Relativity*?" she asked.

"Time Travel?" said Alexandra.

Alice Jane spun around to face her. "Yes," she said.

Jediah sobered. "You'd better fill me in," he said.

Alice sat straight up, her eyes flashing. "In a nutshell, he defined 'space-time.' When you travel through space-time, time goes slower for you than for those you left behind. A person moving through space-time would have no idea this was happening until he returns to those he left behind."

"Oh my God. He actually did it," said Jediah.

"You think he went into space?" asked Alexandra.

Jediah shook his head. "I have no idea what to believe," he said.

"The only thing that stopped Einstein from proving his theory was that he couldn't travel faster than the speed of sound." Alice gave a snort. "Well, *he* wasn't a Sensate."

An uncontrollable sense of doom surrounded Jediah. All the fears he'd had with Teater's wacky experiments now encompassed Alice Jane. Her sense of awe and knowledge of aerospace scared the daylights out of him. He walked over to her chair and knelt, grabbing her hands in his.

"Promise me you won't experiment like Teater did?" he said.

She still looked like she was day dreaming. "It's so exciting. Just imagine, other worlds are at our fingertips," her eyes glazed over.

Jediah grabbed her by the shoulders and shook her. "Alice!"

She jerked.

Her eyes met his. "Huh?"

"Promise me," he said sternly. "I can't go through the not-knowing like I did with Teater. He told me about a hair-brained idea, and I never saw him again for *seventy-eight years.*"

"I'm sorry, Jediah," she said. "I understand why you're upset. Our mother lost her husband. I lost a father and you lost your best friend. The years were long."

He stood and looked down at her. "Then don't make me go through it again."

"I'm not going to promise you," she said, "because I don't want to lie. I'm more excited than I have been in decades. It's the next step in evolution. In space. In mankind."

She stood and faced him, her jaw set in defiance. "I won't tie my hands behind my back. If he accomplished this feat, I want to be part of it."

Jediah stepped away from her. "For all mankind, I hope you're wrong."

He reached over, touched Alexandra, and transported them home.

"I need to check in on Ari," said Alexandra. "Could you put the kettle on for some tea?"

"Sure," he said. "I could use something to help me calm down."

"Use the chamomile," she said. He watched her cross the kitchen and disappear down the hallway.

His arms were leaden as he lifted the kettle from the counter. Had it always been this heavy? After filling it at the sink, he placed it on the back burner and turned on the heat. The flames flickered orange, and then blue as his eyes locked on it. He stood there mesmerized.

The kettle whistled, piercing his ears. He jumped and turned off the burner. Half-lidded eyes turned to bright vibrant ones. Jediah had worked through the kick to his stomach. The Sensate leader had returned.

He lifted the lid of the kettle and dropped in the tea bag. When he looked up, he saw Alexandra supporting Ari.

"Great job, ladies," he said. "Do you need additional help?"

Alexandra shook her head.

Ari said, "I think we're going to make it."

The steam from the tea wafted a scent through the air. Jediah drew it in. The calming effect of chamomile filled his lungs.

"Val gave her the go-ahead today to walk a bit, but only if someone's with her," said Alexandra. "I invited Ari for some tea."

Alexandra held the kitchen chair for Ari as she sat.

Ari let out a huge sigh. "Hot diggity," she said. "We made it."

Jediah's mood improved even more. "Ari, you look beautiful," he said as he poured their tea.

"I owe it all to Alexandra." Ari nodded. "She soaked me, washed my hair, rubbed me down, and brushed my hair a thousand strokes. Tomorrow, she said I'd get a mani-pedi, whatever that is."

"Sshh," said Alexandra to Jediah. "I want her to be surprised."

"Far be it for me to ruin a surprise," he said. "My lips are sealed. How about another topic?"

Ari perked up. "I want to thank you for taking care of me, and for bringing me to your home."

"You're welcome, Ari," said Jediah.

"What does Heartseed mean?" asked Ari. She sipped her tea. "I remember you called your home Heartseed."

"Ari," said Alexandra, "that's a long story, but for now I'll tell you that my great-great grandfather left me a nice piece of land with an arbor on it. The arbor was overgrown with a vine that had tiny white blooms on it. After I cleared away the vines, I discovered the stone supports and the floor were carved with the same vine design. The tiny seed of the vine is round, brown, and has an ivory heart on its side. The vine's name is Balloon Vine, but some

41

call it Heartseed. It seemed a proper name for my home."

"That's a really nice story," said Ari. "I like the name. It suits you."

"Thank you." Alexandra finished her cup of tea. "Umm, that hit the spot," she said.

"Well, ladies, if you are ready to retire for the evening, I'll help Ari back to her room," said Jediah.

"I'm ready," said Ari. "I know it doesn't sound like much, but that walk over here and sitting in the chair have worn me out. I'm looking forward to lying down."

Alexandra took the cups to the sink. "Val said it would take some time for your muscles to regain strength... You're lucky they gave you a physical therapist all those years, or you would have no muscle tone at all. Val thinks you are doing great."

Jediah reached down to assist Ari. He put one arm behind her back and under the far arm. Ari got up slowly, only wobbling a bit. They made it back to her room where Alexandra was ready with the covers drawn. Ari sat and Alexandra pulled her legs around while Jediah held her upright.

"Whew," said Ari, "I'm glad that's done."

Alexandra tucked her in and set the intercom close on the nightstand. "Call me if you need to get up in the night so I can help you."

"Thanks, again, you two," said Ari between yawns. "You're angels."

Jediah grabbed Alexandra's hand as they walked out the door. They closed it just a bit to block the light from the hallway. Ari's breathing was already even. Slumber was a mere minute away.

* * * * *

Ryeth?

Yes, Alexandra.

Did Alice Jane tell you about Teater? she asked.

Yes, he said. *That answers the power surge question.*

She paused. She sensed his concern. *Watch over Alice, would you?*

Believe me, she won't get out of my sight until I'm sure of her intentions.

Thanks.

She closed the connection. Now she could rest.

Chapter Seven

Mid-morning the following day, Alexandra and Jediah were contacted by Val, who requested a meeting of the High Counsel at Balisier, which worked out since Jediah had planned to call a meeting as well.

"How do you think they'll handle the news about Teater?" asked Alexandra.

"I don't know, sweet girl," Jediah said as he pulled her onto his lap.

He loved the way she looked in the morning. Her hair glistened in the early morning sun and reminded him of wheat blowing in the fields. Looking back, the two hundred forty-some years he'd waited for her vanished in a second. He could hardly believe that Teater charmed a stone that caused Alexandra to come into her powers, which led to her coming into his life.

The Prophecy told of her coming. Teater played his part by bequeathing his holdings to her, and ensuring that the mountain that contained Balisier would remain in the right hands.

So much had happened to bring them to this point in their lives. The 'butterfly effect' of the chaos theory, seemed as random as ever, yet today's events could mark a point where life started to become unrecognizable.

He kissed her soft lips. "It's time to take that 'one giant step,'" said Jediah.

"I'm sure this was all supposed to happen," said Alexandra.

"What makes you so sure?" he asked.

"I have no idea," she said, "I just have this feeling that all is as it should be."

"Ready for Balisier?" he asked.

"Take me in the orb, and make the walls clear so I can see as we travel," she said.

"Your wish," the orb appeared, "is my command," he said.

"It's not fair that you can do this and I can't," she said. "I would appreciate it more."

"More?" he asked.

"It's a girl thing," she said.

They arrived in the counsel room where James, William and Val were already seated. They said their hellos and took their seats. Within a few seconds, Ryeth and Alice Jane appeared and took their seats.

Val rose and got right to the point.

"Thanks for coming," he said. "The information I have to share is quite astounding. I thought you'd all want to know ASAP."

"It must be the day for unbelievable news," said Jediah. "We've got a hefty piece of news to share with you too, but since I have no idea how to begin, you may have the floor."

"First, a bit of news on the gas the government used in Ari's gurney," said Val. "It was Xenon as I suspected, so there will be no residual side effects to worry about where Ari and Ryeth are concerned. There were trace amounts of some gold and nitrogen alloy they may have used as an aerosol, but they were in such small quantities, that they won't cause any ill effects."

He cleared his throat, "Jediah, I don't think your news can top this one," he said. "Ari's DNA results were completed this morning. All of you are

45

aware that we have a copy of every Sensates' DNA, except for Ryeth, which we hope to obtain soon."

"All you need to do is ask," said Ryeth.

"Then stop by my office here in Balisier and get that taken care of today."

Ryeth nodded.

"The results of Ari's DNA did not point to a new genealogy branch as we suspected," said Val. "She belongs to one of our own, two to be precise."

He took a deep breath, expelled the air in a quick rush, and said, "Ari is the natural daughter of Teater and Nancy Jane."

Jediah gasped, as did the others. His mind stretched to make the pieces fit together. After Alice was born, their biological father died with yellow fever. Nancy married Teater later, but she only had the one pregnancy. "But the baby died," he said.

"So we thought," said Val. "Apparently she did not."

"If what Ari said is true," said Alice Jane, "she was stolen at birth."

"How could someone have stolen Nancy Jane's baby?" asked Alexandra. "Wasn't anyone around when she delivered?"

"Not really," said Jediah. "Alice was off on her own…" He looked at her as she hung her head. "I was involved in revamping the interior of Balisier…"

He shook his head and offered his lame excuse. "I wanted to have it completed for Teater's return." He snorted. "My mother was playing the I-can-do-everything-by-myself heroic role."

"I remember that," said James. "She was feisty in those days."

"She didn't even want *me* around," said Val. "Nancy Jane actually paid a local midwife to help her with the birth. They only called me afterwards. By that time, they had the baby dressed for a quick burial."

"She even had the grave dug," said Jediah. "We went to the cemetery on top of the mountain and paid our respects. The whole affair was wrapped up in fifteen minutes or so."

"So you never examined the baby?" asked Alice Jane.

"There was no need," said Val. "Still born babies happened all the time."

"The only one who could have switched the baby was the midwife," said Alice Jane.

"That's what I'm thinking," said Jediah, "which makes my news doubly important."

He took a deep breath, let it out, and said, "Teater has returned."

"Holy moly," said Val as he dropped into his seat.

Jediah stood and paced the room as he told the tale of the wandering Teater. He ended with an apology to the group for not telling what Teater was up to, but stated he had given his word. No one spoke throughout the whole tale. He returned to his seat.

If minds whirred as they worked the sound would have been deafening. As he looked from face to face it was apparent the news was too much to grasp.

"I just can't believe it," said Val. "He traveled in space?"

"Einstein thought it was possible," said Alice Jane. She explained Einstein's theories on Space-time in detail, which left them even more baffled.

James said, "He really said he was gone just three days?"

Jediah nodded. "He did."

"That means…" said Alice Jane, "that for every minute he was gone, we aged about six and a half days."

"Unbelievable," said William. "I sit here before you as your eldest Sensate. I can tell you, that in all my six hundred twenty-seven years, I have never been more in awe than I am right now."

James looked around the table and said, "I think we *all* are a bit dumbfounded."

"What do we do next?" asked James.

"We need to give Teater time to grieve," said William, "and Ari time to heal."

Alexandra, who had been quiet throughout said, "Maybe we should put Ari at the retreat with Teater; they could heal and grieve together."

"They both have to be told the truth," said William. "That won't be an easy job."

"It'll work out easier if we are all there as a family," said Alice Jane.

"We will have to take it easy on them," said Alexandra.

"I'll help with Ari," said Alexandra. "She's comfortable with me."

Jediah nodded to Alice Jane and said, "We'll all go to Teater."

"Once we've told them individually, we'll bring them together," said Jediah.

William pushed away from the table. "How do you tell Teater that his dead daughter is alive and that the Sensates stole her from the government? On the other hand, how do you tell Ari that her father just spent seventy-eight years on another planet?"

The room grew silent.

"Gently," said Val. "You do it gently."

Chapter Eight

"You're telling me I have a daughter?" said Teater.

Even though he'd heard the words from Jediah's mouth, he couldn't believe his ears. Their baby had survived.

"It had to be that Riggs woman, you know, the midwife," said Teater. "Her name was Roberta Riggs. I told Nancy I didn't trust her, but she pooh-poohed me telling me that she knew best."

Jediah nodded. "Ah. That's why the name sounded familiar. I only met her once," said Jediah.

Teater was emphatic. "I kept telling Nancy it was bad to depend on a woman who was due at the same time, but she still defended her; said she needed the money," he said. "Nancy said that if all else failed she could give a yell to Val, so I let her keep the midwife."

"It sounds like either her baby died, or another client's baby died, so she replaced it and took yours," said Alexandra.

Teater looked into the purest face he'd ever seen and still couldn't believe she was his great-great granddaughter. The girl was as fresh and beautiful as a spring flower. He sensed her soul. She didn't have a drop of malice. She radiated goodness of heart and mind.

Alexandra's voice was filled with compassion as she said, "I'm sorry the midwife did that to you and Nancy Jane. I wish Ari could have met Nancy, she would have loved her like I did."

"That's kind of you to say, child," said Teater. "There's no doubt in my mind that Nancy loved you. She gave you her powers, didn't she?"

"Yes. I told her I was unworthy of such a gift, but she did it anyway," said Alexandra.

"Nancy knew what she wanted," said Teater. "Once she set her mind to something, there was no dissuading her."

"The same could be said for someone else around here," said Jediah.

Alice Jane nodded in agreement. "Teater, I'm sorry I wasn't here for Mom. She was so independent she made the rest of us look weak."

"Don't you worry none, Alice," said Teater. "Nancy knew you didn't want the life you were born into. She loved you for standing up for yourself, for braving to be different all on your own. From what I see before me, you've done well. That's all parents really want for their children."

Alice Jane hugged him. He loved Nancy's daughter like his own. He turned to Jediah.

"Jediah," he said. "I owe you an apology."

Jediah jumped up. "No, Teater, I owe you one."

Teater shook his head. "My mistake caused yours, so you can't be held responsible," said Teater. "I should have never made you promise not to tell what I was trying to do. I was only thinking of the here and now. I just didn't want Nancy to worry." He smiled to himself.

"I also didn't want to get hollered at," Teater said. "When she got her hackles up, I'd run for cover."

Alexandra said, "I can't believe that. She was always so self-composed and regal. I admired her greatly."

"As we all did, Alexandra," said Teater. "She was a combination of fire and brimstone, and poise and composure… quite a woman."

Teater smiled knowing that even in the end, Nancy Jane had chosen her own path. He would miss her 'til the end of his days.

"So, when are you going to take me to meet my daughter?" he asked.

"She doesn't know about you yet," said Alice Jane.

"So? We'll tell her," said Teater. "If she's anything like her mama or papa, she'll bounce right back."

Teater watched as Jediah looked at Alice who looked at Alexandra, who shrugged.

"Oh, come on…" said Teater. "You know if you don't take me, I'll get there on my own."

Jediah came at him smiling. He wrapped him in a big bear hug and squeezed him tight. "Man, I've missed you Teater," he said. "Welcome home."

"I'll go on ahead," said Alexandra. "Alice, bring Ryeth, you can introduce him to Teater. Jediah, take him in the orb and show him what's happened to our mountain."

She disappeared from view.

"Is she always that bossy?" said Teater.

"Only when she's organizing," said Jediah, "and in that respect, there's no one better."

"I'll see you soon," said Alice Jane, as she left.

Jediah turned to his friend and said, "Are you sure you're okay to go ahead with this?"

"I will be," said Teater. "I'm not one hundred percent, but I'll be okay. I need her."

Jediah created the orb to encase them. It went through the walls of the house to the outside then rose high in the air and gently floated to the mountain that contained Balisier.

"You built a house up there?" he asked.

"I didn't. Alexandra did," said Jediah. "The whole concept was her idea. The house, the old-fashioned windmill – she made it all to go with and complement your arbor."

"Nancy Jane's arbor..." said Teater. "Did she ever see it?"

"Yes," said Jediah. "I brought her up about a month after the baby died. She loved it. She used to come here often. Then as the years went by, she came less and less."

"I'm sure it was hard for her," he said. "I didn't know..."

"No one knew," said Jediah.

"That wife of yours put a windmill on top of the old cistern," he said. "What a great idea."

"I guess you knew she'd find that stone and figure her way out of there," Jediah said with a sideways glance.

"I hoped, I really hoped she would," he said. He thought back to when he planned the whole scenario. It had all come true, just like he saw in his vision. The vision was so strong it'd pushed him to deed the property to Alexandra and leave her enough money to take care of Balisier. Alexandra was vital to the Prophecy. It had been his job to pave the way.

"You'll have to tell me how you enchanted that stone," said Jediah.

"I'm afraid I can't. I don't know how I did it myself." He shrugged, "It just happened."

Jediah took the orb to the front of the house.

"It's a beautiful home, Jediah," said Teater. "If I can't be here with Nancy, then the next best thing is to have you here with Alexandra."

"Thanks, Teater," said Jediah. "I thought you'd like what Alexandra did with the place." He cleared his throat. "Are you ready to go in?" he asked.

"I'm ready to meet my beautiful daughter who has survived the government and who lives to tell the tale," said Teater.

Jediah cocked one eyebrow. "I'll take that as a 'yes'," said Jediah.

Chapter Nine

Ari heard a commotion in the living room. Voices that did not belong to Alexandra or Jediah sounded excited.

Alexandra appeared at her door. "How are you today, Ari?" she asked.

"The physical therapist came and said I was doing great. Dr. Jellan, I mean Val, just left and gave me good news. He said the drugs should only take a day or two to be completely out of my system, and that I should move about as much as I wanted. He also said to continue to eat solid food. He said I'd know when to stop."

"That's good news. Are you feeling well enough to go to the living room?" asked Alexandra.

"Yes. I might not need too much help," she said. "You'll be impressed. The therapist was. I don't think I'll need to call you in the night anymore."

"I want you to be careful. Call me if you're the least bit unsure. I don't mind at all," said Alexandra.

"I will," she said. "I heard voices, is someone else here?"

"Yes. I have three Sensates I want you to meet."

"Do I look all right?" she asked.

"Ari, you could be covered in mud with pickles sticking out your ears, and you'd still be beautiful." Alexandra smiled. "But to answer your question, you look great."

"Okay. I'm ready," she said.

Ari rose, slow but stable and stood next to the chair. She straightened her blouse and smoothed her pants. She walked, straight and tall to the door, turned and said, "Are you coming?"

She read pure delight in Alexandra's eyes.

"Yes, I'm coming," Alexandra said. "You're a sight to behold."

They walked together to the living room. Jediah and the others rose to greet her.

"Ari, take a seat here," said Alexandra as she motioned to a chair. "They can come to you."

She eased herself into a comfortable overstuffed chair. Two men and a captivating female faced her. All were handsome people.

The tallest caught her eye first. He stood an easy four inches over Jediah. Dark and brooding, he gave off a mysterious air. His black hair and darker skin tone set off his almost black eyes. Her breath caught as she remembered him. He stepped forward and offered her his hand in friendship.

"Ari, my name is Ryeth Garmendia," he said. "I'm a new member of the Sensate High Counsel. It's a pleasure to meet you."

"You flew me through the air in a bubble," she said.

"That I did," he said. "I wasn't prepared for you waking up. I had no wish to scare you."

"I'm sorry I fought you," she said. "Thank you for all you have done." She hesitated, and looked at his massive frame. "I'm glad you're on our side," she said as she smiled.

Ryeth returned her smile and stepped back in line next to the beautiful woman with flawless ivory skin. Her violet eyes drew her attention right away.

Ari looked at Jediah's eyes. They were exactly the same.

The woman walked over to Jediah and they both approached her.

"I see you have already made the connection," Jediah said. "Ari, this is my sister, Alice Jane."

"Hello, Ari," said Alice. She bent and kissed her on the cheek. "It's good to know you're safe here with us. Welcome to our small, but selective, group."

"Thank you, Alice Jane," said Ari. "Your name is as beautiful as you are, and with those violet eyes I'd have made the connection to Jediah easily."

Alice Jane stepped aside. Ari looked around the room. All eyes were on either her or the unknown man now standing before her.

An unfamiliar feeling began in her chest. At first, she thought it would consume her body, but little by little the feeling settled. The feeling took hold and grew. As it grew it filled a gaping hole inside that had been dark and gray her whole life. It warmed her and made her want to share it.

She looked deeper into the man. He had strong feelings for her, she sensed it. It flowed from every pore in his body. As she stared at him, his feelings grew even stronger. She was shocked to realize the feelings were feelings of love. He loved her!

Her heart pounded in her chest; her breathing increased. Unable to understand the emotions running rampant through her body, her eyes jumped from place to place and then back to him.

He smiled. She became caught up in that smile. His face lit up like a child at Christmas. The smile shone in his eyes.

She couldn't help herself. She was connected to him, connected by an everlasting cord. The outdoorsy charismatic man had won her over completely. She trusted him with her life. Her eyes took in his dark blonde hair, streaked with gold; his skin, tanned by the sun, the high cheekbones that framed his chiseled face. Her senses told her he was as beautiful inside as he was on the outside.

Ari, I am Teater Higgins, and I am your father, he said.

Her heart skipped a beat as her eyes filled with tears. She couldn't catch her breath.

He knelt before her and took her hands in his. His eyes were intense. She dropped her eyes to his strong rugged hands as they engulfed hers. Tears fell down her cheeks. Ari blinked her watery eyes to focus on the sun-bleached hairs on his arm.

She breathed in and out until her heart no longer pounded in her ears. As sure as she was sitting there, she knew this amazing man before her spoke the truth. How or why she couldn't fathom, it didn't matter.

Her eyes began a slow trail upward until they stared into his.

Yes, she said. *You are my father.* She blinked and smiled.

His eyes brimmed with unshed tears. He reached up and hugged her close.

Among the myriad of emotions Ari sensed flowing through the room, one stood out as the most positive. She was home.

One by one, the intruders to Ari and Teater's homecoming vanished from view.

* * * * *

After they left Ari and Teater, Jediah landed the orb in the arbor.

"He didn't even speak to her," said Alexandra.

Jediah rolled his eyes. "I don't know about that one. I think he was speaking volumes."

"Teater is so charismatic. I can't think of any word that fits him better. I swear he could have the whole world eating out of his hand if that's what he wanted."

"That's Teater for sure," said Jediah. "You could search the world over, and you'd never find one finer. I missed that old coot."

"I have so many questions," said Alexandra. "I know it's not the time, but I'm overflowing with curiosity."

She stepped to the middle of the arbor, flung her arms out wide, and spun in a circle. "I have been so blessed to have you, your family, and Teater in my life."

Alexandra pulled her arms back to wrap them around her chest. She closed her eyes and came to a halt. "What a feeling," she said.

Memiki, your heart is full.

Yes, Kayè, it is, said Alexandra.

Both of my boys have come home. You have saved my daughter. All is as it should be.

Alexandra's eyes flew open wide. She should have guessed, but how was it even possible? Her Kayè was Mother Earth, Grandmother Earth, *and* Ryeth's mother, Onatah.

Yes, it is so.

Ryeth needed you, she said.

It was his rage that blinded him to me. That is no more.

Kayè's touch was gone.

More questions swirled in Alexandra's head. Onatah died centuries ago. Was she talking to her spirit?

"Alexandra," said Jediah. "You look like you're a million miles away."

"I know who the voice is," she said.

"You said before it was Kayè," said Jediah.

"Yes, but I didn't know who Kayè *was.* She's Ryeth's mother, Onatah."

The look on Jediah's face said it all. He was as bewildered as she was. At least a hundred possibilities ran threw her mind as to the why and how of it all. The mother of all Sensates spoke to her.

"Ryeth never said anything," said Jediah as he stroked his chin.

"He just found out," said Alexandra. "She said it was his rage that blocked her all these years. What a shame. Ryeth needed her desperately."

Jediah laughed and shook his head. "You're concerned about why she didn't speak to Ryeth?"

"Yes, so?" She didn't understand what he found so funny.

"I'm wondering how she can speak at all," said Jediah. "She's been dead about four hundred fifty years."

"That occurred to me too, but with all the other incredible things that we can accomplish, does it really sound odd that the essence of a life force can live on after the body dies?" she asked.

"I suppose not," he said, "it's just so incredible."

"You've been a Sensate too long," said Alexandra, "it's no more incredible than making a sphere that can pass through solid stone, and being able to jump from one place to another."

Jediah sat on a stone bench. "Maybe I have become complacent. I certainly have forgotten the awe I had when I first became a Sensate."

Alexandra sat next to her husband. "Everything about being a Sensate is so new and powerful, that sometimes I think anything is possible if we just put our minds to it."

"I keep forgetting that your powers are greater than any other Sensate." He kissed her sweetly. "A new age of Sensates is dawning right before my eyes."

She felt Jediah's arms tighten around her. Nothing or no one would ever change the way she felt. Her path forward seemed clear. No matter what happened, her choices would determine the greater good for the Sensates. If they had to go up against the government to secure their future, her heart was in it until the end.

She felt Teater's touch a split second before his voice.

Hey, guys. Teater here. I'm taking Ari with me to the retreat. We want some time together.

She turned and looked at Jediah with astonishment. He shrugged his shoulders.

Teater, it's good to know some people never change, said Jediah.

We send our love, said Alexandra.

Chapter Ten

Magis was escorted from his cell at Greene County Prison to a room where the guard locked his ankle chains to a ring on the floor. His hand cuffs received the same treatment on the steel table. Months of incarceration had hardened his exterior. The hands that held a football throughout his high school years now showed a lack of care; pretty boys didn't fare too well in prison.

A suit sat opposite him. Older, a little flabby in the middle, but his eyes were keen. Something told him the suit didn't miss a trick.

"Mr. Magis," said the suit. "My name is Dave Edwards. I'm with the Fringe Science Bureau, FSB for short."

Magis picked at his fingernails. "Never heard of it," he said, not making eye contact.

Edwards leaned back in his chair. "Not many have; we like it that way." His voice was droll. He continued with the description and sounded like he was reading from a boring book. "We're a division of Homeland Security, the Sensor Division to be more precise."

Magis thrust his chin out and said, "Yeah. So?"

"I've read your statements regarding what happened to you on your boat when you abducted Alexandra Higgins."

"I don't talk about that anymore. You get nothing here," said Magis.

"What if I told you that I believed you?" asked Edwards.

Magis sneered. "Then I'd tell you they got a white jacket for you just like they got for me."

Edwards rustled through some papers in his briefcase. He pulled three pictures from the case and laid them in front of him.

Magis looked at them and shrugged.

"Do you recognize any of these men?" asked Edwards.

Magis looked away and then back. "Maybe I do, and maybe I don't," he said. "What's it to you?"

"I just wanted you to confirm that none of these men was the man who held you in place as he tortured you," said Edwards.

Magis shifted in his chair. Doing so made the chains rattle against the metal loop on the floor and on the steel table. He leaned forward and glared at Edwards, a sneer resting on his lips.

His eyes narrowed as he spoke. "If you read my statements like you say you did, then you know the guy was real tall with black hair and black eyes," said Magis. "Those guys don't look nothing like him. You're wasting my time. I've got far better things to do than lead a wet-nosed hound dog around."

Edwards scratched the side of his neck, seemingly unaffected by Magis' tone. "I'll take that as a 'no,'" said Edwards.

He picked up the photos and returned them to his case.

Edwards stood and grabbed his briefcase. "You see, Magis, I'm going to capture that black-haired monster and put him away, with or without your help. I just thought you might want to be in on the kill."

Magis scrutinized Edward's face. The suit just might be telling the truth. Maybe he could get back at that unholy demon. "What's in it for me?" he asked.

"Nothing that would improve your current situation," said Edwards. "I don't make deals with guys who treat women like animals."

Magis spat on the floor. He didn't like being played. Certainly not by a chubby over-the-hill suit. "Then what are you doing here?"

"I thought you might like a little satisfaction to keep you warm at night, that is, if you don't already *have* something." He turned to the guard, "I'm finished here."

Magis jerked his chains against the rings, and slammed his cuffs on the steel table. The noise echoed against the concrete walls. Edwards didn't flinch.

The guard opened the door and Edwards left without looking back. Another guard came, unlocked him from the table and floor, and led him from the room.

As he shuffled down the hallway to his cell, anger made bile rise in his throat. The suit had no idea who he was hunting. Hah. He hoped the suit *did* find the black-eyed demon, it would serve him right.

He sat on the cot and stared at the wall. Memories of the worst day of his life came front and center. The harder he tried to force the memories back, the stronger they became. He didn't need to be reminded so vividly; he dreamt of the man almost every night. The black eyes followed him throughout his incarceration in

Wheeling to the Greene County Prison where he awaited his trial.

Where did the suit say he was from? Some Fringe Science government division? The next time he got library privileges, he'd look that one up. It sounded spooky; maybe that's why he was trying to find the big guy; maybe he *was* a demon.

Those thoughts did nothing to calm him. He wiped his sweaty palms on his pants, and concentrated to quell the internal shaking in his chest.

The creature that held him in place and taunted him until his blood boiled had *never physically touched him*. Air had blown around his black leather coat, and Magis could swear his feet never touched the ground; he floated like a ghost. A real live demon had intervened on Alexandra's behalf and almost left him with mush for brains.

Bordering on panic, he looked up just in time to see a huge, bald guy with tattoos on his arms and a ring in his nose walk by his cell and smack his lips at him. Magis yelled an obscenity at him.

An ordinary man, no matter his size, failed to frighten him. He'd already seen worse in real life and in his dreams.

Never had a scheme gone so wrong. Just when the brainwashing of that pathetic Alexandra Higgins neared completion and his pockets were soon-to-be lined with gold, the black-eyed monster had appeared.

If that over-the-hill copper thought mere satisfaction would make him go against that black inhuman abomination, he was wrong. Dead wrong. The suit would have to kill it, burn it, chop its head off and bury it long before he, Tom Magis, would stick his neck out and talk.

The hair on the back of his neck rose. Magis couldn't control the sensation that the demon still watched his every move. He looked around; a chill went up his spine. "I didn't say a word," he said out loud. "Did you hear me? Not a word."

He climbed back on his bed, leaned against the corner, and drew his knees up. There would be no sleep tonight. He felt him; the black demon was near.

Chapter Eleven

Edwards returned to the office he'd taken on the far side of the compound away from the actual FSB headquarters. Four cardboard boxes filled to the brim with unsorted documents were piled on his desk. He loosened his tie and opened the first box.

As he envisioned the job before him, he wondered why no one had catalogued the information before. That alone should have been grounds for Black's dismissal.

The majority seemed to be surveillance accumulated prior to computerization of the bureau. Heck, if these creatures lived longer than the average human, shouldn't all the information be considered? The Millennial and 'Y' generations just didn't get it. If it didn't appear on their computer screen, it either didn't exist or it wasn't worthy of consideration. And heaven forbid that anything learned from a book actually be *applied* toward a solution.

Edwards spent his time in the trenches; doing the manual labor that produced results. That type of work ethic would never go out of style. It may be slower, but it was thorough and considered every detail, no matter how small.

Three hours later he stepped back to look over the results. He'd separated the documents into piles for each individual under surveillance. Documents that contained more than one person were copied and placed in corresponding piles.

A knock on the door interrupted his thoughts.

"Come in," he said.

A drab looking middle-aged woman stepped inside.

"Ruby, I want you to scan these documents into files for each person. Then, I want you to set up a documentation system so we can cross reference the highlighted words I've marked as keywords and set up search parameters."

"Yes, sir," she said.

"This is just the beginning, we have three more boxes to go through," said Edwards.

"I'll get started right away," she said.

"I'm going to lunch. I'll be back in an hour to continue." He grabbed his jacket from the back of his chair, put it on, and straightened his tie before leaving.

Dave Edwards did not head to the commissary. Instead, he exited the building and walked across the road to enter the aviation building. He spied his senior engineer, Ron Anderson, and walked to his side.

"What do we know so far?" he asked Ron.

"We flew a plane over the area in Waynesburg. You were right," said Ron.

"She showed up there?" Edwards asked.

Ron nodded. "We picked up the particle signature," said Ron.

Excitement filled his chest; his hunch was dead-on. 613 was the FSB's proof that teleportation existed in human-like creatures who also possessed an extended life span. She had escaped on Chief Morgan Black's watch, but during the escape, she received a dose of Edward's blue gas that permanently placed a gold particle in her system that he could track.

Edwards came alive. He loved the chase, he loved the game, but most of all, he loved pitting his intelligence against the foe's.

His eyes narrowed. "Game on. 613, your days are numbered."

"Looks like it," said Ron. "Take a look at this GPS recording."

Edwards' eyes followed the plane's scan of Waynesburg. When it got close to the outskirts of the city from the west, he leaned in closer. As the plane crossed over the city, the scan was negative, but when it flew over the mountain where Alexandra Saffle built her home, a bright red spot appeared.

613 was located in the Saffle's house.

"Shut down the passes over the house for now," he said. "I don't want them getting suspicious." He patted Ron on the back. "This is the first real break we've had since 1958."

"I'll shut it down," said Ron.

"I want you to get ready to move our equipment to another facility," said Edwards. "Choose the pilots, maintenance personnel and engineers carefully. I want full dossiers on each before a word is said regarding the operation. You and I will be the backbone; no one else is to know anything; understood?"

"Understood," said Ron.

Edwards turned to leave, but stopped and turned back. "Lock that data up in a safe place; I don't want it disappearing."

"Consider it done," said Ron.

As he walked back to his office, he formulated the next steps in his plan. Extracting every name from the surveillance documents was the starting point. Anyone who came in contact with them would be considered a potential suspect.

A slow smile crept across his face. The key to breaking open this case was anonymity. He'd decided to control the FSB's actions via a fictitious government email. Unlike Morgan Black, he played his hand close to his chest. He would use Black, the self-proclaimed puppet master, to carry out his instructions. Plus, he'd commandeered one of her attack dogs to keep an eye on her and feed him information.

Edwards had considered removing her to a distant section, but thought he might like to keep her closer so he could watch her. Besides, if need be, he could use the venomous creature as a decoy.

They had watched Black like a hawk, knowing her quest for power would be her downfall. When they assigned her the task of watching over the human left-overs from the Area 51 fiasco, they never assumed she would stir it into a live case with military implications.

After removing Black from the active case, he inserted himself. Where Black concentrated on one freak of nature, Edwards planned to capture or infiltrate a whole gaggle of them.

The game they played appeared one-sided. The FSB wanted them to assure a world domination of military power. *They* wanted to remain clandestine. The FSB wanted to use their powers against the nation's enemies; *they* indicated no threat against anyone. Yes, it was definitely one-sided.

Back in his office, he performed a quick Google Map search of the Waynesburg area to figure out his options. The first order of business was to shift his base of operations. When it came time to make his move, he wanted a better vantage point.

The Greene County Airport caught his eye and appeared to be minutes from Waynesburg.

"Ruby," he yelled from his office, "contact Ron Anderson and have him fuel up the Piper Cub, would you, please?"

"I'm on it," came Ruby's reply.

"Tell him to pack a bag as well," said Edwards. "We're going on an overnighter."

A slow smile crossed Edwards face as he located the DNA file on 613 on his desk. Once the Bureau began testing criminal DNA back in 1986, it had taken them nearly twenty years to test and catalog the backlog.

A stroke of illegal genius allowed the FSB to access every newborn's DNA from its routine laboratory workup. Without the public's knowledge, a secret database now existed on every child born in the United States after 1986.

The priority search for 613's DNA match-up lit up the FSB database like sky rockets the day Alexandra Higgins was born. Since then, Alexandra and her parents had been under surveillance with no abnormal incidents until her abduction by Tom Magis.

Four years ago, the surveillance team noted Alexandra's search for ancestors had uncovered a relative in Waynesburg, Pennsylvania. The direct ancestor was Teater Higgins, who died in 1928. The house he owned and its occupants were put under surveillance as a precautionary measure since it had passed to his wife and her descendants.

Edwards leaned back in his chair and crossed his arms over his protruding pouch. The path to this operation had taken place over eighty-years and passed through three, maybe four, generations. It was hard to believe that one woman's fear of her child had placed 613 securely in their hands.

He shook his head and then finished sorting the documents from the second box. His stomach growled. One glance at his watch told him he'd missed lunch for the third day in a row.

Edwards stood, stretched, and threw his jacket over his shoulder. He grabbed his cell from the desktop and looked at it as if waiting for it to ring. Almost on command, the vibrator went off and the phone jiggled in his hand.

He flipped it open and read the screen, 411 was displayed. He pressed the button to answer.

"Yeah," he said

"Nothing new," said a male voice.

"Tomorrow."

"Yep," said the voice.

Edwards closed the phone. 411 was a long shot. But he liked gambling against the odds. It never hurt to have an outlier in the field.

He opened the closet door and withdrew his overnight bag. Maybe he could talk Ron into a thick steak before take-off.

Chapter Twelve

Alexandra awoke with a gnawing need to test the limits of her powers. Jediah lay beside her, his arm thrown over her waist. Instead of rising from bed in the normal fashion, she teleported herself to the foot of the bed.

The action was so quick, she was able to watch Jediah's reaction as his arm fell to the mattress and woke him.

"It's a need-to-know day, my love," she said to her tender giant.

"What are you up to?" he said. "Come back to bed; it's early." He held up the sheet and beckoned her to come back.

"No way, bucko," she said. "Today, we are going to find out what I can do, and what I can't do."

"Why the sudden urge?" he asked.

"It's not sudden at all," she said. "As a matter of fact, I think I've been pretty lax. Maybe after I've lived a few hundred years like you and the rest, I won't be so eager to test new things, but for now, I need to explore, and I want you by my side so I don't end up lost for seventy-eight years."

He sat straight up. His eyes were intense. "You're not thinking of going to another planet are you?" he asked.

"Oh heavens no," she said. "I'm an earth-bound gal. But I do want to try a few things out."

"Okay," said Jediah. "Can we have breakfast first?"

"As long as you make it snappy," she said. "Otherwise, I'll be forced to leave you behind."

In a flash the covers fell to the mattress and Jediah enveloped her in his arms of steel. His arms went empty as she flashed to the kitchen.

She reached for the kettle and filled it with water. Within a minute, he appeared at the kitchen table fully clothed.

"You'd better hurry, or it will be you that's left behind," he said.

She placed the kettle on the stove and concentrated on the molecules in the water. By moving the molecules faster and faster, it was only seconds before the whistle blew.

"Brew the tea, would you please?" she asked. "I'm feeling a little underdressed."

She transported herself to the bathroom, completed her morning toilette, dressed, and was back in the kitchen in under two minutes.

"Not bad for a female," said Jediah with his back to her.

"We have more stuff to do than you fellas," she said with a shrug. "You didn't shave."

He turned around, and a clean-faced husband presented himself.

"Hey, you cheated," she said. "You snuck back upstairs and finished."

"All's fair in love and usurping your wife," he said with a grin and one eyebrow raised.

She reached up and stroked the raised eyebrow. Her heart swelled with love for him. As her arms wrapped around his neck for a nice hug, her brows furrowed as the FSB threat entered her thoughts.

The Fringe Science Bureau seemed to be a perpetual bump in their smooth world of perfection.

The Prophecy loomed before them, making the FSB her target; her goal, defense.

As she pondered the situation, she considered that since the FSB had Ari for decades, they certainly had a huge head start on collecting information. The agent snooping around at Larkspur for four years didn't hurt their knowledge base either. The FSB had plenty of time to dig up dirt.

Jediah's silence on the issue was probably for her benefit - her protection, but he needed to realize that she was fully committed and ready and able to do all in her power to protect the Sensates.

The other Sensates had years of experience over her. Her twenty-two years were a blink of the eye to most. Yet, the Prophecy all but named her as the one who'd save them all. If that was the plan, then they'd better look out because her pappy didn't raise no fool. They would soon learn not to mess with a Higgins.

Jediah kissed her forehead. She looked up into sensual, vibrant eyes. He'd stolen her heart from the get-go. His love strengthened her resolve.

Alexandra took Jediah deep into the forest on top of their mountain. She stopped at a familiar fallen tree and sat.

"I came here when I first learned of my powers," she said. "I could feel the animals. I knew when a grasshopper spat tobacco; I sensed when a fledgling bird left its nest for the first time, and I heard it sing with joy that it could fly."

Jediah looked at her in awe. "I've never had success with animals," he said. "I can sense when they are near, but I don't have the type of connection you're speaking about. How far can you take it?"

"What do you mean?" she asked.

"For instance, can you talk to them? Can you get them to do you bidding? Can you see through their eyes?" he said.

"I never thought to do those things," she said.

The day turned into one where Jediah shared his past failures, and Alexandra attempted to turn them into her successes.

She could start a fire by exciting molecules to move faster. She could see through animals' eyes; make herself invisible to all the people who were at Balisier at the given time, which was a hundred or so; and levitate five or six feet into the air, as long as she really kept her mind focused; otherwise, she fell sideways.

It only bothered her a little that she could not make the orb. She could do all the other things that Jediah and the others could do, yet the orb was one thing that evaded her; that particular power remained in the hands of Ryeth and Jediah.

Still, at the end of the day, she was left with the feeling of dissatisfaction. There was more; she was sure of it.

The following day, after Jediah left for Balisier, Alexandra strolled onto her back deck. Teater's trip to another planet crossed her mind. Of course, she needed to talk to him in great detail, but first, a bit of research was required.

Within an instant, she knew what she wanted to do. It would be impossible for her to attempt because she hadn't prepared the groundwork as Ryeth had. What she had in mind would take years of preparation.

Alexandra ran to the study and picked up the globe. She traced an imaginary circumference using the closest longitude line to Heartseed. She wrote down the countries and the longitude degrees.

Ryeth?

You have lousy timing, he mumbled.

When you have a free minute or two, stop by to see me, she said.

Just me? he asked.

Yes. Make sure we are alone.

Will do.

The connection ended.

Alexandra was on pins and needles waiting for Ryeth's arrival. She couldn't discuss her experiment idea with Jediah; he was still too raw from Teater's incident. If he even *knew* what she was thinking, he'd go off the deep end.

She tried to justify the compulsion to know what would happen if… but she couldn't. Driven by a force unknown, she had to complete the test.

An hour later, Ryeth finally appeared.

"Thanks for coming," she said.

"What's up?" he asked. "I can tell you're ready to jump out of your skin."

"It's that obvious?"

He nodded.

She straightened her shoulders and let her thoughts burst forth. "For reasons that shall go unnamed, I need to have landing points at these places." She handed him the slip of paper that contained the cities and countries from around the world.

He looked at the paper and said, "Do you have a globe?"

"Yes. Come with me, it's in the study."

He followed her into the study, and took the globe in his hands. "I can get you close to two of the sites, but I'm a good hundred miles off the third," he said. "Is that all right?"

"Yes, I think that will work fine," she said.

"Do you want me to take you to the places, or do you want me to imprint them into your mind?" he asked.

"Just imprint them."

"As you wish," he said. He made the transfer.

Alexandra smiled as the sites filled her thoughts. "They're all isolated places, so they're perfect."

"May I ask what you're up to?" he said.

"Not just yet," she said, hedging. "I need to speak to Teater first. He may have done some preliminary work that will save me some training time. When I'm ready, I'll need you by my side."

"Not Jediah?" he asked with a sideway glance.

"No," she said, "it has to be you."

"Why?" he asked.

Dang, she knew there would be questions, but she didn't like having to side-step them. It didn't feel honest. She shrugged her shoulders and said, "Ryeth, I really don't know. I just know with all my heart that I have to do this with you."

"If you feel that strongly, you have my support."

"Thanks."

He vanished but she heard him say, *Jediah's coming.*

She hurried to crush the paper with the cities and countries listed on it, and just reached the kitchen to throw it in the trash when Jediah appeared.

"What's going on at Balisier?" she asked.

"I'm supervising work on a new construction and finalizing a special addition to the tunnels," he said. "Oh, you don't know about those."

"The ones from my dreams?" she asked.

He smiled. "I didn't think you'd remember," he said.

"The dreams you gave me when I first became a Sensate were all so vivid. How could I *not* remember them?" She smiled remembering how the dreams he put into her subconscious helped her to learn about the Sensates as she slept. Every day when she woke, new abilities and powers were at her fingertips. It had been his way of bringing her up to speed.

"Do you remember the sequence of animal icon triggers for the doors?" he asked.

"Just like it was yesterday." She ran through the list of animals in her mind.

"I showed Teater all the changes at Balisier today," said Jediah.

"What did he think?" she asked remembering her first impressions of the Sensates' secure base. Over hundreds of years, they had carved a huge space out of the interior of the mountain. The only access was by teleportation. She still had a sense of awe every time she looked out over the village. The engineering was remarkable.

"Teater was impressed with the latest additions," said Jediah. "He loved the false façade to the rooms where we keep our history and the lists of everyone's abilities, and agreed that although writing them down was dangerous, access to the information would be invaluable if we ever needed to defend ourselves."

"How is he? As a matter of fact, how is Ari doing? I miss her."

Jediah sat on a stool at the counter. "I think they're both doing as well as can be expected," he said. "Jonathan's filling in all the blank spaces. Pretty soon, we'll have to grill them both. Ari could have heard things that didn't make sense to her that could help us in the future. I hate to admit it, but there's probably something to be learned from Teater's mistake as well."

"I don't see his trip as a mistake," she said.

His head shot up and he stared at her. "How can you not?" he asked. "The results were disastrous."

She chose her next words with care. "Yes, the results were unfortunate, but I understand his need."

"Unfortunate? How can you use such an ineffectual word to describe his actions?" Jediah's neck turned pink; his eyes, intense.

His patronizing words stung.

"Jediah." Her voice remained calm and matter-of-fact. "I'm allowed to have my own opinion."

Alexandra didn't miss the small intake of his breath or the slight furrowing of his brow. He continued to stare at her.

In the same calm voice she said, "If Teater senses your disapproval, he'll be less forthcoming with the details of his adventure."

In an unexpected turn, he got up from the stool and said, "Fine, *you* talk to him."

He vanished from view.

She dropped down on the vacant stool. Her first disagreement with Jediah had not gone as expected. Well, that suited her just fine. He'd better get used to her increased need for independence. For certain, there was more to come.

Brushing the incident with Jediah aside, she picked up her phone and dialed Cassie's number.

Although she couldn't talk to her best friend about Sensate things, she *could* talk to her about everything else, and that meant difficult husbands.

When she got off the phone an hour or so later, they had made plans for Cassie and John to visit for a long weekend, which improved her spirits by leaps and bounds.

Chapter Thirteen

Alexandra straightened her shoulders, drew in a deep breath, and strengthened her resolve. Urgency was nipping at her heels as time was closing in. The Prophecy indicated that Ryeth and she would save the Sensates.

There were times when uncharitable thoughts entered her mind regarding the hwihs on her shoulder. The others had so much knowledge and years to develop and hone their abilities. By comparison, months seemed like a gross error on someone's part.

With all things considered, she felt strong, fresh, *and*, she had a plan.

Ryeth was on the lookout for intruders when they last met, so he must have used a locator of sorts. Tired of asking others to teach her a technique, she decided to work it out on her own.

Some of the abilities she had contained parts of what she thought was needed, but she knew it would require distance and speed features, because intruders could be five miles away and driving a car, or thirty miles away and traveling in an orb.

Within half an hour she managed the ability. Once mastered, it took very little resources to maintain. It felt instinctual; as if she'd had the ability all along and only now flipped the switch. With her intruder alert she could protect the privacy of her activities.

Next, she visited Ryeth's three points on the globe to get her landings precise. Two were located in national parks, and the third in a frigid, desolate ice field. Standing in the cold in a tank top and shorts, she felt as silly as she probably looked.

Why she had the distinct urge for this information evaded her, but once she completed the act, the compulsion eased.

The next item required research and knowledge. If Jediah could teach her French in a minute, she should be able to tap the minds of others to achieve her goal. Caltech and MIT personnel had the knowledge she lacked.

With the FSB watching their every move, how could she get to California and Massachusetts to speak to the physicists personally? Tougher than the first hurdle, she set her mind to accomplishing the task. Since she couldn't make an orb, and she didn't want anyone to know she'd left the area, she figured what she really needed was to be in two places at the same time.

Alexandra knew how to make herself invisible to others by blocking her image from their sight. Could that work in reverse? Could she plant an image of herself in another's mind and have it project from their optic nerve not only as a stationary image but also as a live one?

The only way she could see herself was to look in a mirror, so she went to the bathroom and looked at herself in the full-length one on the back of the door.

She thought of Cassie. If this worked and her best friend saw her appear out of nowhere, she would love to be there and see the look on her face. How much fun they would have had with her powers.

She sighed. Cassie must never know. It would put her friend at great risk. Pangs of resentment and loss hit her from out of the blue. She chatted with her on the phone, and they emailed daily, but the pixie non-Sensate with the bouncy curls had to remain on the fringes of her life for her own safety.

If not Cassie, then who could she test her form of astral-projection on? Only one name came to mind. Alice Jane.

She smiled, located Alice, placed the image in her mind's eye, and then forced the image to become live. She even gave a little wave in the mirror as if to say 'hi.'

Just when she thought she'd projected long enough, Alice Jane appeared at her side, doubled over in laughter.

She ceased the experiment. Alice's laughter was contagious. She found herself smiling, but wondering why it was so funny.

Alice stopped laughing, but a huge grin remained. "Alexandra, I don't know how you astral-projected, but it worked," Alice Jane said.

"How did you know it wasn't really me? What's so funny?" she asked.

"You forgot to reverse the image," she said. You were standing on your head."

Her shoulders fell. "Oh," she said.

"Don't be discouraged, it's a fantastic ability," said Alice Jane. I'll go back and you try it again. Let's see if the 'other you' can do anything else."

She repeated the procedure, but reversed the image, acted like she was walking and spun around. Alexandra mouthed, "Can you hear me now?" as a joke, and then reached out to slap her reflection before she severed the connection.

Alice Jane re-appeared, excited and full of information. "The walking looked like marching in place, it had no depth," she said. "When you spun around, the image blinked, because you stopped looking in the mirror for a second. I couldn't hear you, but, on the other hand, the slap seemed so real, I ducked."

"It sounds like astral-projection has its limitations," said Alexandra.

"Yeah, but it could come in handy in a pinch," said Alice Jane. "Tell me how you did it. I'd like to give it a try."

Alexandra shared her method. An excited Alice Jane vanished. She could only imagine what Alice had in mind.

Bent on perfecting her technique, she continued pondering her missteps. Could she watch herself in the mirror and save the image in her mind? Was it possible to save an image just as she saved the imprints from other people's minds?

Alexandra closed her eyes to concentrate. Searching through her mind, she located the mechanism that allowed her to save imprints. It seemed to be a fairly simple process, so she copied the mechanism and replaced the imprint with an image from the mirror.

A split second before she located Alice Jane to try it, she reconsidered. An additional refinement was necessary.

If she could save an image, then why not a moving image, or a memory, or a scene from a karate movie?

She admitted it sounded a bit far-fetched, but, what the heck? It was just Alice Jane's laughter that she would have to suffer through...

Alexandra ran to the den and turned on the TV. She rummaged through her DVDs until the found Bruce Lee's, *Enter the Dragon*, and fast-forwarded to a fight scene where the camera was on him. To keep it short, she imagined the scene of him preparing to attack, and flying through the air with a jump kick. Concentrating only on him and not the background, she imagined just his three-dimensional form.

Now she was ready to test her revised mechanism on Alice Jane. If everything worked as planned, Bruce Lee should appear directly in front of Alice Jane and come at her with his best head kick.

After reminding herself to flip the image upside-down, she reined in her concentration and forced the moving image into Alice's mind and waited.

Alice Jane appeared before her in the skimpiest bra and bikini panties she'd ever seen. Her hand was on her hip and she was definitely copping an attitude.

"Uh, I caught you at a bad time?" she said to Alice Jane, and then burst out laughing.

"The next time you send Bruce Lee to my bedroom," said Alice Jane, "please make him taller than three feet."

"Oh," she said, still smiling.

Alice Jane went to her bedroom, jumped on her bed, grabbed a pillow to cover herself and said, "How the devil did you do that?"

Without waiting for a response, she continued. "I can assume you know what I was planning for Ryeth, ergo, the get-up. I was just getting ready to put the image in his mind when Bruce showed up," she said, laughing.

"I see…," she said. "Did Bruce move?"

"Yes. Had he been the right size, I would have sworn he was real," said Alice Jane. "I'm glad I didn't send the image to Ryeth. I'm now thinking of a more wicked one." Her eyes were filled with mischief.

"Before I tell you how to do it," said Alexandra, "I was thinking that maybe you and I could keep this mechanism between the two of us; what do you think?"

Alice Jane nodded. "Spoken like a true sister."

"Also, let me try it on you one more time to see if Bruce can man-up."

"Sure, go for it," said Alice Jane.

Alexandra turned away from Alice Jane and concentrated. Re-sizing the image meant a 50% increase to the focal length. She made the correction in her mind's eye by doubling the size of the image. She placed the revised moving image in Alice Jane's mind.

"Little sister, that was super amazing! I thought you would have to be actually looking at the movie to make it happen, but you have that part of the movie in your head. Dang, I'm really impressed."

Alexandra plopped on the bed. "Once I tell you how to do it, you have to do it to me so I can see how it works, okay?"

"Anything you ask….," said Alice Jane. "I can't wait to try this on Ryeth. I want to be around to see the look on his face. Hah! It will be great to be one-up on him."

"Sounds like a great plan," said Alexandra. "Here's how I did it."

Chapter Fourteen

The roar of water plunging deep into the mountain's chasm failed to extinguish Jediah's confusion. Not even the hum of the hydro-electric plant that powered Balisier got through to enter his thoughts. The confident leader of the Sensates sat on a boulder trying to make sense of the changes to his world.

Over the years he came to love that spot in Balisier. Onatah either teleported there or made an orb – he'd have to remember to ask her – but it definitely was she who located the internal cavern and deep chasm within the mountain many centuries ago. Her place of refuge, the waterfall inside a mountain, became the Sensates' safe haven, and his special place for pondering.

The unfamiliar emotions that surfaced lately regarding his new wife were not normal for the typically even-tempered, peaceful, and controlled leader of the Sensates. His marriage of a few short months was drifting into uncharted, rough waters.

He reviewed the past weeks for any disagreements or hesitations on her part and could find no reason for the difference in their home life.

What happened to his lovely Alexandra? Still young and beautiful, she now possessed a sharp edge to her character. She was changing, evolving and he had no idea into *what*. He didn't see it coming. He got out of bed in the morning, and there it was. He sensed the difference, and it was growing.

Granted, a lot was going on in their lives, and if he added her personal stint with Magis to the heap, there could be reason to have a change in attitude. But didn't trials and tribulations draw two people who loved each other closer? His Alexandra seemed secretive and elusive. It felt like she was sheading a skin and growing into something unrecognizable.

So deep in thought was he that he didn't sense Teater's arrival until his friend placed a hand on his shoulder and startled him.

He looked up into kind and gentle eyes that knew him like no other.

"What's with the moaning and groaning?" asked Teater. "I felt your anguish so -,"

"You came running like you used to?" said Jediah. He picked up a handful of pebbles, stared at one while his mind focused on Alexandra, rolled it between his thumb and forefinger, and then threw it in the clear water where he watched it until it fell so deep it was lost from his view. As he picked out a second pebble and started the same process, Teater interrupted him.

"I'm still your step-father," said Teater, who watched his ritual. "But most of all, I'm your friend."

Jediah had to admit the man was both. In actuality he was older than Teater by approximately a hundred years or so, but because they stopped aging around thirty-five, they looked the same age. And because he'd fallen in love with his mother, Jediah always thought of him as older.

"It's me that should be comforting you," he said to Teater, tossing another pebble into the bottomless pool. He scrutinized the remaining ones in his hand, selected one, and dropped the others on the ground. He set the last pebble on the boulder next to him, brushed his hands together to knock off the dust, and then wiped them on his pants.

"The only comfort I need," said Teater, "I'm finding in the company of my daughter. She's quite a girl."

Jediah heard the pride in his voice. "She's endured a lot."

"You don't know this yet," said Teater, "but I'm going to tell you just a snippet of what she was able to accomplish."

Teater walked back and forth; excitement filled his eyes. "I don't understand how she did it, I probably never will, but she was able to filter the drugs from entering her mind."

Jediah paused and set his own dilemma aside while his mind processed Teater's words. Ari, a girl with no more than a tenth grade education, filtered the blood in her body and didn't allow it to affect her mind. He didn't think scientists were able to do this *outside* the human body.

Teater added to Jediah's disbelief. "The rest of her body was affected, but not her mind. She said it took all her energy to do it. Can you imagine that?"

"No," said Jediah. "I can't get my mind around it at all." Through self-preservation, she'd devised a way to appear drug-induced without alerting the FSB? Ari's feat was extraordinary to say the least.

Still filled with exuberance, Teater continued. "Between that filtering ability and her cries for help, that's all she could manage during captivity," he said. "She remembered an incident where she was scared and found herself in an outside corridor, but she had no idea how that happened."

Jediah shook his head, completely dumbfounded that a Sensate could achieve so much on her own. Ryeth honed his abilities alone, but Ari developed her abilities alone *and* under captivity. Maybe Alexandra was right, they had become complacent with their abilities. After hearing this bit of knowledge, he had to wonder if their isolation stymied the development of their abilities.

Left to her own devices, Ari found a solution that allowed her to survive intact. "Val said she was amazingly clear and had a sound mind," said Jediah. "He said she was quite sharp."

"She is sharp," said Teater as only a father with a puffed up chest could do, "and extremely fast on developing the 'normal' set of Sensate abilities."

"I assume you've been coaching her?" asked Jediah.

"Some, but not as much as Jonathan." He winked at Jediah. "Those two seemed joined at the hip."

Jediah smiled. Through all the good and evil, life went on. Jonathan matched Ari in demeanor and intelligence.

"So what's got you seeking the solitude of the chasm?" asked Teater.

His thoughts quickly returned to Alexandra and his inability to understand the change in her. "Your descendant," he mumbled.

"Alexandra? You've got to be kidding. She's an angel, to be sure."

Jediah looked up at Teater sideways. "I'll agree on that one, but she's changing."

"Oh, I see," said Teater.

Jediah stood and stretched to his full height. "No you don't," he said. "She acts like she can't wait for me to leave the house."

"She's flexing her muscles?" said Teater, his eyes twinkling.

"What do you mean by that, you old goat?"

"Have you been hovering over her every move?" asked Teater.

Jediah shuffled, a bit uneasy regarding the question. "I wouldn't say hovering. I make sure she doesn't get in over her head."

"Uh huh," said Teater. "Maybe like a parent instead of a husband? It could be that she needs something different than what you're offering."

"You're stuffed with hay." Jediah shifted his weight. "What do you know? You've been gone, remember? You don't know how it was with us…how it *is* with us."

The old goat's eyes softened as he said, "Some things never change."

Teater left as he had arrived. Jediah returned to his seat on the boulder, his thoughts still unclear.

Maybe there was some truth in Teater's words.

* * * * *

The air contained a hint of sweetness from the last cutting of hay that lay stretched out over the hill to dry. Teater loved the family's retreat farm. It was just rural enough to feel isolated, but close enough for supplies.

He and Nancy Jane had spent many nights cuddled on the hill watching the stars. Now that he thought about it, it was those nights, looking and dreaming about those stars that probably got him in trouble. Well, he couldn't change the past, so he decided not to dwell on it.

Instead, he shifted his thoughts to Jediah and Alexandra. Jediah was probably feeling a bit like he did when he entered into his first serious relationship. His was a bit strained from the get-go.

When he first 'noticed' Nancy Jane that way he was sixteen, and Nancy looked to be a woman of thirty-five. She was a Sensate guide, and he, an admiring fledgling. The next phase of their relationship, when he knew she was the love of his life, he'd become a fully grown man of twenty-eight, and Nancy, still his mentor, remained thirty-five, but his feelings were no longer those of a student. Luckily, they were separated by miles and he had a wife and two boys.

He remembered a tortuous decade or so later, when he returned to Waynesburg. Both he and Nancy Jane now appeared the same age, but his wife in Wheeling still lived. In his attempt to hold back his feelings for Nancy Jane, he'd thrown himself into his work. He tore through updates to Balisier like a hurricane, and as time passed he and Nancy Jane became very close friends.

Years later, after he got news of his wife's death in Wheeling, he made his feelings known to Nancy Jane. He wanted her to see him as more than a student or friend. Although Nancy Jane returned his feelings of love, the transition from one role to another was difficult. They'd had more than one battle before they emerged as a twosome, each on equal footing.

Yep, Jediah had a row to plow, but he was sure, once the field was planted, he'd emerge a better man.

Chapter Fifteen

Ari awoke with a start. As her mind cleared and she assessed her surroundings, she relaxed. It would take time for the horror of her captivity to recede. Waking up for decades under the watchful eyes of her captors had required meticulous concentration.

She smiled as she remembered building the ability in her mind. It was the 'trick' she mastered in 1958, the very first day of captivity.

She'd quickly learned that as long as her eyes were closed, those watching her assumed she was sleeping. They spoke softly as they monitored her, but she could still hear their whispers and knew what they were thinking.

Their thoughts scared her. They watched her from behind glass mirrors and talked about her without using her name. They called her 613. Men and women talked of becoming her friend, but they only wanted to get her to do what they wanted.

She was afraid of what they would do to her after she fell asleep for real. She didn't like them and she didn't trust them, especially when they said they were going to hook her up to machines so they could see into her mind.

Ari had worked quickly to separate the areas of her mind so that only she maintained control. She worked the fingers of her hands to determine the area for touch, made noise to discover the part she used for sound, and continued until sight, smell, and taste were located as well.

When Ari heard them talking of putting drugs into her system to keep her under control fear gripped her until she thought of its transportation through her body.

Her blood was tough to isolate because it went everywhere inside her. When she ate and drank, her blood filled with a cloudy mixture that fed and watered her cells. She memorized all the different parts and their functions so that if anything new was added, she could stop it from passing into her head.

The red-headed girl of sixteen grew more confident. Even though she was scared of her captors, she was more afraid of losing control of her mind while she slept. If that happened, she knew she'd be lost for good. The safeguard needed to operate on its own, like a light switch that was always on.

It was like breathing, which happened whether she controlled it or not, and like the beating of her heart – automatic. Ari concentrated on locating the trigger for those two functions in her mind and was elated when they both headed to the same area. She used this area to turn her trick 'on'.

It was a cinch after that to set her waking state to always wake with her eyes closed so she could assess what was going on around her and keep her captors at bay.

All those changes to the way her mind controlled her body were no longer needed. Hesitant to remove what had kept her safe, she put it off for another day. Today, her eyes flew open wide.

Oh, how she loved the Saffle retreat. Compared to her jail, it was a slice of Heaven. A breeze ruffled the sheer draperies that covered the large section of windows at the far end of the room. They billowed like an angel's dress, soft and heavenly.

In all her wildest dreams she never envisioned life could be so wonderful. She stretched, sat up, and then fell back into the mounds of feather tick pillows. Visions of the gorgeous landscape filled her head. The flowers around the main house were blended in wondrous hues, the grounds were immaculate, the stables well-kept, and the white fence that surrounded the entire estate seemed to say, 'enter with love and appreciate me.'

She cringed as memories flooded her mind from her captured years. Tubes, needles, going in and out of consciousness, people poking and prodding, hushed voices, and zero modesty.

Wasted years of an almost wasted life. If Alexandra hadn't heard her cries for help, she'd still be forced to exist in that sterile, drugged state, with her eyes closed and hearing the metallic clink when her jailers hit the rails of her bed.

Closing off the unpleasant thoughts, she smiled as they turned instantly to Jonathan. If the days at the FSB were at one drastic end of the spectrum, then her time at the retreat and with Jonathan were slamming at the other. What an utter delight he was. She'd never once considered that people could be so caring and charitable.

As she hugged her arms to her chest and closed her eyes, a vision of the Ultra Sensate came into view. If she had to give him a one-word descriptor, she supposed it would be 'neat'. He kept his sandy hair in a precision cut parted on the side, with nary a strand out of place. Wearing button down, form-fitting shirts with khakis, he looked like he stepped out of a catalog. Ah, his smile. Little ripples of joy caused gooseflesh to run up her arms.

She rubbed her arms and laughed at her silliness.

Yes. Neat. That was Jonathan Gellner. She could hardly wait until she knew him well enough so she could mess up his hair.

To say he made her giddy would be a massive understatement. She remembered Teater's caution to take life slow, especially since she'd missed her natural boy/girl formative years, but golly, Jonathan was such a boon to her soul she couldn't stop the feelings that emerged.

Arizona hoped with all her might that the attraction wasn't just what all girls get for all guys when they reach puberty. Alice Jane had been kind enough to chat with her and even brought over some books on the subject that she'd read from cover to cover.

It was all too much to consider. She threw the covers back and hopped out of bed. The world was far too glorious to be seen from a bed, or gurney, for that matter. Onward to life… and to Jonathan, who should be arriving in half an hour.

She emerged from her suite of rooms and entered the conservatory for breakfast just as Jonathan arrived. He flashed that perfect smile, which displayed straight-even teeth and the most sublime dimples a girl could wish for.

"Good morning, Ari," he said, "you look refreshed and ready for a new day."

"Who wouldn't?" she said as she held out her arms and spun in a circle, "this place is Heaven."

She stopped spinning and pointed to the fruit, croissants, bacon, eggs, and muffins displayed on the sidebar. "Look at this," she said, "I love it here."

Jonathan shook his head. "Ari, your exuberance makes the world a better place. When I see your delight, it reminds me not to take things for granted that have become common-place."

"Tell me what you mean," she said.

"Fill your plate and join me at the table, then I'll tell you," he said.

They both filled their plates. Instead of sitting at the main table in the center of the large glass dome, she took a seat at one of the four bistro tables with two chairs near the edge of the conservatory where they could enjoy the view of the property.

Once seated, he answered her question. "We are Sensates who have extended life spans and we can go through many lifetimes. Because of this, we accumulate wealth. When you have wealth, you enjoy a different life-style and some things become common-place or expected."

"I see," said Ari.

He took her hand in his and looked into her eyes. "The point is; you make me remember the pleasure there is to be had in the little things of life."

His touch started an unfamiliar feeling in her stomach. Her throat constricted and she felt like she couldn't breathe. Unable to handle the emotions, her eyes darted around, but came to rest on her hand in his.

Breaths came in small pants as she felt the heat rise from her neck and flame on her cheeks.

She quickly removed her hand and turned away. The first thing she could think to do was to take a bite of eggs, but once they were in her mouth, she wasn't sure she could swallow them, so she chewed and chewed until her throat opened up and allowed the eggs to pass by.

She grabbed her orange juice and took a gulp as her breathing returned to normal.

What the heck was going on? If this was that puberty stuff, she wasn't ready. There was no controlling the weird things that happened to her body. She squeezed her toes together inside her flats and flexed the muscles in her legs. Her hands were wringing together in her lap, and then they began to fidget with her napkin.

In an instant she made up her mind. From now on, she'd select a seat at the big table. He was far too close for comfort.

To her relief, when she looked up, Jonathan was concentrating on his breakfast and acting like nothing happened.

He was the first to break the silence. "I've asked Val to join us today." he said.

Whew, things were back to normal. She could breathe, eat, and concentrate. She took a breath, sighed, and said, "Why? I thought all the drugs were out of my system."

"They are, but I was wondering if your blood filtering technique could be taught to others. Today, I will be the guinea pig and you will be the teacher."

"Jonathan, that's a great idea." She considered her words, and said quickly, "Oh, I don't mean that's it's great for you to be a guinea pig, I meant…"

He broke in. "I know what you meant," he said while laughing, "I think it's great too if your ability can be passed on to others. It would be a fantastic defense mechanism in case of…" He stopped.

She patted his arm, "Yes, I know, you can say it: in case we are captured. It would be a great way to stop intrusion and allow us to be in control."

Ari stood and paced in a small circle. She couldn't think clearly while he was so close and wanted to remove the boundaries from their conversations. "Jonathan, you mustn't worry that your words will bring unpleasant memories to light. I don't want that between us."

She turned to look at him. "You have become my best friend and confidant. I need to be able to trust people in order to feel whole again."

"I understand," he said. "I will honor your request."

"What request?" asked Val from the doorway. "She shouldn't have to ask for anything. Haven't I told you to allow her anything she wishes?"

They both turned to see the cantankerous imp of a doctor smiling at them.

Quick to her friend's defense, Ari said, "Oh, no. Please don't think I was complaining. Everyone has given me more, so much more, than I could ever have asked for..." Her thoughts were empty. What could she ever say to thank everyone for their care and attention? They gave her life - and freedom.

"Don't worry, Ari," said Val, "I was just messing with your compadre," he motioned to Jonathan. "Believe me when I say, you have made it more than apparent how grateful you are for your freedom."

He crossed the room, set his medical bag on a chair, and embraced her.

As his arms surrounded her, she knew words were not required. Never again would she fight a battle alone. She was surrounded by those of great moral fiber, and she was one of them – a Sensate – and that would never change.

He gave her a nice squeeze, and then released her to shake Jonathan's hand.

"It's always good to see you," said Jonathan.

"Likewise," said Val. He turned to Ari. "So, what do you think of our idea?"

He had to ask? She'd give her life for her new extended family, and it wasn't because of the rescue, it was because of the love that surrounded her from morning to night.

She smiled. "If it works, it will be a wonderful addition to the Sensates' bag of tricks," she said. "I'm all for it."

Val nodded. "Ari, I've been researching, and I wonder if you wouldn't mind a bit of experimentation too?"

"Sure," she said, "whatever you need."

"What are you thinking?" asked Jonathan.

Val rubbed his chin while nodding. "My thoughts are this: I'd like Ari, and then, in turn, us, to remain conscious and functional if drugs are in our systems. Also, I'd like to refine Ari's technique to require less concentration and, hopefully, to enhance the mechanism so that the drugs don't have any effect at all."

Jonathan's eyes grew wide.

Ari sat down and rubbed her head. "Do you really think that's possible?"

Filtering the drugs from her mind took all her concentration, but at the time, she didn't know all she knew now about maximizing and minimizing her abilities, or even how to compartmentalize them. The Sensates were schooled with techniques and short cuts. She was a novice, actually, less than a novice, compared to them.

Val shrugged and said lightheartedly, "That's what we intend to find out. The only damper might be that if we are already unconscious, we might not be able to initiate the mechanism, and I don't know if the technique is something we can put into effect as a permanent part of our mental abilities."

"Oh," said Jonathan, "you *have* been researching."

"Gee, I would never have thought to take the idea to such lengths," said Ari. "It's great to be part of such a fantastic group. You guys continually wow me."

Val looked at both of them. "So, let's get started."

Chapter Sixteen

Alexandra withdrew the folded paper from her dresser drawer that Jediah gave her before they were married. She opened it and re-read the lines she now knew by heart:

> One from pain and one from strife,
> Join together guarding life.
> Crossing boundaries, breaking rules,
> Both are marked as ancient tools.
>
> One alone and schooled in lies,
> Anger, scorn, and hate the guise.
> Taught by others to be cruel,
> Hence brought forth the timeless duel.
>
> In the heart where all hope died,
> Grows the truth from deep inside.
> All required is hope and trust,
> Break the tide; turn hate to dust.
>
> None will know and none can see,
> Plans of secret hold the key.
> If one fails, the last will fall,
> One that's close could doom us all.

All the pieces fit except one. The Prophecy clearly spoke of Ryeth, Ari, and her, but last part regarding the secret plans was still unclear. One thing was distinct: Either they had a traitor among them, or one of their group was going to make a grievous error.

It was hard to believe that someone from their group could make a mistake of that magnitude. The youngest, excluding herself and Ari, was a practicing Sensate for well over a hundred years. The whole community's commitment to secrecy was a covenant they lived by; their honor and moral code was certainly above question.

Both items seemed a far reach as a solution. She would have to maintain a vigil against the threat until it became known. Only then could she take action against a traitor or take steps to cover up an error.

Alexandra walked out to the arbor. It was the only place where her jumbled thoughts morphed into clear concise paths. As she reached the threshold, her mind found peace.

The tiny flowers of the Heartseed vine had turned into small pods that looked like Chinese lanterns. They were new and green now, but within the next month, the pods would dry up and turn brown. That's when they produced the seeds she loved so very much. Her father, who had loved wild flowers of all kinds, shared his love, thereby creating hers.

When the pod matured, it would contain many round, dark brown-colored seeds, each clearly marked with an ivory heart on one side. When she was little, she would collect the precious seeds and hold them in her hand; sometimes, she carried them around for days. She smiled thinking that she never really knew what happened to them after that... her mother probably cleaned them off her night stand or dresser, long-since forgotten by her, and planted them somewhere.

She pulled a pod off the vine and held it in her hand. It reminded her of Balisier; a protective place with many hearts inside. Teater came to mind as she wondered if the symbolism was on purpose.

Alexandra's mind cleared and focused on an important item. Her solution to the Prophecy, assuming she could obtain the information from the astrophysics engineers, and that she could pull it off, would require tremendous power. Where had Teater gotten the power to travel light years away? Power was the key.

Alexandra closed her eyes and assessed the combined power available within the Sensates group as compared to her own. She knew she could draw extra power from the Sensates, but would that be enough? She *had* to get information from the astrophysicists.

A quick Internet search gave her three possible subjects. Dang, if she could make an orb, it would be a cinch to pop on over, locate the subject, and perform a knowledge transfer. Any other method could compromise her identity.

Disgruntled and edgy, she recalled Jediah's instructions. The mechanisms the Sensates used were tied, in a great part, to their emotions. She recalled thinking it could be a great desire, or need, but she tried that, and it didn't work. It seemed clear that what worked for one may not work for another.

Alexandra attempted the orb by various emotions. Love, which was very powerful, didn't work. Neither did compassion, charity, or patience. Although she hated to call up hate, anger, and envy, she did it anyway, and was pleased they didn't work, but sad she still didn't have the right trigger.

A good amount of time passed as other options passed through her mind and she tried them as possible solutions. She discarded many as hopeless without even testing them.

Irritation pricked at her skin and she began to pace. She was just about to give up when the soft melodious voice of Onatah entered her mind.

It is your greatest gift, memiki. Jediah's is serenity, Ryeth's is confidence. What is yours?

Her heart fell. She didn't know the answer. Cassie always said she was an 'old soul,' but that couldn't be right. Try as she might, no answer came forth. Struggling to look inward, she sighed and shook her head.

Kayè, I don't think I have a 'greatest gift,' she said.

It is not prideful to know one's self, said Onatah.

Introspection was hard. Alexandra wasn't sure where to begin. Heck, she couldn't even come up with a decent resumè because she thought it was too much like boasting.

Dang it. She clenched her teeth. Okay, she could do this. She was organized. As a matter of fact, she was so organized that her kitchen cupboards looked like items on a store shelf. Her need for an organized household probably bordered on a psychological disorder, yet every evaluation she ever received praised her organizational skills.

She was honest. That trait came from her father.

Over-concentrating, her thoughts went to silliness. She looked down. It was her feet. She had great-looking feet. Sliding her sandal off, a perfect size six and a half foot presented itself. No toes were over-sized. She had no bunions or corns, and the whole foot was proportional. A foot model; if the Sensate thing fell through, she would become a foot model.

Taking a cleansing deep breath, she picked up her sandal and plopped down on one of the stone benches. While putting her sandal back on, she chided herself for wasting time with foolishness.

Back at it with a serious mind she said, "I'm a good person. I believe in treating everyone fairly and equally. I have morals that I live by that are high, by most people's standards. I do not think poorly of others; my thoughts are clean."

A lightning bolt hit her. Oh, for heaven's sake, she was a 'Pollyanna,' a do-gooder. She supposed people even said she was 'as pure as the driven snow.'

Alexandra raised her chin and smiled. *Thank you, Kayè*, she said as her orb appeared.

It shimmered pale blue and silver. It felt so right. With tiny modifications, she was able to make it visible to others, solid, or transparent.

Excitement filled every part of her being. Alexandra Higgins could make an orb, and it was beautiful. It sparkled like glitter and made her feel like a princess, well, at least it did until she looked down at her jeans and t-shirt. She wriggled her toes in the sandals.

Creating it was one thing, operating it was another. With no steering wheel, brakes, or gas pedal, she wasn't sure how to begin. Her eyes glanced at the arbor, and then beyond. Far away were trees and above was the sky. She gasped.

She quickly dissolved the orb. As her heart raced inside her chest she had one thought: Teater. Her heart still pounding at the walls of its cage, she carefully walked to the house and shut the door.

What if she had zoomed upward into the sky without thinking? She could have lost control and dropped to earth like a stone. Boom. No more Alexandra.

She shuddered. It was better to learn control *inside*. Chills ran down her spine. Caution was critical.

Once inside, she re-created the orb. The sparkling light bounced off the walls of the living room like a disco ball. Jediah's and Ryeth's orbs didn't do that. It was probably a girl thing; perhaps Onatah's orb sparkled too. Maybe that's how she was able to see inside the mountain.

Mine was green and gold, said Onatah. *I am proud of you memiki.*

Before Alexandra could reply, Onatah's touch vanished. It was wonderful to know she was near.

Re-focusing on the orb's mechanics, she started slowly by inching it forward with the couch as the destination point. It floated with small jerks at first, but as she grew more confident, it became smoother. When she neared the couch, the arm disappeared, and then re-appeared behind her. It went through things all by itself. It didn't need anything from her in order to pass through.

Although she considered the pass-through thing odd, she continued by moving from room to room just like she was walking there. Nothing weird happened, so she continued experimenting.

Back in the living room with second story cathedral ceilings, she decided to spin the orb to see how fast she could make a turn. Left, right, up, down, all worked as expected, but somehow she thought of a fighter plane making curlicues and circles in the sky.

Alexandra thanked her lucky stars that no one was there to see that one. She learned too late that her feet were *not* attached to the bottom of the orb so she bounced around inside like some goof going over Niagara Falls in a barrel. She came to a halt splayed across the bottom of the orb on her stomach.

After a cup of tea to calm her nerves, she took a small breather to consider the next orb experiments. Why had she been totally protected from falling out of the orb, and Ari's touch caused such fluctuations in Ryeth's? Was it because Ari was a passenger? Or because Ryeth's orb had been stretched to the limit to accommodate the gurney and it was thinner, making it more flexible? Either way, she was glad she maintained the orb and didn't fall out.

Going through the wall onto the deck was next. She focused on the deck and started the orb moving. When the wall loomed before her, she jerked and closed her eyes, awaiting the impact.

None came. She opened her eyes to see the orb had stopped just before entering the wall. She set her lips firm, plotted her course onto the deck, cast a devil-may-care attitude, and zoomed through the wall.

Jubilation coursed through her veins as she made it to the deck. "No guts, no glory," she said.

Making the orb invisible, she then slowly moved through the deck railing and stopped, suspended some twenty-feet off the ground. It was different than when she was with Jediah. With him, she was awed. By herself, she was exhilarated. The feeling was unbelievable, scared, excited, thrilled, and satisfied. She was hanging in mid-air, all by herself.

After practicing all over the yard and passing through the forests on the mountain, Alexandra was ready to brave the unknown.

She flew over Waynesburg, soared over the hills to watch the cars and tractor-trailers pass by on the interstate, went high into the clouds, and then finally positioned herself a few hundred feet outside the side of her mountain.

Going through the solid granite and limestone walls of a mountain would be the next test. She wasn't certain of the interior placement of the village, so instead of slamming into the walls with no specific spot in mind, she decided to glide gently through and see what happened.

A split second before the attempt, she thought to at least tell Alice what she was up to, but tossed the thought out with the wind. She was either up to the challenge or she wasn't.

She moved with great care closer and closer to the mountain. The orb touched the outside, and then disappeared within. She inched closer; her arm and foot disappeared. While holding the position, she stuck her head inside the mountain. She saw her foot and arm, and when she looked backward, she saw the mountain, but not the part of her body that was still on the inside.

So that's how it works, she thought. She moved the orb forward until she was completely inside the stone. Her orb remained intact; except for her, it was as empty as it had been on the outside of the mountain. She continued forward, broke through to the interior of Balisier, and then made her way to the desolate counsel room.

On her trip back home, she decided to test speed. She moved to Ryeth's place in the Pocono Mountains, whipped back to Wheeling and checked out Oglebay Park, and then, as if the devil were on her heels, she sped to the arbor at Heartseed. It wasn't as fast as teleporting, but it was pretty darned close.

Confidence filled every pore as her orb dissipated. She was *woman*! *Hear her roar*!

She looked around and supposed she should back it down a decibel or two, but at that very instant, confidence reigned supreme.

Chapter Seventeen

Once Alexandra's jubilation over creating the orb subsided, her thoughts turned to Teater. She touched the carving on the bench of the arbor and followed the vine's path with her finger. As she sat on the bench, her eyes went to the center stone, and she remembered the intricacy of its internal design. Teater had enchanted it as well as the stone that aided her to get out of the cistern.

Although a scant seven months had passed since her quest for Teater, she'd aged greatly in mental years. The school girl life she led the years following her parents' death seemed long ago and far away.

She stood and walked the short distance to the windmill. It covered the cistern where her adventure began. Her fingers reached inside the pocket of her jeans and withdrew the stone. It lay it in the palm of her hand.

Teater, are you free to visit me? she asked.

Always. He appeared next to her, reached out, and embraced her in a hug.

"So much has been happening," she said, "I just need to rewind the clock. I don't want to miss anything." She looked into his eyes, and realized what she'd said. "Oh, I'm so sorry, I wasn't thinking when I spoke."

"It was a turn of a phrase, child, nothing more," he said. "Don't think a thing of it."

She held out her hand to display the stone. "You changed my life," she said.

He picked the stone from her hand and as he turned it over, he smiled and said, "Imagine that, it worked."

His face clouded over. "Nancy and I planned it together. We figured it wasn't right to completely change an outcome, but we thought we could give you a little help."

"Well, it worked," she said. "It took everything I had that day to stick my hand into that hole in the cistern's wall. Once I did and touched that *warm* stone, I nearly passed out. I was scared and curious at the same time. It wasn't until later that this," she pulled her shirt aside to display the hwihs, "came on my shoulder."

"It's *you*." Teater held her at arm's length, looked at her deeply, and then held her tight against him. "Did Nancy know?" he asked.

"Yes."

"It must have given her great satisfaction to know that she and I helped to bring you into this world." He released her, but kept one arm around her shoulder.

"Let me show you." She transferred all her memories of Nancy Jane to Teater.

He stepped away from her and looked across the yard to the arbor. A few seconds later, he grabbed her hand and led her there. When they arrived he let loose of her hand and sat on a bench.

Alexandra sat next to him as he stared off into space, his face unreadable.

A few minutes passed, his face changed, and then held sadness. His shoulders slumped as he let out a long sigh. Teater brought his head up as he looked into her eyes.

"She was beautiful," he said, "inside and out."

Alexandra felt his pain as her own memories brought tears to her eyes. It broke her heart that Teater never got to say 'good-bye' to Nancy Jane.

"I couldn't agree more." She rubbed his shoulder.

"So?" he said, the sadness gone, replaced by genuine kindness. "What's going on in that pretty little head of yours?"

The confidence she had earlier left her. Maybe it was too soon to ask. She hedged a bit. "How did you enchant the stone?"

"Jediah asked the same thing. I'll tell you like I told him, I don't know. Nancy and I talked about it, and when I placed the stone in the cistern, I wished really hard that when you touched it, it would activate your powers so you wouldn't die."

"That's all?" she asked. It had to be more than that. Everyone made wishes...

"Well, I kissed the stone, but I doubt my kisses are *that* powerful." He winked at her.

"Initially, it seemed to help me come up with a plan to get out of the cistern," she said. "Hours later, when it rested on my nightstand, it glowed this beautiful shade of blue."

"Really?" he asked.

"I couldn't believe it either. It was the oddest thing I ever saw. Then, when I held it, it almost seemed like it was challenging me to hold it longer. That's when it stung me and left the hwihs on my shoulder. I didn't know whether to flush the darned thing or keep it forever."

"I see you kept it." He held it between his thumb and forefinger. "I'm surprised you didn't run for the hills, screaming the whole way," he said. "It seems harmless enough now."

He turned the stone over, gave it a good look, held it firmly in his hand, and then handed it back to her.

"I don't think that's all you wanted to ask," he said. "Whatever it is, don't chew on it any longer. Spit it out."

He had such a way of speaking that Alexandra felt she'd known him forever. Her words came easily and not rushed. "There are two things I'd like to know, if you can share them. The first: tell me about your life. I was so drawn to you in my genealogy research, mostly because I needed to understand why you left your family in Wheeling. You just walked away…"

His vibrant eyes dimmed as Alexandra sensed the painful memories filling his thoughts. He turned and picked a Heartseed pod from the vine, and held it in his large hands; it looked small and fragile.

With small movements, he peeled the outside soft shell away to reveal the tiny round seeds within. From a distance she saw the heart shape on the sides had not yet become prominent on the unripe seeds. Teater's gaze focused on the seeds as he began his story.

"I can still remember my mother's tears as she hugged me and then ran into the house. My father pulled me up behind him on Old Sal, our best horse, and we made the long journey to Waynesburg." Teater gave a small laugh. "Sal's rump was much wider than her middle section and I can remember the ache in my thighs from riding such a distance with my legs stretched around her."

He continued. "Dad didn't talk much on the trip, and I tried hard to be the man he wanted me to be, so I didn't say much either. He dropped me off at the Madison's with barely a word in my direction, but I noticed how his voice caught in his throat as he told them that I 'was a good boy and to treat me as such'. Dad put his hand on my head, messed my hair, got on Old Sal, and rode out of view."

Teater smoothed his hair and centered the binding at the nape of his neck.

"The first few weeks were hard because I missed my family," he said, "but I soon had enough hard labor to keep my mind from wandering. My body filled out, I became strong, and I learned how to manage the pangs in my heart."

He fingered the seeds in the palm of his hand and rolled them around a bit before continuing. "Toward the end of the summer, I began hearing a voice in my head. It was soft and yielding. I knew right away it was female. Although I should have thought to lose my mind, I began to look forward to the voice. Somehow, it filled a void that made me whole."

He stood and began to pace, and almost without thinking, he placed the seeds in his pants pocket.

"I was clearing a stump in the far field when a beautiful woman seemed to appear out of nowhere," he said. "I didn't see her coming, and my view from the ridge was pretty far. She introduced herself as Nancy Jane Saffle."

Teater's eyes became wistful as he continued. "Her hair was fixed in the latest fashion, her clothes were stylish but functional, and she had the smallest feet I'd ever seen on an adult encased in beaded slippers. I was mesmerized."

He twirled what was left of the stem of the pod between his finger and thumb and stared off into space.

"As time went by, she told me that I was a Sensate, like her and many others. When I came into my powers, she was there to guide me. Over the next several years I was introduced to Jediah who became my best friend. It was only then that I realized exactly what it meant to be a Sensate. I also found out that I had visions of the future, but not of all things – only about you and my part in the Prophecy."

He returned to sit next to her. "By the time I left Waynesburg to return to Wheeling, I had fallen totally and completely in love with Nancy Jane. It mattered not that she was older, or that I had a destiny to fulfill. I couldn't help myself."

He shrugged. "My vision compelled me to seek out and marry Mary Wilkinson and to have two sons."

He looked away, gave a sigh and continued. "The birth of my second son, Lawrence, ensured your arrival. After my boys were grown and I had amassed enough money for their well-being, I was compelled to return to Waynesburg and prepare Balisier for your arrival. Once Balisier was under control, the chain of events required by my vision had been fulfilled."

Teater looked up, met her eyes and said, "It was one of the most difficult tasks of my life – to leave Nancy Jane when I loved her so, and to begin a life with another woman, yet I remained in Wheeling when my heart was elsewhere."

A wicked smile crossed his lips. "When my time in Wheeling was up, I *ran* to Waynesburg as fast as I could. It was unfortunate I had to leave my Wheeling family. And yes, to all concerned, it would have appeared that I just got up one day and vanished; but my love for Nancy Jane had no boundaries."

Alexandra watched as peace washed over his face before he began again.

"Over the next several years we maintained a platonic relationship, although a blind man could have seen our love."

Teater now looked almost boyish. His eyes lit up and his face broadened in a beautiful smile, complete with his charismatic dimples. Had he wings, he could have been a Heavenly angel. Love radiated from every pore and surrounded him in a silvery aura. She realized his love had grown strong and pure through completing a selfless act. An act that ensured the continuation of their small but select group.

Teater said, "It was only after Mary died of old age that Nancy Jane and I were free to love each other. It was a long time coming, and I think that's what made it all the sweeter."

Unable to contain her emotions any longer, Alexandra hugged him. "You have given up much for our group," she said.

He rustled her hair. "You might think so, but it was just a pittance compared to all that I gained through loving Nancy Jane."

Teater stood, retrieved the tiny seeds from his pocket and cast them into the wind.

It felt like he was spreading love.

He looked at her and said, "So, what's the second thing you wanted to ask?"

She hesitated only a second before asking, "Would you tell me about your trip?"

He released a heavy sigh. "I thought that was it," he said. He stood and paced the arbor. "I haven't spoken about it to anyone. Part of me felt it was my punishment to carry the story to my grave, the other part still wants to share it."

As his words filled the air, her mind pictured a solar system like the Milky Way, the Andromeda Nebula. She learned of his love of astronomy that began in 1924 when he read an article published in *The New York Times* by Edwin Hubble. Any time not spent with his family, or later, when working on Balisier, was spent soaking up knowledge of the stars and galaxies.

"From what I've been reading and watching since I got back," he said, "I missed a lot of space history."

"I'd bet any one of those fellas that landed on the moon would trade places with you in an instant," she said.

"They probably would at that." He smiled.

"Where did you go first?" she asked. "Surely you didn't just plunge into space headed for Andromeda."

"No, I made small tests first, because I wanted to stay near, but no matter how much I tried to suppress it, I was drawn to a particular place in Andromeda. I can't explain it," he said. "I will tell you one thing – I've decided not to share the steps I took to get there; mostly because I'm not sure of the ramifications of my actions. I was compelled to go there as surely as I was compelled to assure you got to Balisier."

Alexandra sensed the churning of Teater's emotions. He was conflicted regarding his actions.

"If it's any consolation," she said, "I know how you feel. I've been compelled to learn, know, and *do* things recently. I don't know why and sometimes it makes no sense, but I *have* to do it. It's like I can't complete any other function until I squelch the compulsion," she said, as she brushed an imaginary speck off her jeans. "Jediah's not too happy with me."

He looked at her with wide eyes. "You *do* understand." He stood and paced. "Alexandra, you're not attempting anything rash are you?"

"No, I don't think so," she said. "But I have this desire to learn astrophysics – in depth – right now – today."

"In what regards?" he asked.

She caught the slow delivery of his words. His voice held caution. She stood and walked to the opposite side of the arbor. She sighed, turned to face him, and then spoke.

"Space-time, calculations, that kind of stuff." She shook her head and said, "I know, it doesn't make sense. That's why I thought I'd ask you about your trip. I think I want to know about the going and coming, and how it felt, and how long it took, and whether or not you were aware of the passage of time…" She paused. "I'm babbling." She made a chagrined face and sat down.

"Do you want to travel in space," he asked.

"No." She shrugged. "See? It makes no sense."

"Have you talked to Jediah?" he asked.

"Are you kidding?" she asked with rhetoric dripping from her words. "He's still grumbling about you." Her hand flew to cover her mouth.

"Oh," she said as a pained look crossed over her face. "I did it again. Things fly out of my mouth without thinking. I'm sorry."

"Listen Alexandra, if you're going to keep apologizing for everything you say, we're never going to get anywhere. You should be able to say whatever you want as my granddaughter… ah, let's leave the great-great thing out of it, shall we?" He smiled a crooked smile.

Emotion swelled in her chest and caught in her throat. She smiled and ran over and hugged him tightly.

"Teater, I've missed you," she said.

"Missed me? You didn't even know me, child," he said as he returned the hug and patted her back.

"Oh, yes I did." She sniffed. "Believe me when I say I've missed you... but, I've not missed you near as much as I needed you." Tears fell down her cheeks.

He consoled her and in doing so, forever sealed the bond between the two.

Alexandra sniffed and wiped the tears from her eyes. She looked up into the bluest eyes she'd ever seen. "I have to ask you one more thing," she said.

Teater leaned his head sideways and said, "You know you can ask me anything."

"Didn't Jediah try to talk you out of your... ah, escapades?" she asked.

"Sure, he talked 'til he was blue in the face, but as I said, it was an obsession, I *had* to go. Nancy understood my compulsions, Jediah didn't. He hammered on me day and night, even up to the very instant I left."

His shoulders sagged, "If I had known what I know now, I believe I still would have gone." He stared at her. "*That's* how much I was forced to go. I couldn't stop myself. I tried to put it out of my mind, but I was helpless against it. Nothing, short of death, could have stopped me."

Teater hung his head.

As strong as the compulsion to learn astrophysics was, Alexandra had gone along with it, knowing it was for the good of the Sensates. She couldn't imagine fighting against it, for the need was there twenty-four hours of every day and beckoned her forth with an unknown power. Her need was as great as Teater's, and like him, she moved forward.

Later, Alexandra questioned Teater about every facet of his travel; he answered her questions, withholding nothing. By the time he left, the only thing he hadn't shared was the landing sites and the planet itself. He'd told her 'one fool in the family was enough.' She took his word on that.

Chapter Eighteen

One thing that Nancy Jane failed to tell Alexandra during her mentoring phase was that both Nancy and her great-great grandfather received premonitions.

Alexandra figured that either Teater thought she already knew or he'd let it slip, but a little inkling told her that Teater never let anything slip that he didn't want to. As far as she knew, those premonitions hadn't passed on to her, and for that, she thanked her lucky stars.

The force that drove her was quite different than a premonition, for she had no idea what the future held.

For the past week she woke every day with an incessant need to accomplish one thing or another. Today, her head pounded. It had a thirst for knowledge. As soon as Jediah left to continue the work on the tunnels, she plastered herself to the computer screen.

A map of the Albright Technical campus displayed before her. After clicking a few buildings, she located one that might contain personnel whose mind she could peek into.

When she considered what she was about to do, feelings of regret stepped in front of her and prevented her path onward. Regret stopped her just long enough for her to rethink crossing the Sensate moral line. If Jediah and the others could 'monitor' people in the FSB, surely she could gain a bit of knowledge.

It was possible that Alice Jane might have the information she required, but Alice had a powerful mind which included Nancy Jane's mind block. Plus, Alexandra required total secrecy, and if Alice discovered what her plans were, the Prophecy could be compromised. So, she had little choice in her information gathering; she had to obtain it any way she could. The rationalization completed, she began.

She placed an astral-projection of herself on the deck in a lounge chair, reading a book. Jediah couldn't know her plans either. Scanning her image and finding it very convincing, she made her orb, glanced in the mirror to make sure she was invisible, and vanished.

Building #37 of Albright's campus contained the Astrophysics Division and Aerospace Computational Design Lab. It seemed a good place to start.

The campus was alive with activity. One by one she peered into the minds of the professors in the various departments. In no time at all she located a professor who just might fill the bill, but when she performed a deeper search of his mind, she found he had only touched on space-time in his studies, and had no particular interest in retaining the information.

Her in-depth search took her through seven labs and thirteen lectures, and still she could not locate the mind that contained the information she desired.

After several hours and what seemed like a multitude of minds, her own mind turned fuzzy. Ready to leave, she glanced over her shoulder at a sign that said, *Mosser Institute for Astrophysics and Space Research*. Though she was feeling a bit like she was going on a wild goose chase, she squared her shoulders and decided on just one more series of minds before she headed home.

To her disappointment, the information she sought could not be found in any of those professors' minds either. But, while observing a lecture, she was drawn to a young man who didn't seem to be paying too much attention to the topic.

She moved closer to see what he wrote on his pad. Circles. The infinity sign. Sometimes he drew the circles clockwise, sometimes counter clockwise. She sensed his mind racing in all directions even though his outward appearance was one of boredom.

Curious, she entered his mind. Facts, figures, theories, experiments, and computations whirled at an astounding rate. The pace was so quick it caused a sharp pain in her temples to match his speed. She winced, but maintained the connection. When things in his mind repeated, he started a new circle, which began a new way to consider his assumptions. Alexandra found the man's cerebral functions cluttered, yet astounding.

She scanned his mind for space-time. A wealth of information slammed the edges of his thoughts. He'd worked through what seemed like a limitless amount of calculations based on Einstein and Haley's observations. Everything she needed and more was located in this man's head. He not only had eidetic memory, his genius was incredible.

A sharp pang caused her to flinch as she sensed he was deeply troubled and lonely. His gift separated him from those he considered normal. The gift made no sense to him, so he detested it *and* the inability to control it. She searched his heart and found no malice other than for his gift. His one desire was to be normal and have peace of mind. That touched a nerve. *This* she understood.

Alexandra imprinted his mind, for if his wonderful theory worked, she wanted to pay a visit later and thank him for his contribution. He could very well be the first non-Sensate to contribute to their cause.

She smiled. The information surged forth and transferred into her mind. As she withdrew from his inner thoughts, she noticed his student identification card wedged between the pages of a book. His name was Enoch Farmer. From deep within, Alexandra made a wish for Enoch... that he received his own wish for peace of mind.

During her trip back home, which took mere seconds, her spirits soared. The weight of the compelling urge for knowledge left her. The edginess she almost accepted as a new normal, was no longer present.

As she looked over her exquisite kitchen, a pang of regret filled her heart. She missed her adoring husband. The time spent on research and gaining knowledge showed in her personal relationship with Jediah. With a compulsion driving her actions daily, little time was spent on the building blocks of her marriage.

That would end right now. By the time the orb disappeared in the kitchen, a plan had formed in the new wife's mind.

Baked steak, mashed potatoes and gravy, and creamed peas greeted her husband as he entered the kitchen that evening. Jediah grabbed a fresh roll, hot off the rack. The pleasure she sensed coming from him did wonders to refill the void in her heart.

"Ummm...," he said. "My favorite meal."

As he leaned over to kiss her cheek, she swung around into his arms and met his lips with hers. His arms wrapped around her. Their kiss deepened as their senses co-mingled. Jediah stepped backward and opened his eyes. Alexandra watched the astonishment flash on his face as he realized they were in a sparkling silver and blue orb floating a mile above Heartseed.

"You figured it out," he said.

His unguarded pride was visible on his face, which made her ashamed for not giving him the attention he deserved.

"I had a little help," she said, as she lowered her eyes.

Jediah placed a finger under her chin and raised her face to his.

"Ryeth?" One adorable eyebrow raised on her husband's face. She reached up and touched it until it returned to normal.

"Ryeth? Why would you think it was him?" she asked.

"Because he's the only other that can make one. I thought that would be evident," he said.

Alexandra was caught between feeling like a total idiot and feeling a bit slighted that Jediah didn't even think to be a bit jealous that she might have gone to Ryeth instead of him.

His confidence in her and their relationship amazed her. She's seen many couples destroyed by jealousy and envy and she was glad she didn't foster those emotions, but somehow, she was a bit disappointed that Jediah's only emotion seemed to be the raising of that one eyebrow.

So, she did the only thing that she could think of to get rid of the disappointment, she messed up his hair as she said, "No, it wasn't Ryeth, it was

Onatah. She told me it was 'our greatest gift' that enabled the construction. When I still couldn't figure it out she told me it wasn't prideful to 'know' oneself." She took a deep breath.

"That was an easy one. It's your purity, your goodness," he said smiling. His eyes looked deep into hers and then widened. "You didn't know, did you?"

"No, I – I don't know. It was embarrassing. I try to be the person my parents would be proud of. I have angry thoughts like everyone else. But when Onatah said that to me, you know, about being prideful, my heart sang." Geesh, she mentally kicked herself… this looking at oneself was tough stuff.

Jediah hugged her so tight she thought she might burst.

"Introspection, sweet Alexandra. You don't do it very well," he whispered in her ear.

"Does anyone?" she said, leaning back and questioning him with her eyes.

As the sparkling orb landed in the kitchen and dissipated, mouth-watering scents filled the air.

"I suppose not," he said as he ran his fingers through her hair.

Chapter Nineteen

Deputy Chief Morgan Black read the email marked 'confidential.' A new sheriff in town had assumed her position as Chief. She didn't question the authenticity, since she was aware of the FSB security measures.

The demotion still grated on her nerves. Through no fault of her own 613, that blasted freak of nature, had disappeared on her watch. It could have happened to anyone, but luck had turned against her.

Singed from the demotion and the loss of J.T., her favorite boy-toy, her life had taken a spiral downward and soured considerably. Attempts to replace J.T proved unsuccessful time and time again. The insatiable need for an almost-alpha male left her tense and hungry.

Her fingers twitched on the keyboard as she scrutinized the email and couldn't tell if the author was male or female, but she could tell that the new Chief expected no questioning of his/her authority.

Her orders were to maintain surveillance on the Saffles along with several of their friends, and to document the process and any new leads in a daily email to be delivered no later than 1600.

She couldn't believe her eyes. This was the new head of the division? An introduction via a scrawny email? It contained no hint of caution for her past acts, no reprimand for her to stay within the guidelines – nothing.

The new chief appeared to be a patsy with no backbone. Her new assignment was a piece of cake. Sinister eyes narrowed as a smile crept across her face. She'd be back in her old job in no time, for this chief didn't have her tenacity, her commitment, her inner strength.

Fingers flew fast on the keyboard as she set up the required surveillance, and placed herself on the roster to monitor those in Wheeling.

Unknown to her superiors, Black had an ace up her sleeve. 613 may have escaped, but she wouldn't be at large for long. After the disappearance of the three detainees she marked for termination, she implanted a tracking device under the skin of 613 as an insurance policy. Black 'accidentally forgot' to log this piece of information in 613's file.

With a range of five miles, she needed to be close to catch 613 on the monitor. The weekend following her demotion, she followed her hunch on 613's whereabouts. As she suspected, she turned up in Waynesburg, first at the Saffle's place on the mountain and later at their farm south of the village of Waynesburg where she remained.

Unwilling to trust this information to another agent, Black took elaborate technological steps to ensure she could monitor 613 from her desk at the FSB. She rented an apartment in Waynesburg centrally located between the Victorian house, the mountain home, and the farm. The monitor was located there. After writing a short program that sent her emails whenever 613 changed locations, Black returned to Wheeling, WV to begin her surveillance.

She took stock of what remained at her disposal. Years of documented surveillance, live phone taps, and a small bevy of agents. No way was she down for the count.

* * * * *

On her third day of surveillance of the Hudson household, Black determined that there couldn't be a more boring family on the face of the earth. The woman, Katherine, stayed home most of the day, cooking, cleaning, and gardening, and only ventured forth to go to a near-by Kroger's to replace supplies.

The man, Ralph, left precisely at 7:45 A.M. each weekday and returned home at 4:15 P.M. He owned and operated Hudson's Accounting and had five accountants working for him. They handled corporate accounts mostly, but also managed a few prestigious charities. When he arrived home, he either helped in the kitchen or gardened before supper.

The daughter, Cassandra, managed the museum at Olgebay Park, and was so bouncy and happy, that had her curls been blonde, she could have been mistaken for one of the Bobbsey Twins. She was twenty-two and the closest friend of Alexandra Higgins-Saffle, whose abduction allowed an even closer look into the suspected relatives of 613.

Like her father, the daughter left every morning, but at 8:45 A.M., and returned home half an hour later than the father at 4:45 P.M. She arrived just in time to set the table, sit down, and offer the prayer before the meal.

They were gag-able, thought Black. If someone wanted to *really* punish her, they would make her a member of that drab, milk toast family.

Brown checked her watch, 4:40 P.M., her day was almost over, for once the family's lights went out at 8:00 P.M.; they clustered around the TV and didn't leave the house.

She scanned the avenue. Within a few minutes, the bright yellow Smart Car rolled into view. Could the girl have chosen a more sun-shiny color? Her whole persona reeked of 'mommy and daddy's good little girl.' Except for the rack on the girl, she could have been a perfect Stepford child.

The tiny car pulled into the driveway as the garage door rose. Within a minute, the garage door closed.

She reached to start the engine of the black SUV, but out of the corner of her eye she saw a car pull into the Hudson's driveway. Before the driver had a chance to get out of the car, Little Miss Sunshine ran out the front door of the house, down the walkway, and leaned into the driver's window.

Black's interest was piqued. The girl actually had a boyfriend, and by the length of the hello kiss, they were very well acquainted.

Finally, the girl leaned back enough for the driver to open the door. He got out, hugged Cassandra Hudson, and with his arm around her, walked her to the door. They both went inside.

Picking up her voice recorder, she pressed the record button and said, "Suspect Cassandra Hudson entertained a male, Thursday the 14th in her home. Unable to get a good visual. Will investigate. Late model black Lincoln has Ohio license plate HNS 4632."

Black kicked off her heels and pushed the seat back in the SUV to allow enough room to stretch her legs. She cracked the window and lit a cigarette. How late would the fellow stay? Surely the Hudson's wouldn't permit a sleep over.

She looked at her watch, and made a bet with herself. Nine o'clock; he'd leave by then.

Almost on the button, at nine the front door opened and closed, and the man got in his car and left. Perfectly respectable. She expected nothing less.

The lights in the house started to go off one by one. That was her signal to leave for the night. She'd check the license plate in the morning, as far as she was concerned, the night was young, and T.J.'s Sports Bar was open until two. Maybe she'd find some lonesome frackin' fella to share a beer with...

Chapter Twenty

The Piper Cub glided to a smooth landing at Greene County Airport and taxied to a parking spot near the terminal.

Dave Edwards and Ron Anderson exited the plane and headed for the administration building. Edwards stroked his chin as he read the sign for the building. Not only did it house the airport facilities, it also contained the municipal offices as well.

Behind the airport terminal, a sign indicated the Evergreene Technology Park was under construction and by the looks of it, neared completion. As fate would have it, he had walked smack dab into the luckiest scenario possible. If he couldn't succeed with this much good luck, he doubted he ever would.

Edwards looked at Anderson. "Do you believe it? Unless the earth opens up and we get swallowed whole, this set up is perfect."

"Tell you what," said Anderson, "even though it's late in the day, while you're setting up our facilities, I'm going to take a walk over to that Technology Park and see what I can find out. We could kill two birds…"

Edwards nodded, then turned and walked into the building feeling happier than he had in months. He took a seat in the lobby and using his cell phone arranged for a rental car to be dropped off. He checked his watch, it was just about five.

He heard the door to the building open, glanced at the man entering, stood and nodded. Without a word spoken, they disappeared behind closed doors.

Half an hour later, Edwards exited the building and noticed Anderson heading toward him waving the keys to the rental. A quick trip east on Route 21 brought them to an older EconoLodge. Edwards pulled in and groaned. Home definitely looked better than a motel.

Around 6:30 P.M. the gentlemen emerged from the hotel wearing jeans, tennis shoes, and casual short-sleeved shirts. They drove to a nearby diner and took a booth near the back of the establishment.

After ordering, Edwards cased the room. The occupants appeared to be mostly locals, and the ones sitting close had children in highchairs.

"What'd you find out?" he asked Anderson.

"I can have 2800 square feet of industrial space under my control within a week," he said.

Edwards nodded. "Good. My contact with the National Guard says they routinely do air mobility training out of the airport using helicopters." He winked at Anderson. "They've been routinely flying over the area in question for years." He grinned from ear to ear.

"You know," said Anderson, "I've never had an operation go this smoothly. Ever. An airport, a National Guard unit, a state-of-the-art technology center," he looked around the room and then back to Edwards, "I'm waiting for the other shoe to fall."

"If it'll make you feel better, there's still a lot of time for things to go wrong," he said.

"Okay, I'll shut up," said Anderson.

"How long do you think it will take for you to retro-fit the particle sensors on the helicopters?"

Anderson, paused, then said, "Under a week, I'd think. I'll need to get some equipment set up first. I can have it flown in, a day to set up, and then if the bird is accessible, it should only be a matter of hours for installation… Yeah, a week on the outside, if all goes *really* well, a few days."

Edwards considered the options. "Bring the thermal imaging sensors along and hook them up too. It might be nice to see how many people we are dealing with."

"How many of the, ah… how many do you think there are?" asked Anderson.

"I don't have any idea," Edwards said shaking his head. "I don't know if they're aliens, humans, some type of hybrid, or a natural evolution of mankind. So, I don't know what to call them either."

"You know, that woman, 613," said Anderson, "never aged." Awe showed plainly on Anderson's face.

He would have to curb Anderson's interest in 613's abilities. Interest could turn into other feelings and compromise their mission.

"Can you imagine the fallout from that one fact if it ever got out?" said Edwards. "What woman wouldn't want to reach her sexual prime and remain that way? What old geezer wouldn't want to remain in his best physical condition?"

"Everyone would want it," said Anderson. "You'd have it all. There'd be no more I-wish-I-knew-back-then-what-I-know-now." He paused. "Doesn't sound like such a bad thing."

"Yeah, almost omniscient," said Edwards, "until you think of it in the long stretch, population explosion, food shortage; and what about those who don't have the ability? They would do anything to get it, creating a whole new set of crimes."

The waitress delivered their meals. For a time, Edwards was lost in thought.

"Dave," said Anderson, interrupting his train of thought, "have you ever wondered whether or not we're doing the right thing?"

Edwards' face grew hard. Chills ran up his spine. He sipped his drink, calmed his emotions and said, "No. It's not my job to determine the right or wrong of it. My job, *and yours*, is to follow instructions and ensure the safety of our nation."

"That's just what I was thinking," said Anderson. "Safety. They've apparently been around for a while, and none of the stuff you were speaking about has happened. Do we really have anything to fear from them?" asked Anderson.

He wiped his mouth with his napkin and threw it down on the table. "Blast it, Ron. Keep your idle thoughts to yourself. Besides, if we don't assess their powers to see if we can use them for defense, someone else will."

"Defense?" said Anderson.

His eyes narrowed. Anderson had the innate ability to ferret out his inner conflicts and bring them to the surface quicker than anyone. He could feel the heat beneath his collar. He would not let his inner conflict between right and wrong determine the course of his career.

"Shut up, Ron," he said trying to control his indignation. "Don't take our friendship into uncharted waters. I don't need to be reminded of my humanity. We both carry the same heavy burden."

"Eating," said Ron as he scooped up a bite, "not talking." He took the bite and chewed.

Edward's deep sigh cut through the still air. He forced his thoughts to concentrate on the task at hand. In his own mind, if something isn't causing a problem, it should be left alone. But, within the boundaries of his job, he wasn't permitted the luxury of a conscience.

However, that dark-haired, dark-eyed devil that Magis described might be a different side of the coin. If their powers could also control someone's mind and hold their body rigid, shouldn't they be feared?

What other powers did they have that he or the FSB had yet to uncover? He made an assumption at that point. Rather than blindly accept, he would fear the unknown. He would assume the worst.

The question of whether or not to sequester these people was bigger than him; bigger than the FSB. Why was such an important decision left with just a small division of Homeland Security? Why not the whole Homeland Security team or the government? Why wasn't the President involved? Did the President even know?

He had to stop the random thoughts from running rampant through his mind. Blast that Anderson; he didn't need to be reminded of the consequences, he'd been unable to sleep through the night since this job fell into his lap. Was he in charge because he was competent yet expendable?

Why couldn't he just eat in silence? The food was already laying in his stomach like a lead weight. Lead weight. He'd give anything to be retired and fishing right now.

A bit calmer, his thoughts returned to the situation at hand. Security. The least amount of people to know about this mission, the better. The fallout from Area 51 taught the government hard lessons. So it was up to him and his team to make sure this operation went down in top secret history as a successful mission. Only those with the highest security level would ever know what happened.

If he failed in recapturing 613 and capturing the bulk of the others, the whole lid would blow off and probably end up in an all-out secret war between the FSB and them, whatever *them* was.

If he didn't fail, no, he refused to go there. His mind couldn't wrap around a world where a seemingly benign group of people were forced to do horrendous things.

It was too big for one man to control the strings. How had he become that man?

At the end of the meal, he sipped his coffee and looked at a sheepish Anderson. "Omnis, we'll call them Omnis."

Chapter Twenty-One

Balisier was quiet in the early morning. Those living there were not yet moving about. Jediah led Alexandra to the façade of a newly constructed building. The design was similar to many of the others, except the limestone, instead of being stained an earth tone, was bleached lighter to emphasize the veins of the stone. A similar technique appeared on very few others.

The interior of the new building was one large room, and one room on the second floor. Leaning against the wall was the sign for the new shop, which read *Escape Travel*. Boxes of brochures were piled next to the sign. Pictures of beautiful destinations leaned against the walls in various positions, awaited hanging.

Jediah placed his hand on the wall. The complete stone wall slid sideways and revealed a hidden room. Although the wall was made from stone and a foot thick, she didn't hear a sound as it moved.

"The wall face contains sensors that read palm prints for identification," said Jediah. "Only William and I can open this door, and only we three know of its existence. The interior of the door is filled with clay so the interior space can't be detected by ground penetrating radar or heat sensors."

The exact plan or need for the construction design evaded her, but Alexandra said nothing.

They stepped inside the room. As the door closed behind them, the interior lit and displayed a room that looked like a library, bank vault, or data research area.

One wall contained what looked like safety deposit boxes, yet they had no locking door on the front. The front displayed the name of a Sensate, the year born, and the year the Sensate ceased to be. They were stacked in chronological order based on the date of birth.

"What's inside?" she asked.

"Open one and you'll see."

She searched the boxes until she located her own, and pulled the drawer open. Inside she found a blank questionnaire form. As she thumbed through the questions she realized, that once filled out, it would be an autobiography which contained the thoughts, abilities, and specific powers of the Sensate.

She looked to Jediah, a million questions on the tip of her tongue. Before she could single out and formulate one, he spoke.

"When you were captured, we felt lost. We had no way of knowing what each Sensate was capable of doing, or how they could help. For centuries we kept our secrets by not writing anything down, always afraid of discovery."

"I can understand…," she said trying to grasp all the implications and sensed there was more to the story.

"But it also tied our hands behind our backs when we needed to amass the power to save one of our own." He hung his head. "We were slow. When we needed action, instead of flying to the rescue, we had to first access what we had. That information should have been at our fingertips."

"Wow, what a revelation that must have been." She looked at the information stacked in piles on the desks: family trees, areas of expertise, specialty powers, one-of-a-kind powers, and attached to each power was the mechanism that made it work.

Two desks contained state of the art computers. The genius of the idea hit her. They were cataloging the Sensates powers into a database for easy retrieval.

Jediah knew by the look on her face that she'd caught on to the process and said, "We can also try combining powers to create new ones. When you were abducted by Magis, we found out that Reslyn has a 'touch' power that allows her to act as a conduit. We were able to use power from one Sensate to enhance the ability of another."

A feeling of doom entered her mind, "What happens if this information falls into the wrong hands?" she asked.

"The paper from the questionnaire contains a chemical that blackens if the smallest amount of a specific gas is introduced into the atmosphere. Anyone entering this chamber without a proper hand print or the matching DNA signature, we just added that one," he said with a wink, "will set off a chemical reaction and ruin the printed information."

The process was exquisite and seemed perfect for their needs. William and Jediah certainly covered all the bases. Eager to know more, she asked, "The computers...?" She motioned toward them.

"They would receive a similar reaction to the chemical, but it reacts with a different trigger. Our hard drives are laced with an acid. Once triggered by the chemical gas, it reduces the information to a gelatinous substance; it looks like gray goo."

Alexandra's mind was blown. She thought the FSB had been tricky, but not nearly as slick as the Sensates.

"It's ingenious," she said. "It's a shame all the hard work would go down the drain if this was discovered, but knowing the accumulated knowledge won't fall into the wrong hands is really, quite reassuring."

Her eyes traveled once more over the massive undertaking before her. The hands-on knowledge base could be used by guides who assist new Sensates, by individual Sensates who wish to attempt abilities that others possess, and by their High Counsel to thwart opposition as in the case of the FSB.

She hugged her wonderful, amazing, hunk of a husband. He was the grand protector of the Sensates, and he took that job very seriously. "You and William did a fantastic job," she said. "Have the questionnaires been uploaded?"

"We are almost done. Just a few stragglers to finish up. Yours is one of them," he said as his eyes lit up. "Watch how sweet this process is..."

He grabbed a questionnaire and fed it into the scanner. A giant screen came to life on the wall. She watched as the contents scanned and the information was stripped from the image. The screen changed to one where all abilities were mapped out in flow chart fashion and linked to various trigger mechanisms. The latest additions were highlighted.

It was an encyclopedia of extrasensory perception, complete and unabridged. The information piqued her curiosity. How did her powers and abilities match up with this depiction of uniqueness? The knowledge alone of all the mechanisms displayed before her boggled her mind.

"You've been busy, I see," she said, not taking her eyes off the screen. "Whoa, this is really something else. I don't think I have words to even describe how I'm feeling, let alone express to you how important this information is."

His arms encircled her from the back and closed around her waist. She felt his lips on her neck as she spoke. "Honey, you've created the Sensate holy grail."

"It's pretty darned impressive if I do say so myself," he said.

"I certainly won't disagree." She turned to face him. "It's truly a great accomplishment; how did you think of it?"

"Once we started, it all just seemed to fall in place. Before we knew it, it morphed into this gargantuan piece of history. William was really against it in the first place, and I had to talk to him until I was blue in the face. But now, you should see him. He acts like a proud papa who had his first son. He wants to show everyone."

"William?" she said, "I don't know that I've ever seen him as happy as you're describing. That sounds like an accomplishment itself."

Jediah winked at her as he said, "It just might be."

A thought struck her. "Jediah…," she said while pondering the possible answers to the intended question, "wasn't Teater the leader of the Sensates before you?"

"Yes, he was. But when he failed to return, I was selected as the engineer of choice to carry on his work at Balisier."

She felt his eyes on her.

"Why? What are you thinking?" he asked.

"He's very powerful, isn't he?"

"Yes," he said, "next to you and Ryeth, I would say it would be a close call as to who was third, Teater or me." He bent to look in her eyes, but her face was looking down.

When their eyes met he said, "But you didn't answer *my* question, did you?"

"No, I didn't, and I'm not sure I'm ready to answer it even now. I'm still working through the process, and I want it to be more concrete before I get your opinion on its flaws."

"Alexandra Saffle, you are a minx." He kissed her nose.

"You're not angry that I don't want to tell you just yet?" She queried his eyes and face for the answer before he spoke.

One eyebrow raised as he smiled at her. "You're a competent Sensate and a good person who doesn't take risks lightly. I trust your judgment and will give you my total support in whatever you need me to do."

His voice and the message she heard was music to her soul. "I thought you resented me," she said, her voice barely above a whisper.

"No, love." He kissed her with passion. When he ended the kiss he said, "I thought you didn't need me."

Her heart jumped, did back flips and danced all at once. "Jediah, you are my rock; my safety net; my shelter in the cold." She laid her head against his chest and hugged him tight. "I couldn't exist without you."

Chapter Twenty-Two

The Prophecy consumed most of Ryeth's thoughts, and yet he wasn't sure where he could benefit the Sensates the most. If the truth be told, the hwihs on his shoulder that marked him as one to ward off the Prophecy, didn't feel like it truly belonged to him.

Before meeting Alice Jane, which encompassed centuries, he cursed that he might actually become involved in the blasted thing. After all, he wasn't a *real* Sensate, not like them.

His ethics were loosely woven and showed excessive wear and tear. The sense of family and community he possessed made up only a very small fraction of his life, unlike the healthy society that inhabited Balisier. He measured the majority of his existence by what he could do for himself, not in what he could do for others. There were no others.

Until Alice Jane. A sigh escaped his lips. If Alice Jane weren't so tied up with the Sensates, he could walk away and never look back. Heck, up until a few months ago, all he'd really wanted to do was snatch Nancy Jane's power from under their noses and walk away.

The most recent occurrence to shake his world came in the vision of his mother, Onatah, whose ties to the Sensates were unconditional; she had created them all. He was her last remaining direct offspring. All the others were descendants off the main branch.

Everything that stared him in the face was topsy-turvy. It all seemed out of phase; almost as if things were supposed to turn out another way. Estranged for nearly five hundred years from the group within Balisier, left him feeling more of an outsider than a son.

Ryeth tried to summon a better feeling of comradery with the Sensates, but the closeness was just not there. It was a suit that was too tight; the sleeves were too short, the cloth too shiny – even thinking about it, he grew terribly uncomfortable.

Alice Jane felt as he did. A smile eased onto his lips. Now *there* was a fine woman. Her independence pleased him, as did the rest of her. Although there were times when his skin crawled with the weight of the Prophecy, he was still the most comfortable he'd ever been in his life.

He had freedom, the love of a good woman… yes, she *loved* him. He was certain of it. Hmmm, what a satisfying thought.

The urge came suddenly. Ryeth bounded down the stairs and out the back door. His cantilevered deck overlooked a mountain range; visibility was an easy twenty-some miles. He created his orb and sailed upward, around thirty thousand feet.

At that altitude he knew he had enough oxygen in his seven-foot orb to last about twelve hours, but at that height, planes were a nuisance, so he only stayed long enough to feel separated from Earth before dropping lower.

He mapped out a voyage that revealed some of the most extraordinary scenery on the planet, but when they passed before his eyes, they mattered not; Ryeth was lost, deep in thought.

Hours later the orb landed and disappeared. His eyes rested on the tall and majestic shagbark hickory, his pawcohiccora. She stood erect; her arms reaching to the heavens; her roots firmly planted in rich soil and her bark loose, offering part of herself to those in need. Her limbs drooped, heavy with pods containing hickory nuts; she was a mother in full bloom.

Throughout the centuries, the rift created due to his parents' deaths helped to fuel the separation from his mother's people, and later, all people. His past had cost him in many ways.

Anger. Hatred. Revenge. Holding onto them was like drinking poison and expecting the other person to die. Wasted years; wasted energy; wasted life. Giving up the things that drove him for centuries made him question who or what was underneath?

Uncertainty consumed him. He considered Jediah a worthy opponent; his strength came from his character, his honor. The cantankerous Sensate, William, seemed to have his strength centered on wisdom and deep-thinking. Alice Jane's strength came from independence and self-satisfaction. And Alexandra, from miles away, reeked of goodness, purity, and compassion.

Trying to discover one's true self, Ryeth considered, was pretty heavy stuff. The items that filled his persona soured his stomach. In his present condition, he *wasn't* worthy of the hwihs on his shoulder.

How did one turn the tide of his life?

He looked deep inside. The resentment he felt for the Sensates came from not being part of them, from being on the outside.

The envy bred hate and further fueled the revenge. He had maintained that cycle and poisoned his insides for centuries. The act had not harmed them at all, only him. This was not the act of an intelligent man; it was the act of a hurt one.

Knowledge of his past wasn't enough to stop his poisonous cycle. He had to look deeper to find the truth. He sensed it happened at the same time the cycle started, so as hard as it was, he opened his mind to re-live, in detail, the day Nootau entered his life.

He remembered not being able to shake the notion that something bad was going to happen. The prickly feeling crept up the back of his sixteen-year-old-neck since early that morning.

Always aware of his surroundings, he saw his mother working at the edge of the field near the house, and his father on the opposite side near the forest.

As he bent over the garden row, a shrill Indian war cry broke through the peaceful air.

Ryeth turned to see an Indian brave standing over his slumped father wielding a knife in the air. He heard his mother's piercing scream as he ran across the field toward his father.

His giant strides consumed the distance quickly, and as he reached for the brave, his mother ran between them.

Ryeth's eyes locked on the brave, whose eyes grew wide. The brave shoved his mother away, and with a horrified wild look in his eyes, turned and fled into the woods.

His mother slid down, her knees buckling.

"Ma!" he cried; his heart clamored in his chest. He caught her in his arms and saw the knife sticking out of her stomach.

He gently lowered her to the ground, holding her close to his chest. His father lay lifeless at his feet.

"Oh Ma, stay with me!" he sobbed.

She spoke softly, "Ryeth. Remember…"

He watched in horror as she grabbed the hilt of the knife with both hands and pulled the blade out. As her lifeblood flowed she slumped to the ground. Her breath was labored. She held up the knife and whispered something so softly he couldn't make out the words.

"Ryeth." She gasped. "A great future awaits you."

"Don't talk, Ma. You'll be all right." Panic gripped him.

"Listen." She took several short breaths.

"When all is threatened, give this knife to one whose heart is pure."

Her breathing was shallow; her words almost inaudible. He leaned closer. She lowered her lids. As her chest rose slowly, he heard her whisper, "Don't forget."

Ryeth choked. "Ma, I'll do whatever you want."

She closed her eyes. He clutched her tight, tears streaming down his cheeks. She opened her eyes with one last effort and gazed at her son. He watched as her eyes grew dim, and she faded from his life. He heard her final words in his mind, *All is as it should be.*

The wound to his soul back then was apparent. The loss of his parents festered and oozed the same poison he drank for centuries to keep the hate and envy alive. All the toxic emotions aided him in survival, but were no longer needed. Releasing his rage allowed his mother access, but that alone was not enough. Hate and envy needed tossed out as well. The Sensates deserved that as a minimum; he deserved it as an act of self.

Ryeth remembered the man his father was; his strength, goodness, sense of fairness, and honesty. He pictured his beautiful mother, with her all-knowing eyes, gentle manner, and how she possessed wisdom beyond her years. He understood that now...

As he looked up from beneath the canopy of the pawcohiccora's leaves, he sucked in a great breath of air. When he blew it out, any reserves he had regarding the Sensates and his association with them dispersed in the breeze.

It wasn't necessary for him to meld completely with the lives of the other Sensates. He could aid them when necessary and count on them if he needed them. As long as he remained separate from their group he could maintain the type of lifestyle and ethics he desired.

He knew he was different; not an undesirable different, but a necessary one. His extraordinary abilities, skills as a survivor, and looser ethics positioned him as the Sensates' guardian against outside interference and corruption. Wasn't that exactly the role he already assumed? Without realizing it, he fell into the part naturally. It's where he fit, and where he was comfortable. An exaggerated sigh escaped his lips.

Hello, my son.

Ma, he said. Her voice was a caress; his name on her tongue, a blessing. A vision formed in his mind. The form grew from the mist. He recognized the shape of her doeskin dress. As it grew clearer, her beautiful face appeared. Long braids hung down her shoulders; her eyes, a warm brown. She reached out her arms, then pulled them close, crossing them on her chest. She projected her love and he received it in full.

He was blanketed in unconditional mother love. His heart surged and filled his chest.

They spoke of his life, and how, even though it blocked her from him, it enabled his strength, confidence, and survival.

Unable to withhold the question, he asked, *Ma, how are you here? How can you speak to me?*

I do not know the 'how' of it, I only know that when my life ended my spirit spread across the fields and woodlands. Many of your winters passed before I could make my voice heard to others. Though I could not reach you, I was always with you, my son.

Ryeth closed his eyes to still the emotions building inside. How it must have hurt her to watch as he struggled with his powers when she was unable to help.

I feared for you when the boar caught you by the arm and when you were tied to the stake. My heart broke when you were lonely, and sang for you when you danced holding the fish high above your head.

Ryeth smiled at the memory of the first fish he beckoned from a stream with his mind; he knew then, that as long as he lived, he would never go hungry.

Mother and son wiled away the remainder of the day. They talked of many things, of all things, of Alice Jane, and of their part in the Prophecy.

Chapter Twenty-Three

Most of Teater's days were filled with extensive visits with Ari. The remainder he spent in pondering.

The trouble with pondering was that it was filled with so many what ifs. In order to get beyond them, he pushed the 'what ifs' and regrets from his past aside and forced his thoughts only to the future.

Visions that used to come a mere two or three times a year, now came almost daily. They repeated the same message time and time again. Knowing exactly what was needed in no way boosted his confidence that it actually was possible.

He was responsible for the massive amount of power Alexandra would need for her part in the Prophecy. Though the vision gave him insight, he didn't know how she would use the power.

The vision didn't have to warn him of the need for secrecy. Any dolt could understand the consequences. In obtaining the power, not only would he bypass their honor codes, he also intended to bypass moral codes. If the others knew of his actions, unkind thoughts in his direction would be the least of his problems.

Once the plan came together, his die was cast. In the past Nancy Jane coupled her powers with his to perform the enchantments. This time, he was alone.

Teater transported to the site where his vision indicated the final confrontation would take place.

Leaves tinged with yellow and red hues signaled winter's approach, and the end of the Prophecy.

Once he assured no one was near, he sat amid nature's splendor and cast his first enchantment, and then touched one of the six stones surrounding him. He sensed the power leaving his body as he grew weaker. He swayed. His body slouched and his finger pulled away from the stone.

Teater became aware of his breathing first. With each breath, his energy returned, bit by bit. He blinked his eyes and in a few seconds, he was back to normal. His watch indicated 11:47 AM. The drain of his power knocked him out for a little over an hour.

Without thinking, he reached for the stone. When he touched it, it glowed blue. As soon as he removed his finger, the stone returned to normal coloring. The enchantment worked, but had a nasty side effect. The others would suffer the same loss of power and recovery. He would have to accomplish his feat while they slept.

Teater wrestled with the underhanded nature of the act, but when he considered the options, it ended up a one-sided judgment call. Stripping their powers did not compare with the loss of the Sensates' way of life. Hard decisions were necessary.

He transported himself back to the retreat.

The smiling face of Ari and Jonathan greeted him from the bistro table in the conservatory.

"Dad, you almost missed lunch," said Ari.

If he lived hundreds of years, he knew he would never tire of the word 'dad'. "What are we eating?" he asked.

"Jonathan's mother's chicken salad on rye, potato chips and pickles," said Ari.

"Sounds great," he said. He pulled up a chair and joined them.

Ari made him a sandwich and placed it on his plate while Jonathan added a handful of chips and some bread and butter pickles.

He leaned back in his chair and crossed his arms over his chest. "I feel like a king," he said.

"Don't get too used to being waited on," said Jonathan. "Ari already told me that this was an equal opportunity household. Everybody serves everybody else."

Ari flushed to the roots of her hair and busied herself rearranging the chips on her plate.

"There's nothing wrong in asserting your independence, Ari," he said, "nothing at all. As a matter of fact, I think it's a darned good thing you have that independence. It makes you the person you are. It also kept you safe."

Jonathan cleared his throat and looked her way. "I like you just the way you are. Don't change a thing."

One glance at the way Ari and Jonathan looked at each other was enough for Teater to realize he was the third wheel in the room. He finished eating, thanked his chefs, and walked to the stables.

He saddled Jediah's stallion, Ob, and rode out to check the fences. It wasn't long before the responsibility for the Prophecy filled his mind once again.

Jonathan and Ari. Jonathan was an Ultra and very powerful in his own right. Would Ari forgive him if things went wrong? Would any of them forgive him?

The once leader of the Sensates was glad he was leader no more. Although his path was crystal clear, the baggage that went along with it weighed a mighty ton.

The ride on the sleek black Persian failed to settle his mind. He made his way back to the retreat and unsaddled Ob.

The magnificent stallion stood before him, a symbol of strength and obedience. He compared himself to the horse and found himself wanting.

To steal power from those who trusted him was wrong. He knew it, yet he couldn't help himself, and he knew that his actions must remain a secret, if only to keep their small club intact. It would destroy the confidence the group had in their leaders if it were discovered that he'd done something so underhanded. All he could hope for was forgiveness. He cringed at the irony. All he did lately was ask for forgiveness, even when he couldn't forgive himself.

Later he crawled into bed and fell asleep with conflicting thoughts.

A mental clock went off inside his head at three in the morning. He was conflicted no more. Teater dressed and went out into the cool fall air. A breeze cut into his light jacket reminding him of the lateness of the season.

He transported to the stones.

As he sat in front of the second stone, he cleared his mind of all extraneous thoughts and concentrated on the mission. Teater touched the minds of the four Ultras to ensure they were all fast asleep. He performed the enchantment as he had done for himself, but this time he used a different mechanism to extract and transfer the power one at a time from Alice Jane and Jonathan. He placed their power in the second stone. It glowed blue against the dark sky for a few seconds and then returned to normal.

Extracting the power from Reslyn and MacAila, the remaining Ultras, he followed the same procedure and placed their powers into the third stone.

Teater paused to monitor all four Ultras until he was certain they had no more ill effects than he had. He breathed a sigh of relief and continued.

He wrung his hands together with grave misgivings of the next transfer. This one was critical, and he had no wish to wake the large uncensored Sensate. When he carefully touched on Ryeth's mind and noted he was well into the REM part of his sleep pattern, he smiled with the tiniest sense of security.

He took a breath. His heart pounded in his ears. Ryeth's power was almost as great as Alexandra's; if Ryeth woke, discovered his intrusion and the stripping of his power, he might be forced to defend himself. Teater would lose.

Maintaining secrecy regarding the enchantments was key to its success. The secrecy part seemed odd to Teater, for if the process was explained to the Sensates, even Ryeth, they would give up their power willingly, especially if it wasn't a permanent condition. Why he had to steal what was freely given puzzled him immensely.

With very soft footsteps, he traveled through Ryeth's mind. He performed the enchantment and placed Ryeth's power extract into the forth stone. A final touch to Ryeth's mind ensured he left undetected.

He relaxed his shoulders and shook off the tenseness. Glad to have that one completed, he calmed a bit before he went on to the next.

Only Jediah's power remained. Teater's vision didn't extend into the one remaining stone. It would obtain its power in due time. With the enchantment of the fifth stone to transfer Jediah's power complete, his job was done.

A fast re-check of all the Sensates stilled his worry regarding their safety and his stealth.

He felt dirty. The acts he had performed were against all he believed in and had turned him into someone who could no longer be trusted. Hope was all that remained; hope that he had done the right thing and that if the enchantments didn't work, that he would be forgiven.

He stood, dusted off the back of his pants and returned home. His obligation for the Prophecy was fulfilled.

Chapter Twenty-Four

As fast as the crates were unloaded, Anderson and his team had them unpacked and put into their proper space.

Edwards watched their facility take shape. He called his National Guard contact and nodded his head with satisfaction.

He yelled to Ron, who was headed in his direction anyway. "The bird's coming first thing tomorrow morning. You gonna be ready by then?"

"Yeah, I think so." He pulled up a folding chair next to the make-shift table Edwards had erected for his laptop. "I've got to tell you. I really didn't think things would come together so quickly."

"Pretty sweet, huh?" said Edwards.

"I can't speak for the accommodations which," he made a face at the folding table and chairs, "so far, are pretty crappy, but the technology stuff has been spot on." He leaned back on the folding chair, lifting the front feet off the ground. The chair creaked with stress. He sat it back on all four with caution.

Edwards scrunched up his face just waiting for Anderson to hit the floor. "I wouldn't do that again if I were you," he said. "Another ten pounds and you would have landed on your backside."

"Ain't that the truth," said Anderson. "So, what do you want me to install on the helicopter?"

Edwards rubbed his chin. "The particle sensor, thermal imaging sensor, and a thing a buddy of mine was supposed to send in from Langley. I think that's it in the box marked 'fragile'." He motioned to a small white crate with red lettering.

"What's in it?" asked Anderson.

"Supposed to be the latest in GPR, I think he said."

"What's GPR?"

"I forget," said Edwards. "He said he put all the documentation, instructions, and the schematics for the wiring in there. It's just something he wants us to test for him. As a favor, I told him we'd do it."

"Hmm," said Anderson, "it could put us behind a bit. I wasn't planning on any favors."

"Ah, if you can't get it up and running with the others, we'll add it on the next fly over," said Edwards.

Anderson stood, shrugged his shoulders and said, "We'll give it our best shot. I'd better get going if I'm going to get this business up and running."

He turned and walked toward the white crate. Edwards watched as he pulled a knife from his pocket and cut the straps. Anderson searched through the crate until he stood and waved a handful of papers at him.

Edwards turned his thoughts back to the printout attached to Ruby's email. If her database was correct, the immediate circle of friends of the Omnis could be as small as five or as large as twenty-five, if they considered those who attended the recent festivities.

613, who they'd held since 1958, was handed to them on a silver platter by the girl's mother, and Black enabled her to get away. 613 *had* to have

160

teleported out of there. Why she had taken the gurney with her remained a question.

As the thought struck him, he typed an email to Black and instructed her to present him with a mockup of what 613's room would look like if she were still in it. Then, he instructed her to pinpoint the severed connections for the IVs sensors, and any wires that were attached and mark the areas on a three dimensional drawing and send it to his email ASAP.

The next disturbing fact that faced him was teleportation. He knew Homeland Security had had their fingers involved in teleportation since 1993 when IBM Research published a paper on quantum entanglement. Although teleportation had taken place with photons, his need wasn't to teleport, but to stop teleportation from happening.

He placed a call to The PhD who had been involved with the IBM Research team, introduced himself, and explained to the good doctor what he hoped to accomplish. Forty-five minutes later, he had a possible solution.

"Hey Anderson, stop by my desk when you have a minute," he yelled across the floor. Anderson, whom he supposed was against yelling, merely waved and nodded.

Edwards continued his research, but now he was headed in a different area: multiphase diffusion lasers. When he took on the assignment, he considered the latest in technology, but had no idea he would be getting in so deep.

He heard Anderson clear his throat, and looked up to see him sitting alongside the desk.

"Look over my shoulder at this gadget. I need you to figure out how many we need in order to have the laser field encircle the Saffle's house and surrounding buildings."

Anderson's eyes bugged out. "Holy moly, Dave. Have you gone completely off your rocker?"

"Are you asking for more help?" said Edwards. He kept his tone flat and unemotional on purpose. It was one of his great joys in life to witness Anderson when he became unhinged.

"More help?" he said, shaking his head. "All you ask me is if I need help. Buddy, you need a strait jacket."

"You're not the first person to suggest that to me this week," he said. "I can have some additional engineers here tomorrow. How many do you need?"

"Fine. Get me two to start, and put an additional one on notice," said Anderson.

"Say, Ron, you're looking a bit frazzled. Are you getting enough sleep?" asked Edwards.

Anderson stood, glared at him and said, "Tonight we're going to sit down after supper and you're going to tell me what's going on. You know I don't like to be in the dark." He turned to leave.

Edwards grinned. "Will do, Mama."

Anderson gave him an obscene gesture and went back to his side of the room to complete his numerous tasks in the shortest time frame possible.

Edwards spread a map of the area over his desk. If his PhD was right, it just might work. Especially if they used the element of surprise and had the helicopters appear from different directions all at the same time. Once the Omnis were immobilized, they could be drugged like 613 and held indefinitely.

Edwards scratched his partially bald head, swore, and then patted his comb-over back into place. He had to find out how many Omnis he might be dealing with so he could prepare holding rooms – that is *if* his plan worked.

A slow exhale escaped his lips. His eyes roamed over the large space as it began to take shape and came to rest on Anderson.

He would never understand the man. Anderson had refused to accept a post as chief in another section, stating he preferred to maintain the working relationship with him. No amount of money could buy that type of loyalty or friendship. The informal duo would have a lot to talk about over supper, and for many hours afterward.

Chapter Twenty-Five

Three days later, the helicopter was ready to make its first pass over the Saffles' mountain home. Edwards notified the National Guard to begin the training runs at 1300.

Edwards and Anderson huddled over the computer screens. The pilot turned on the tracker. He took off heading east toward the Monongahela River, turned north as far as Interstate 70, and at Little Washington, turned south to follow Interstate 79 to Waynesburg. The other eight helicopters would follow the same flight plan at five minute intervals.

As the pilot neared Waynesburg, Edwards clenched his fists. The mountain came on the screen. The width of the scan covered the mountain completely. As the helicopter flew directly over the Saffle house, nothing happened. No red blip.

Edwards released his pent up breath through clenched teeth. The muscles in his hands relaxed as he realized his error.

"These don't make any sense," said Anderson. "The particle scans didn't pick up any indication of 613. I thought the trace particles in the gas were permanent."

"They are," said Edwards. "She's not there." He swore under his breath. "It's my own stupidity. I wasn't thinking. I'll have the National Guard repeat their training tomorrow. They'll need to change the flight plan to include the Saffle's other properties in the area in their scans. They have that old Victorian on the outskirts of Waynesburg, and that multi-acre horse ranch with the mansion south of the city."

He turned to the table where the maps were spread out. "If the helicopters leave the airport and head east, they can turn north at the Fairgrounds; fly over the mountain home first heading north, turn west to Wheeling, then return to Waynesburg via the quarry, cross the farm, turn north and cover the Victorian near the University, then back to the airport."

Anderson, who looked over his shoulder and followed the path, said, "That should do it. It will be a lot of maneuvers at once. Should we cut down on the amount of helicopters, especially since this is the second run?"

"Yeah," said Edwards, "maybe just two."

"If we don't locate her, aren't we treading on illegal thin ice?" asked Anderson. "We'd have no reason to sky-drop a Seal team on *any* of their properties without probable cause."

"Yeah, I guess things were going too good. I'll wait to kick myself in the butt until we see if 613 shows up tomorrow. Could just be a minor hiccup."

Edwards flipped his attention to the thermal imaging scans. As he reviewed the flight path, he caught a heat signature that looked out of place on the Saffle's mountain. He pointed it out to Anderson. "Do you see any reason for the heat signature on the eastern side?"

"It's fall, people clean up brush and burn it," said Anderson, "but the temperature isn't right, and it's much too large."

Anderson viewed another screen. "I don't see any activity on the mountain on the visual scan," he said, "I think the stone of the mountain is hotter there. Look at the vegetation in the area. The trees there have already turned golden and some a hundred feet away are still green."

Edwards stroked his chin. He looked at Anderson, who seemed baffled as well.

"Pull up some historical data from Google maps," he said to Anderson. "Take a closer look at that area and see if the changes are apparent in the spring as well. I want to know if the trees get their leaves there first, and whether the snow melts faster."

Anderson's fingers flew across the keyboard.

Edwards searched forestry GPS sites, and when he made his determination, he glanced at Anderson, who was making some fast calculations on a pad.

Half an hour later, when Anderson looked up, Edwards said, "They've got something big in there, don't they?"

"Yes, I think so, and if I'm correct, it's some type of power plant," said Anderson.

"How in the dickens did they manage that?" he asked, not expecting an answer. "Do you think it's nuclear?"

"No, nothing of the sort. Wrong heat signature, but a marvel nonetheless," said Anderson.

Edwards watched as Anderson walked around as if on air. He clenched his teeth and pressed his lips together as he sensed Anderson's admiration.

Anderson seemed unable to contain his jubilation. "Whoa ho, you've *got* to give them their kudos. "That," he said, pointing to the screen, "is one heck of an accomplishment."

Edwards couldn't believe what Anderson just said. He sounded like he was in awe of the Omnis. Edwards narrowed his eyes and kept his tone level.

"Let's not forget our mission," he said.

The smile left Anderson's face in a flash; no longer did his eyes have a glint of fascination. "I've got to get busy," he said.

"With what?" asked Edwards.

"Remember that favor your buddy sent you?"

"Yeah," said Edwards.

"It's a GPR unit."

Edwards looked at him and shrugged.

"It's a radar unit. Ground Penetrating Rader, GPR for short," said Anderson. "*It* has the capacity to find out just what's inside that mountain and give us some pretty good intel."

Following Anderson's train of thought, he could feel the satisfaction building in his face. Edward's lips moved upward into a half smile. Fate appeared to be shining on him once more.

"Why wasn't it hooked up for this pass?" he asked. Drat. Earlier intel meant a better leg-up on the opposition.

"A piece was missing, and I didn't find out until I was installing it this morning. The piece is due in first thing tomorrow. If you plan the training session about the same time tomorrow, it shouldn't draw attention. I can have the installation complete and the software loaded by then."

This whole scenario was turning out to be quite an adventure. First, he was handed an assignment that dealt with people who could teleport; next he discovered those people had built a power plant inside a mountain.

As much as he found the thought disgusting, he played with the notion to pay Magis another visit - just to tell him thanks for aiding in uncovering the existence of the Omnis. Without Alexandra's escape from Magis' clutches with no means of getting home, the FSB might not have moved as quickly. Coupled with the DNA confirmation, they had enough to begin the siege.

Another weird thought crossed his mind. Alexandra lived in Waynesburg, and a mere ten minutes away, lived Magis, safely ensconced in the Greene County Prison. He wondered if she knew her abductor was that close.

The snap of a laptop closing caught his attention. "I'm looking forward to tomorrow," he said to Anderson."

"Me too," said Anderson, "I doubt I'll sleep a wink tonight.

If the look on Anderson's face proved anything, the man was telling the truth. Anderson looked like a kid on Christmas Eve with big eyes of wonder.

"Get that goofy look off your face," he said as he scowled at Anderson.

"Why should I?" he asked. "We're entering into a new era, and I'm happy as all get out to be here on the front lines witnessing it in person. I can't believe you aren't excited."

"It's not my job to be excited," he said, a bit chafed that Anderson showed so much pleasure. "It's my job to follow instructions and keep our country safe from all harm, both foreign and domestic."

"Fine, you think about it your way, and I'll think about it mine…," said Anderson, "and I'm thinking that if they've been in Waynesburg long enough to excavate an area from the inside of a mountain of solid rock, build a power plant with no apparent entry, and have in no way threatened or harmed anyone, I can certainly be excited and enthralled with their existence."

As much as he tried, he couldn't fault Anderson in his reasoning. He was having trouble not joining a crusade for them as well, except that one dark-haired, dark-eyed devil kept him on track.

They had power. Mind bending power. And they could use their power against others. The fact that they hadn't didn't lessen their threat if they did decide to use them. Heck, for all he knew, they might bend the will of key personnel and change the course of governments. Maybe they already had.

Where did they come from? The power plant evidence proved their habitation of the mountain was very long-standing, maybe fifty or as much as a hundred years. Generations of them. They were multiplying. Was this their only facility or did they have others? Were they wide-spread as in global?

Thoughts of this magnitude gave him a headache. He could already feel the acid pumping into his stomach. Why did this have to happen on his watch? Why now? Seven or ten years down the road it would land in some other son-of-a-monkey's lap. Fate, kismet, or just plain bad luck. Whatever decided the ups and downs was definitely not on his side.

Why did he have to be the one to bring them down? He knew he didn't have the stomach to force the will of another. Put bad guys in jail, sure. Protect the country from terrorists, he was front and center. But this? Injecting people to knock them out, and holding them with no cause?

Yeah, he wouldn't sleep much tonight either, but he'd be danged if he'd tell Anderson that.

Chapter Twenty-Six

Since her demotion over the loss of 613, Black maintained almost the same interaction with her team. The only differences were her much smaller office and the inability to call the major shots. It was the second item that stuck in her craw.

As if that wasn't bad enough, J.T. was no longer accessible to calm her nerves. He'd been transferred to another unit in the FSB. Gone were the lusty insinuations at the office, which made for *very* long days, and the sating of her sexual appetite.

J.T. was the closest she'd ever come to idolizing a member of the male species. He had the physique of a Spartan and the stamina of an Eveready Bunny. He had suited her to a 'T.' She blew out her frustration in a loud sigh. It would do no good to miss what was gone.

Strict attention to her path going forward was required if she was going to serve crow to the higher-ups at the FSB, so she wiped all thoughts of J.T. from her mind.

Per the email from her phantom boss, she put together a team to carry out the mapping of 613's room and took a break from the Hudson surveillance to make sure the Dayton team understood her instructions.

As the technicians brought in a gurney and simulated 613's presence in the room, the 3D designer recorded the dimensions in his program.

Black kept a close eye on the designer's work and was surprised to see a pattern emerge from his drawing. Her pulse raced as she admitted the addition of new blood in the investigation was warranted after all. Left to her own devices, she would have missed an important piece of the puzzle.

There was one item Black figured she might never know: whether 613 left on her own, or was she taken like the others. If the other three were strapped down and had IVs like 613, would their beds have disappeared too?

Without being in command, the small details were out of her grasp. Only after the whole mission ended would the final report bring those tidbits to the light of day. Even then, if the operation ended with little green men inhabiting the planet, she'd never know. Black sighed. Her failure seared her butt in the fire, no one else's.

She turned to the 3D designer and said, "Send me a copy of that when you're done. I need to send it to the boss ASAP."

Back at her desk she composed an email to her boss. She re-read it several times to ensure it contained facts, no acid, and a tad of flattery. Just enough to let him/her know that the results of the drawing were informative and perhaps beneficial to the ongoing investigation, and that she was ready to help in any capacity.

A few hours later the 3D drawing appeared in her inbox. When she opened it, she was amazed at the outcome; the re-creation was unbelievable. In no way was she responsible for 613's escape. The technology that removed her and her gurney from the FSB was beyond their comprehension and technological ability. This was the work of an alien race or people from Earth who possessed superior abilities. If her boss came to the same conclusion, her exoneration was right around the corner.

Black attached the drawing to the email, sent it, and hoped the boss was a male and easily manipulated.

At 5:30 P.M., she left work and headed home, eager to check on 613's whereabouts. The girl's dot on the screen showed that almost every afternoon she ventured out of the home and traveled further each time. Today, she walked to the center of Waynesburg, and strolled the downtown section.

A glint sparkled in Black's eyes as an idea came to surface. She checked her calendar, logged into the FSB's employee site, and requested two weeks off. If only her new boss co-operated. She left the screen open as her thoughts went wild formulating what seemed like a perfect plan. Less than ten minutes later and much to her surprise, her request was granted.

Black's confidence soared. She grabbed a brown wig and dark glasses and placed them into a small suitcase. Next, she added enough clothing for a week, her laptop and binoculars. Finally, she placed a call to rent a car. Before leaving the apartment, she checked the cartridges in her Glock, returned it to her shoulder harness, grabbed a second clip and some additional ammo, and placed them in her handbag.

Elation filled the ex-Chief. Her vindication was near; she could almost taste it. Once she brought 613 back singlehandedly, they would have to reinstate her. Although she'd taken two weeks' vacation, a week was all she needed; she'd start with actual eyes on the subject and go from there.

Since Interstate 70 went directly through Wheeling, she dropped off the interstate and booked a room at the Hampton Inn. It was late; she decided to have a quick bite at the sports bar across the street and check out the local bubbas. She liked the men in Wheeling. They held the door for her, called her ma'am and, on the whole, were pretty talented between the sheets. She could use some country company; it just might improve her disposition.

As it turned out, as soon as she sat down at the counter and ordered a drink, a fella sat down next to her.

He leaned close and said, "I watched you walk in the door, and I thought, 'now there's a pretty lady, probably the prettiest in the room.' So I decided to stop by and tell you that. I won't bother you no more. You have a nice evening now, ya hear?"

The man turned and walked away.

Throughout his speech, Black hadn't taken her eyes off the stirrer in her drink, but when she sensed his departure, she glanced in his direction.

He was middle-aged with a full head of white hair, a bit pudgy in the middle, and carried himself away with a tired, sauntering gait. The inner part of her personality that she considered weak would have smiled, thanked him for his kind words, and asked him to join her for a drink; but the personality that controlled her waking hours wouldn't acknowledge his existence, let alone thank him.

An hour later, and after she'd determined no male in the place suited her, Black tossed a tip on the bar and left.

Tomorrow would come soon enough. She planned to spend the whole day surveilling the Hudson household. To date, she hadn't checked out their typical weekend activities, so a Saturday would give her a better picture of their lifestyle.

* * * * *

Black rose at 6 A.M. and strategically parked her car near the Hudson's home by 6:45.

With her high-powered binoculars, Black caught the daughter move the curtains aside to peek out the window. A few minutes later, the white Lincoln pulled in the driveway. The curtains fluttered again as the Lincoln's door opened and out stepped the boyfriend.

The license plate lookup indicated the car was a rental from the Pittsburgh Airport area, and rented by the Fox Chemical Company. Listed on the rental agreement were the names of six employees who could utilize the car. Among them was the owner of the company, Michael Fox, a chemical engineer currently residing in Washington, PA. Fox's record was pristine, and indicated he graduated with honors from Ohio State with a Masters in Chemical Engineering.

There was no way of knowing which employee was utilizing the rental, or if it was Fox himself. The other names checked out squeaky clean as well.

Black reached for her binoculars, but halted to catch the bouncy girl running into his arms. The boyfriend caught her, and using her momentum, swung her around.

The scene was dipped in chocolate syrup and had a cherry on top, thought Black. Disney could have written it for one of their princess movies. Before her teeth decayed, Black put the binoculars to her eyes. She'd dallied too long; the man's face was turned away. She followed him up the walkway, but his vision was centered on the girl and he never gave a backward glance.

Black pulled down the visor mirror. She didn't like the reflection with the sneer on her lips, so she softened her appearance, checked her make-up, and then slung the visor back in place so hard she broke a nail.

Swearing, she dug through her purse for a file. Time wore on so long with him inside, she completed all ten nails, and, had she been a contortionist, she could have done her toes as well.

What in Hades was he doing in there? Praying? Having breakfast?

Her eyes narrowed considering her next move. She decided in an instant. Other agents could monitor the boring Hudson household. With a quick note to her team, she assigned the task to a lesser agent, started the engine, and pointed the car toward Waynesburg.

Chapter Twenty-Seven

After the missing part of the GPR was installed, Edwards crossed his fingers that 613's red blip would re-appear on their particle tracker. He received the thumbs up gesture from Anderson, and notified the National Guard that the helicopter's new technology was ready to test.

The waiting game started anew. Both Edwards and Anderson were intent on the computer screens. Anderson focused his attention on the GPR screens, while Edwards' key to the operation centered on locating 613. If the lost Omni didn't show up, he wouldn't have the evidence required by law to support the continuation of the air surveillance. He could be shut down before taking another step.

The helicopter rose out of the airport, made a large circle, and approached Waynesburg from the southeast. As it passed the Saffle's horse farm, a bright red dot appeared.

Edwards gasped. "Anderson, she's there, at the horse farm." His breath hissed through his teeth. Satisfaction released the tension in his shoulders. "We're back in the game."

"Can't wait for it to pass over the northwest area. I'm on pins and needles over here," Anderson said.

Edwards continued his watchful eye on the screens as the helicopter flew beyond the farm and entered the city. He held his breath then gasped as the screen displayed a second red blip when the helicopter flew over the Saffle's Victorian.

"Blasted mother of a monkey," said Edwards, his eyes as wide as saucers, "there's a *second* blip on the particle scanner." He rubbed his chin as part of the puzzle found its proper place.

"Anderson, 613 had help," he yelled, then jumped when he turned to find him standing next to him.

Racing through his mind were a million possibilities, but only one held his attention. 613's escape was a two man job, which meant two Omnis existed.

Two who could teleport, and if the 3D drawing from Black was believable, they used a sphere about seven feet in diameter, to take 613 and her accomplice away. That blasted sphere alone possessed incredible technology. It was invisible, could maintain breathable atmosphere and pass through solid walls, maintained the ability to float to avoid floor sensors, and could accurately bypass the rooms' ambient temperature sensors. The technology or innate ability was impressive.

Was Magis' black-eyed demon the other Omni? From Magis' description, the over-sized Omni certainly had mind control over his victims. Was it possible for him to make a sphere with just the power of his mind?

A nit-picking thought hit home - if 613 needed help that meant the escape hadn't been Black's fault. The technology for the escape was well beyond whatever technology the FSB had at their disposal to detect. The creature who ordered the extermination of three human lives without batting an eye didn't deserve a reprieve.

He returned his thoughts to the screen and wondered if the particle gas spray he'd installed without Black's knowledge was inhaled by any more Omnis when they removed 613 from the gurney. An inward smile brightened his thoughts – he would've loved to have witnessed that.

"Holy catfish," said Anderson. "Look at that screen." He dropped into his chair, his wide eyes plastered to the images.

When Edwards peered at the Ground Penetrating Radar screen, he was dumbstruck as well. The mountain was hollowed out. The length was enough to hold a few football fields, if not more. Thermal imaging picked up rows of tiny hot spots. Layers of square and rectangle shapes filled the screens. His breath caught in his chest as he peered at the GPR's 3D screen and realized that the inside of the mountain contained a whole town. Some of the heat signatures looked to be vegetation, but the remainder was the real kicker - an easy hundred or so moving people signatures.

His mind came to a halt and refused to absorb any more. Edwards had to look away; he'd stumbled on the tip of an iceberg, for there was much more beneath the surface than he ever imagined.

Caution, the type associated with massive danger, gripped him by the throat. As he stood staring at the screen, he felt alone, singled out from the masses. There was no one to pass the buck to, this one was on his shoulders. Reflexes and instinct took over.

"Anderson, shut it down," he said in a voice barely above a whisper. "Get everyone out of here. Send them home; I don't care what you do with them, just get them out of here now." As he spoke his hands were busy shutting down the screens.

Anderson jumped into action. With quiet authority that came from years of military experience, he addressed each man individually.

Edwards watched as Anderson carried out his instructions in a thorough and efficient manner. He heard him tell the guys how much he appreciated their good work. He gave them the rest of the week off with pay, and as the last one left, he closed and locked the door behind them.

The information overload was beyond Edwards' comprehension. He dropped into his chair and leaned back. The repercussions of the discovery was enormous. What would happen to the sleepy town of Waynesburg nestled between the Appalachian Mountains? How many of the inhabitants were Omnis? How much had they infiltrated over the years? How many government officials were Omnis? Did the Omnis in Waynesburg represent a small sector of a larger group? Were they global? And, as his thoughts moved to self-preservation, he wondered if they were watching him? The thought sobered him.

Edwards was unable to wrap his mind around knowledge of this type and could conceive of no humane path forward, so he decided to do nothing. As far as he knew, only Anderson and he had any idea what lay beneath the limestone mountain.

"Grab any discs, flash drives and laptops and put them in the car. Put any printed readouts in that barrel over there." Edwards pointed to a used grease barrel. "We'll roll it outside and light it."

Half an hour later, the two stepped into the car. Edwards gripped the steering wheel and headed out of town. He took a road east and pulled into a golf course parking lot. Benches were placed along the tree line to watch returning golfers play the last hole. He walked to the farthest bench and sat down. Anderson sat beside him.

"What are you going to do?" asked Anderson.

"I haven't the faintest idea. I know what I *should* do, and that's my job. I can't help remember that movie, *A Few Good Men*. When it came down to it, the soldiers were supposed to protect those who could not protect themselves."

"Yeah, I remember that," said Anderson.

"They followed orders, yet were found guilty of 'conduct unbecoming' and given dishonorable discharges. It's a paradox. Sometimes, there is no real solution."

Though the men appeared to watch the scene before them, their eyes were vacant. The peace and quiet were lost on the two who sat so immersed in thought that they could have been in a hectic subway station.

The more Edwards considered the situation, the more he knew it was his responsibility to follow through on the operation. Men of his caliber made decisions that affected millions of unsuspecting people every day. Forty years of 'seeing the larger picture' prepared him for the unthinkable, the dirty, the creepy stuff from the dregs of humanity – but never for this.

Vibrations in his pocket upset his thinking process. He retrieved his phone and noted the call was from 411. "Yeah," he said into the receiver. "I understand… no, I have it under control from here… sure. Later."

Edwards pressed the button to end the call and said to Anderson, "Loose ends."

Anderson nodded.

Before he could return his phone to his pocket, it buzzed. He gave a huff when he read the request on the screen. As he authorized the vacation, he said to Anderson, "Black won't be in the picture, she's requested a vacation. What luck."

They both returned to their contemplative state. After a few minutes Anderson offered up a bit of thought. "Those Omnis must have been there for hundreds of years," he said. "The excavation alone must have happened over time, and then the buildings, so intricately laid out…"

"Where do you think they put the stone?" asked Edwards.

"Oh, you probably weren't looking, but when the helicopter approached from the southwest, it passed over a quarry."

Edwards picked at his cuticles and gave an almost imperceptible shrug. "They really had it figured out, didn't they?"

"I'll bet if we researched the quarry ownership we'd find out it belongs to one of them," said Anderson.

"Probably so…"

The question foremost in his mind didn't revolve around the Omnis as much as it encircled him. The decision of to-stay-or-not-to-stay.

He could easily wrap the information in a nice package with a bow, hand it to his superiors, and walk away, let some other poor fool handle it. But, if the next guy turned out to be someone like Black, would there be a greater loss of life?

Someone was going to go after the Omnis, and Edwards preferred it was, at least, someone with a conscience. His die was cast; he would stay and complete the operation; that way, he controlled the fallout.

He reached in his pocket and pulled out the car keys. "Ron, I have to do my job." The statement resounded his work ethic and pride in his career, but the decision didn't come easily. His stomach was shredded. From now on, he would not back down or waver. He would remain firm, even though the decision could cost him greatly in the years to come.

"Whatever you decide, I'll back you up," said Anderson.

"I know that, my friend," he said, smiling, "but that's about the *only* thing I know."

He stood, looked at Anderson, and sighed. "What do you say we grab a cheesesteak and some fries at that ice cream place we passed? I could really sink my teeth into something familiar."

"Sounds good," said Anderson. "Their ice cream is homemade; I saw it on the sign."

"Homemade." He pursed his lips and rubbed his chin and said, "Homemade is good."

Chapter Twenty-Eight

Spinning, turning, she grew larger and larger until the whole world lay before her feet. Alexandra woke in the early morning, the final part of her puzzle complete. Fate, kismet, karma, or some other unforeseen force opened its arms and shared her future.

Before she threw back the covers, she reached for Jediah. Her hand came up empty, but the bed was still warm. Savoring the last remnants of clarity before beginning the day, she soaked up all the information she could remember from the dream. Her path was now crystal clear.

The grand scheme was too big, certainly too big for a twenty-two-year-old, yet she didn't question her actions. Confidence filled every pore as she flew into action.

Scant minutes later, after verifying Jediah was gone for the day, she was in her orb: destination – the apartment of the young troubled scientist, Enoch Farmer.

The imprint she had of his mind brought up his location. She took her orb to his apartment building outside campus. After checking the hallway to make sure she wasn't noticed, she landed the orb, took a deep breath, and appeared outside his door.

She entered his mind to make sure he was alone. He was dressed, ready for the day, yet sitting on the edge of his bed. Alexandra sensed his conflict. Enoch was unsure how to begin another day, and wondered if he would make it all the way through without the overpowering sense of isolation impeding his way.

Her hand rose. It hesitated, but only for a millisecond. She rapped on the door, straightened her shoulders and prepared herself for what lie ahead.

She sensed his uneasiness as he walked to the door, and his unwillingness to answer.

Alexandra knocked again. The door opened. He appeared shocked to see her.

In an attempt to ease his mind, she held his gaze and spoke. "Enoch, my name is Alexandra and I need your help."

Enoch looked up and down the hall and said, "What do you want?"

"Can I come in?" she asked. "You aren't going to believe a word I say, so I'd rather not be overheard." She shuffled her feet, afraid he would shut the door. "If you prefer, I'll leave."

He looked down the hallway once again, then at her, before stepping aside for her to enter.

As he closed the door behind her, she looked over the sparse contents of the room. Reference books littered the floor, opened to various areas of interest. Computers lined a make-shift counter against the wall. A black leather sofa looked brand new and out of place in the work area that once sufficed as a living room.

Enoch motioned to the sofa. "You can sit there," he said. "Do you want something to drink?"

"No thanks."

He pulled a desk chair from the counter and rolled it to face her. "What do you want from me?"

"I'm not sure where to begin," she said. "I've never done this before, but if you consider the last eight months of my life..." she looked up to see she was losing him. "I'm sorry, I'm rambling."

She decided to take another tack. She read his mind: he wanted her to leave him alone.

"I can't leave you alone," she said. "Many people's lives depend on my actions."

Okay, crazy girl, time for you to leave. He started to rise from his chair.

"I do suppose I should leave, but I need your help."

Yeah, right. I can't even get out of bed in the morning and you want me to help you? Good luck with that. He stood, looking down at her.

"I have days like that too. Not every day has great beginnings," she said. Alexandra sensed he was going to ask her to leave, and then, quick as lightning his eyes told her he caught on.

He sat back down and looked at her, his eyes intense. *She knows what I'm thinking? Nope, can't be. It's a shame she's crazy, she's cute.*

Alexandra blushed. "Thank you," she said. "I promise I'm not crazy."

"Are you reading my mind?" he asked, his eyes as big as saucers.

Yes. I can talk to you this way too.

She watched as shock, then euphoria spread over his face.

We call ourselves Sensates, she said. *We have been in existence for over two thousand years.*

His eyes lit up, which transformed his face into that of a handsome, intelligent young man, instead of one with a tortured soul.

"Tell me more," he said.

Alexandra searched his heart and discovered he possessed a high code of honor; his integrity, above question. With warning bells going off like sirens in her head, she made the decision to trust him.

"This may take some time. Do you have to be anywhere?" she asked.

"Nowhere that's as important as being here with you right now." He leaned forward, his elbows on his knees. "Tell me, Alexandra, how can *I* possibly help you?"

He smiled. His personality spun in a whole new direction. This Enoch was charismatic, charming, outgoing and excited for the day to begin. In his element, where many things were possible, he transformed into a clear-headed, insightful genius.

She stood, stepped away from the sofa, and walked into the middle of the room.

She motioned for Enoch to come and said, "Please come and stand next to me."

Enoch rose and walked near.

She grabbed his hand and pulled him next to her side. Alexandra sensed his hesitation as she said, "Showing you will be much faster than talking."

Her sparkling blue and silver orb appeared and enclosed them in shimmering light.

To his credit, Enoch maintained a calm demeanor on the outside, but his mind emitted awe by the boatloads.

She grasped his hand tighter, and moved through the wall to the outside the building and rose high above the campus.

"Are you an alien?" he asked.

The question shouldn't have surprised her, but it did. She wondered why the thought never occurred to her when she met Jediah. Not even an inkling of her thought processes entertained that notion. Was Onatah an alien? Could they all be alien hybrids?

Now was not the time for her to question the Sensates' origins. In all honesty, that should have happened months ago. For now, she stored that question for resolution at a later time.

"No, we are all descendants from an Iroquois Indian named Onatah," she said. "I will answer any and all of your questions, but as we travel, I want to tell you a story."

Enoch glanced at the orb and then back to her. "You have a captive audience; proceed."

She laughed at his pun and began her story with the death of her parents while she was in college and continued to the present day. As she told her tale, she would sometimes stop in some secluded place and demonstrate an ability.

Several hours later she ended by landing in the arbor built with love by her great-great grandfather.

"I suppose you are as starved as I am," she said.

"Maybe for food, but certainly not for knowledge," he said. "You have filled in gaping holes in my thought processes that have plagued my existence and been the cause of many nights spent without sleep. There's a strong chance you have saved me from a mega crash and burn."

"Maybe you can return the favor," she said.

"Now that I understand your problem, I'll certainly try," said Enoch. "As I understand it, you can extract any data you wish from me, however the application and perhaps creativity are beyond your comprehension."

"Precisely," she said. "Let's go eat." She hesitated. "You know, I've broken a vow to all the other Sensates. I've told an outsider about our existence and I don't know what will happen if they find out."

"Let's hope that never happens," he said, "and if what you are considering actually takes place, your lack of discretion will vanish in the wind."

Once the two were sated, they continued with refining calculations, addressing communication needs and solidifying the process.

Before she dropped him off at his apartment, she asked, "Are you sure you don't mind getting involved? Some things aren't quite legal…"

Enoch took a few seconds to think over her question. "Alexandra, no laws have been written for what you are about to do, so that should be the farthest thing from your mind. Protecting the Sensates and their way of life is worth any risk. I am honored that you came to me, and proud to assist you."

He lowered his head and continued. "Thank you for my sanity. I was floundering quite badly when you knocked on my door this morning."

"I know, I sensed your anguish." She hugged him. "I don't sense it anymore. So, we're on for the remainder of the week?" she asked.

Enoch smiled and said, "Count on it. You can always consider me a friend."

Warmed by his heartfelt words, she created the orb and transported him home, an easy task. Living with subterfuge of the Sensates would be another matter altogether.

Chapter Twenty-Nine

Ryeth sensed the change in their world. Something major regarding the Prophecy had shifted. As he questioned the shift, he heard his mother's voice, *All is as it should be…*

He shook his head. Conversations with Onatah about the Prophecy, while informative, left Ryeth with numerous questions regarding his part. She made it clear that his job was to locate the 'one that's close' who could ruin them all. Although she had some semblance of the future, she couldn't see anything with clarity.

Since he had access to Balisier, he created an orb, made it invisible and entered. He spent time with every Sensate on the premises, listened into their conversations, and got a sense of the personality of each without their knowledge. He still didn't have a clue.

He made a quick trip to the FSB headquarters in Dayton and checked in on Black. Although she seemed reconciled with her demotion, he sensed she was more concerned over the loss of her 'boy toy.'

The woman disgusted him. Ryeth couldn't believe J.T. actually hung around *that* long. The man was well-built, handsome, had a good job, and according to Black, a woman satisfier. Why J.T. wasted time on her was a mystery.

Ryeth followed her around for the majority of the day and found out that the new head of the FSB division remained anonymous. The only contact Black had with her boss was via email.

Jediah?

I'm here, Ryeth, what's up?

Are any of our group hackers? he asked. He sensed Jediah's concern.

No, not in the way you're asking. We have several that are very computer savvy and who have written security programs, but it really isn't our way to go where we shouldn't.

Drat, that blasted moral dilemma thing again. He felt his ire beginning at the nape of his neck and pushed it back down.

Thanks, I'll come at it from another direction.

Can I help in any way? asked Jediah.

I'm trying to figure out who's the new head of the FSB. I'll give a holler if I need you.

He broke the connection when he realized adhering to their principles would always be a struggle. He understood them – even admired them, but *no way* did he want to be them.

There had to be a reason for the shift he'd sensed. Perhaps the other with the hwihs had answers.

Alexandra, is there anything you need to tell me?

He smiled as he sensed her indignation. *How did you know?*

Ryeth sent her an image of himself with his chest puffed out and made his voice deep and resonating. *I am Ryeth, Sensate with hwihs on shoulder. Do not mess with me or I will appear with long black leather coat.*

Her humor rolled through his mind.

I'll meet you at your tree, she said.

When he appeared at her side she said, "You are incorrigible. Far worse than Jediah."

"What have you been up to?" he asked.

"Oh for heaven's sake, do I *have* to tell you?"

"No, you don't have to, but if it has anything to do with the Prophecy, I think you should."

She walked up and down the path and stomped her feet in the dirt, refusing to meet his eye.

"Blast it, I absolutely *hate* getting caught doing something bad," she said. "It's bad enough to do the bad thing, but to compound it…"

A picture of a young girl with her hand caught in a cookie jar went through his mind. He said, "Stealing a cookie is not so bad."

"Ryeth, it's much worse than stealing a cookie."

Ryeth sensed her defeat as she plopped down in the moss next to his tree. "Okay, little girl, out with it."

"I told someone I was a Sensate." Her words exited her body like they were propelled. "I made an orb, flew him all around, told him about all of us and the Prophecy, and then dropped him back at his apartment."

His hand flew to cover his mouth in mock astonishment. "You're going to get thrown out of the club."

"Oh stop it. It may not be a big thing to you, but I gave my word… and I broke it."

Ryeth sobered. "Alexandra, sometimes we have to break our word for the greater good. We can't adhere to a set of rules all the time, especially when decisions to protect others have to prevail. You must have had a good reason."

"Yes, I did." Her words were a whisper.

"Did you do it for the Prophecy?" he asked.

Alexandra's shoulders relaxed just enough to let him know her tenseness was fading.

"Of course. I needed his mind. Not just the part I could take, but the creativity to use what I had taken. I just don't have his ability to apply the knowledge; I don't have his experience. I had to trust him. And he's a good man, Ryeth. He needed me as much as I needed him."

He looked at her out of the corner of his eye. "You know what you have to do to avert the Prophecy, don't you?" he asked.

"Yes. I don't know how, but a little at a time, things become clear to me. I know what I have to do. I don't know when, but I know how and where."

Ryeth looked at the girl sitting at the foot of his majestic tree and realized how very small she was by comparison. A huge amount of responsibility rested on her shoulders. She was the core around which everything revolved. Even his part was secondary to hers, a mere Sensate of a few months; compared to his lifespan it didn't even qualify her as a novice.

His part was to support her at all costs. Above his precious Alice Jane, and above his mother, regarding the Prophecy, Alexandra came first.

"Like you," he said, "I've been receiving pushes to do certain things. I had a long talk with Mom; she really is a wonder. When I think of the years I missed with her just because I carried around so much mental garbage, I could kick myself."

"I'm so happy for you Ryeth. Without knowing it, Onatah was a source of strength for me during my darkest times. That her spirit survived throughout the centuries is miraculous. I'm proud to know she is part of me."

He fumbled a bit, but then decided to ask, "Can you tell me what you're planning?"

"I don't think so," she said, "not because I don't want to or I think you're unworthy, it's because I think others aren't supposed to know. It might upset the balance of things and stop the solution from working."

She scratched her head and shook her full head of hair as if it might somehow rearrange everything and have it make sense.

She stood and looked up at him. "So you don't think I'm terrible for telling?"

"I don't think you have a bad gene in your whole body; you are completely free of malice."

He reached out, took her in his arms, and hugged her; he knew, if it came to it, he would give his life to aid her.

She stepped back. "Thanks, Ryeth, I needed that. I'd better get home, Jediah's on his way. Tell Alice Jane I said 'hello.'"

"Will do."

She disappeared from his view. That conversation was a revelation. If Alexandra knew her part, the time of the Prophecy couldn't be far off.

Before he went in search of Alice Jane, Ryeth took a few minutes to check in on the nighttime activities of his favorite FSB agent.

The vision through her eyes indicated she was driving across Interstate 70. He caught a road sign; she was heading east and currently 17 miles from New Stanton, PA. She was heading in their direction. Ryeth sensed a feeling of total satisfaction coming from the human deviant.

An uneasy feeling crept up the back of his neck as he entered her thoughts.

Her mind was occupied formulating plans for a recovery operation. It entailed Black and a small hand-held canister of xenon gas.

Black's plan was to simply walk up to the front door of the Saffle's farm house, and when she was face to face with Ari, spray her with the xenon gas. Black counted on her disguise of a wig and glasses to be enough for Ari not to recognize her. Once Ari was disabled, Black would drive Ari back to Dayton.

After his last experience with the FSB, Ryeth was well-versed in that particular gas. His eyes narrowed; the belly-crawling creature was at it again. Pushing further into her mind he came upon her initial plans, which she intended to act on sometime within the next two weeks.

He blinked and caught his breath as he realized Black had implanted a tracking device in Ari.

Blast it! It was a gaping loophole the unsuspecting and honorable Sensates failed to uncover. Again, they played by one set of rules, while Black and the FSB played by another more ruthless set. He couldn't have the device removed from Ari without tipping his hand.

Luckily, the tracking device had a limit of five miles and the base unit was centered in Waynesburg. All he had to do was get Ari out of the village when the time came.

He orbed to Black's apartment in Waynesburg to check out her set up. On the table of the sparsely furnished room were the house plans for the Saffle farm, a hand-held gas mask, and the canister of xenon gas.

The canister was small, about three inches tall, and came equipped with a directional nozzle. Ari wouldn't have a chance.

A menacing scowl spread over Ryeth's face. The woman was toxic, and he had to admit, sneaky. She had no plan to alert the FSB of her discovery. Re-capturing Ari was her means of getting her old job back.

As the knowledge of her actions settled in his mind, he considered her a nuisance, nothing more. She hadn't set the date of her mission, but he was sure it would happen before her 'vacation' ended.

All he could do until then was wait and watch Black every minute of every day for the next two weeks.

Chapter Thirty

The weekend of Cassie's visit to Heartseed had at long last arrived. Although Alexandra enjoyed the evening of the housewarming with Cassie and John, it wasn't the same as plopping down on a bed and sharing the intimate details of their lives. She would have more time to spend personally with Cassie.

Cassie's parents had even stepped in to become pseudo parents after her own parents' deaths. To say she owed the girl her eternal love seemed an understatement. The buxom girl with bouncing brown curls warmed her heart and recharged her soul.

Alexandra's heart leapt for joy as she heard the security buzzer for the gate at the bottom of the mountain and buzzed them in. She had a good five minutes before their arrival, so she ran to the freezer and made fruit smoothies for four.

Jediah, they're here.

Coming, love, he said and appeared at her side.

"My beautiful wife, you are simply beaming," he said, grabbing her from behind and giving her a welcoming hug.

"Get out the fat straws for the smoothies, would you please?"

"Yes, ma'am."

She looked over her shoulder to see her dutiful husband snap to attention and retrieve the straws from the cupboard.

"Oh, I'm sorry, I don't mean to bark commands, I just want everything to be perfect," she said.

"I know you do," he said. "I often forget how close you and Cassie are. I'm sure you miss her a lot."

Miss her a lot? If there ever was an understatement that was it. It wasn't just the missing of her physical person, it was so much more than that. Cassie and her family were the tether that kept her grounded after her parents' accident. With no close relatives, or siblings, at eighteen Alexandra was left alone in the world. They were the only family she knew for four years until she met, and fell instantly in love with Jediah.

Jediah and the Sensates took over where her parents left off. They supplied security and opened their arms to her, providing a full complement of pseudo aunts, uncles, mother and father.

But even with all that the Sensates meant to her, it was not the same as her life-long friend, Cassie. She could be herself without being judged. She could talk to her about everything... not so anymore. Alexandra had a whole section of her life that Cassie would never know existed.

The loss saddened Alexandra. Try as she may, the hurt remained, for she could never have that closeness with Cassie again.

"This weekend will hold me for a while," said Alexandra, "but you are right, I miss her terribly."

She placed the smoothies on the counter, put a straw in each and went to the front door to greet her guests just as the doorbell rang.

Squeals of glee shot through the air as the two ran into each other's arms, quite unaware of the two men shaking their heads.

Their conversation continued as the four walked into the kitchen.

"Smoothies for all," said Alexandra.

"Oh, let's enjoy them on the back deck," said Cassie, "we may not have many beautiful days like this left this year."

"The colors coming up your driveway were something else," said John.

"The whole trip was gorgeous," said Cassie. "Just a few days ago everything was still green."

As Cassie stepped out onto the deck, Alexandra saw her look around in wonder. "Wow, if you would have kept this all to yourself and not shared this autumn splendor, I might never have forgiven you."

Alexandra said, "I can't wait to see the view when all the leaves are down."

She led Cassie to a far point on the deck, out of hearing of the men.

"I've invited some people to dinner tomorrow," she said. "Alice Jane and her friend, Ryeth, and two other distant relatives of Teater's that I located just recently."

"That sounds nice. Are you cooking?"

"Are you kidding? No way. I want to spend time with you and John. I'm having it catered, so I can relax. As a matter of fact, I've hired help for the whole weekend."

"I can remember a gal, not too long ago, who wouldn't spend a drop of that 'blood money,'" said Cassie.

"I don't have that money anymore. I used most of it to build this house, and the rest, I gave to St. Jude's." Alexandra remembered all too well the compensation given to her by the coal company for causing the sink hole that swallowed her parents and home. "I'm using Jediah's money."

"What about the money Teater left you?" asked Cassie.

"Saving it," she said. "You never know…"

A fall breeze whipped Cassie's curls around; when they settled, she was as gorgeous as before, not a hair out of place. "Give me the scoop on Alice Jane's friend."

Alexandra had to grab her hair and hold it so the breeze didn't cover her face with hair. She pulled a strand from her lips before she spoke. "Well, you first have to admit that Alice Jane is no slouch in the looks department," said Alexandra.

"Well, heck, yeah," said Cassie. "That's a given; she's stunning."

"Then imagine a tall, dark, brooding male, four inches taller than Jediah, and reeking pheromones similar to those of the Pied Piper. *Then*, you might have one tenth of an inkling what Ryeth is like."

"Oh my…" said Cassie, placing her hand on her chest. "If your description is for real, I can't wait."

"It's real. You will not be disappointed."

Tangent thoughts of a different disappointment crossed her mind. Two times before the pregnancy test had been negative. This time, her body was sending signals.

She grabbed Cassie's hand, and yelled to the guys, "We'll be right back."

Maybe the timing was off before, but with Cassie at her side, Alexandra felt more positive than ever.

"What's going on?" said Cassie.

When they reached the bathroom, she shut the door, reached into the linen closet, and pulled a pregnancy test from behind the towels. She held it up and said, "This."

"Do you really think you might be?" asked a super excited Cassie.

"Yep." Her heart beat so loud she thought the guys might hear it on the deck. She sensed Cassie's excitement, which increased her own.

"How long does it take?" asked Cassie.

"Three minutes."

"Get to it… I'll watch the time."

Three minutes never felt longer. After wetting the strip, she placed it on a paper towel on the sink. They turned their backs to the strip as they watched the clock. When three minutes were up, they spun to see the results.

Alexandra was stunned, unable to speak. She heard Cassie say, "Allie, you're going to be a mommy."

Excitement filled the air. Cassie cried. Alexandra cried. They hugged and danced together at least a million times before they heard the knock on the door.

"Everybody okay in there?" asked Jediah.

"Be out in a minute," said Alexandra. "Cassie's bra strap mal-functioned."

Cassie pushed her arm and whispered, "Why does it always have to be my clothing that goes south? Can't it be yours this time?"

"Ssh, goof, he'll hear you," she said. Jediah's footsteps paced back and forth.

Cassie whispered, "How many times over the years have I pretended to have a bra mal-function? I'll bet it's been 10-15. You really need to come up with a better story. I don't think my mom *ever* believed you."

"What are you yammering on and on about?" Jediah yelled. "Get your lovely butts out on the deck."

"One more sec," she yelled through the door, 'we'll meet you on the deck." Alexandra listened at the door. Finally, his steps grew softer as he returned outside.

Alexandra turned to her sweet friend and kissed her on the cheek. "I'm going to have a baby!"

She performed a celebratory dance with her arms held high over her head. Cassie joined her. After they re-checked their makeup, the two friends hurriedly hid the evidence and returned to the deck.

"Sorry we took so long," said Alexandra to Jediah, "sometimes we just need a bit of 'what used to be' to fill our buckets. Won't happen again," she squeezed his arm, "my bucket's full."

"Mine too," said Cassie. She walked over to John and looked up at him. "My bucket is brimming."

Chapter Thirty-One

The following day, Cassie, John, Jediah and Alexandra relaxed on the deck, played euchre, hiked a few trails, and had crossbow competitions.

About four they separated to opposite sides of the house to get ready for the dinner party.

Alexandra and Jediah entered the deck to see John arrived first. He was leaning against the far post talking on his cell. When he caught sight of their approach, he ended the call.

"You have got to be the fastest dresser in the east," said Jediah. "In my defense, I did stop to smell and admire the roses on the way."

Alexandra blushed and felt the hairs rise on her arms. "He *did* smell the roses," she said, "and he actually cut some red knockout ones for our centerpiece. Anything else inferred from his statement was purely false bravado."

"Ouch, woman, you cut me to the quick," said Jediah, faking a wound to his heart.

She laughed. "Just keeping you honest."

The gate buzzer sounded. Jediah stepped into the house to open the gate.

"Cassie tells me Alice Jane has a significant other," said John.

"Yes," said Alexandra, "they seem well suited. You'll like him; he's a man's man." She stopped to think, then said her thoughts aloud. "As a matter of fact, if I were to consider all the men who are coming today, I'd categorize them as alpha males. But Ryeth, he'd be the alpha's alpha."

"Whoa, that's some statement," said John, "you better not let Jediah hear you."

"I'm sorry, I didn't realize I said that aloud." Her chest rose and fell quickly; her face flushed.

"I won't tell if you won't," said John.

"What won't you tell?" said Cassie from the doorway.

John turned to Cassie and said, "That you are the most enticing woman I have ever met." He took in the view before him and smiled.

Cassie went to his side. His arm wrapped around her shoulders as he kissed her cheek.

The sight of her best friend so in love with John made Alexandra feel warm inside. Somehow, it eased the longing for Cassie, knowing she had a shoulder to lean on.

John had appeared in Cassie's life just about the same time Jediah entered hers, though she doubted John made the same type of impact.

Jediah came back onto the deck, followed by Teater and Ari.

Alexandra noted John's reaction to Ari's ivory face, cool blue eyes and flashing red hair. It was hard *not* to be drawn to the magnificent beauty.

"John and Cassie," said Jediah. "I'd like you to meet Teater and Ari Higgins, fifth and fourth cousins of Alexandra's. They, themselves, are cousins and newly acquainted."

The buzzer went off again. Jediah excused himself once more and went to release the gate.

Teater stepped forward to shake John's hand. Alexandra welcomed Ari with a hug.

"You've chosen a beautiful day for your dinner, Alexandra," said Teater.

"Thank you," she said. "I ordered it specifically for us."

"You can do that?" asked John.

"I certainly can," said Alexandra, "I keep Mother Nature on speed dial."

"Yeah right," said Cassie, "just like you did for our Senior Picnic in high school. That record for the most rainfall in a twenty-four-hour period will *never* be broken."

"That was a horrible deluge," said Cassie. "Remember Wheeling Hospital's walls caved in on their new building? If you had any control over Mother Nature, you wouldn't have allowed that to happen. So, to quote James Gardner in *Murphy's Romance*, 'take another tack, Emma.'"

Alexandra noted the blank looks on Ari and Teater's faces. "I don't think everyone watches as many movies as you and I do, Cassie. But I will admit, that if you haven't seen James Gardner's films, you are missing a slice of life that you need to recapture."

"I'll put him on my list of movies to see," said Ari.

"Say Ari," said John, "that's a beautiful name."

"Thanks," she said, "it's short for Arizona. I think I was named after some distant aunt."

Jediah cleared his throat from the doorway, "I'd like everyone to meet my sister, Alice Jane, and her friend, Ryeth Garmendia."

Alexandra walked over to them. She hugged Alice Jane, and received a hug and a kiss on the cheek from Ryeth. She stepped back, and while they made the rounds to greet the others, Alexandra reflected on her relationship with Ryeth.

She loved him, just like she loved Alice Jane. He was strong, smart, and reliable, not to mention that he also wasn't bad to gaze at. His walk was like that of a panther, calculated and sure.

When the thought hit her, she became instantly at peace. Ryeth was the older brother she'd always wanted. No wonder she was proud of him and understood his moods, they were of the same direct lineage.

So struck was she with emotion, she needed an outlet. She stepped over to Ryeth and touched him lightly on the arm. When he turned she whispered, "I love you."

She sensed his astonishment, then his understanding. "I love you too, Alexandra. We are one and the same." She patted his arm.

As she looked at the others on the deck, she spied Cassie motioning to her to come over to John and her.

"What's wrong?" she asked Cassie.

"I just wanted you to know that you didn't disappoint me with Ryeth. What a hunk. He and Alice Jane look like they stepped out of a magazine. They could easily be a New York power couple."

"What does he do?" asked John.

"I'm not really sure," Alexandra said, "although I think he's independently wealthy."

The evening was off to a great start, she thought. Friends, family, a beautiful evening, a fantastic meal and a baby on the way. Life was *very* good.

* * * * *

Ryeth heard a familiar voice as he walked through the room. As he stepped onto the deck, he located the man whose voice he sought. Their eyes locked for a brief second as he realized the man had eyes on him as well.

He reached for Alice Jane and after greeting their hostess, escorted her onto the deck toward the drink bar.

He entered the man's mind without so much as a second thought and located proof of the man's treachery.

John Ryan, or J.T. as Black called him, was an undercover agent for the FSB.

The knowledge gave Ryeth no satisfaction whatsoever. Cassie was Alexandra's best friend, and she was totally in love with the worm.

Although the guttural low life had real feelings for Cassie, the thought did little to suppress his loathing for the man who also maintained a relationship as a 'boy toy' to Black.

Considering the intrigue, Ryeth thought he just might not be bored.

Jediah, Teater. Cassie's friend, John, is Black's sleeping partner and an agent for the FSB.

He sensed both men's increased alertness.

You're sure? asked Jediah.

Yes, Ryeth answered.

Tell Alice, said Teater. *Have her listen to his every thought.*

I'm going to excuse myself, said Jediah. *I'll get Jonathan busy checking out the house for bugs. We're aware of those at Larkspur, but this is a new wrinkle.*

Too bad for Cassie, said Teater.

Too bad for everyone, said Ryeth.

Both Black and John Ryan made a sizable wrinkle in the Sensates' security. Though Ryeth considered Ryan the most severe threat, Black's plans required squashing as well.

The High Counsel was aware of Ryan, but Ryeth kept Black's intrusion secret. He wanted the pleasure of thwarting her efforts all to himself. As his eyes narrowed, a slightly wicked smile formed on his lips.

Chapter Thirty-Two

As soon as John and Cassie left for home, Jediah whisked Alexandra out of the house. He took her to the secluded place in the woods near their home she'd discovered while learning her powers.

He turned her to face him and said, "John Ryan is an FSB agent. Ryeth recognized him from his surveillance on Black."

Would the FSB never leave them alone? She walked away and sat on a log. "What a mess. Poor Cassie," she said, then considered her words. "She can't ever know he was using her to get to us. She *loves* him."

"Jonathan swept the house and found seven bugs. Of course, we're leaving them where we found them."

"I don't like walking on eggshells in my own home," said Alexandra. "It's invasive and cruel."

Jediah paced across some fallen leaves. The crunch seemed deafening in the stillness of the woods.

"Alexandra, I've kept quiet about a lot of things, wanting you to find your own way without my interference. But I sense the Prophecy is getting closer and I don't know what your plans are."

She dropped her head. There was no easy way to tell him that she could not confide in him.

"Jediah, I really don't know what to say. If I tell you that I am certain of my path, will that be enough for you?"

He dropped his arms and shoved his hands into his pants pockets. Her heart ached because she couldn't share many things with him, especially since they had vowed to have no secrets. Her inner self was afraid the outcome could be altered if they knew.

She only had one chance to save them all, and if she failed, all would be lost.

"I can tell you this, Jediah. We each have a part to play. If any one of us fails in our responsibilities, we put our whole community in the hands of the FSB. I have been driven to complete my part. Ryeth has felt the same compulsion. I don't know what his part is, nor do I know yours or anyone else's. I'm locked on this path and I'll see it through for the good of all Sensates." She stood, reconciled. "I can tell you no more."

"Thanks love, I understand. And now that you've brought it to mind, I can tell you that I have felt driven beyond belief to secure Balisier and our people; it's why I spend so much time away from home."

He sat on the log and pulled her onto his lap. His natural serenity washed over her as she ran her fingers through his hair and then rested them on the nape of his neck. Love for this man and his people surged through her veins. She would protect them no matter the cost.

Instinct pulled her hand to rest on her stomach. What of their baby? She imagined how delighted he would be to learn of their child growing inside her. Her thoughts soured with the betrayal of not telling him.

If her plan worked, there would be no need for apologies; if it failed, apologies wouldn't begin to erase the damage done.

"We have to trust that we all do our part," she said.

He smoothed her golden hair, then took a few strands and twirled them around his finger. "It seems unfair that you have so little experience being a Sensate and you must carry the majority of the load."

"But I'm not shouldering it alone," said Alexandra. "Balisier is a fortress like no other. The FSB doesn't know we exist; they're grasping at straws. As far as proof, they know of Ari. I'm a 'maybe' on their list."

Jediah's arms tightened around her. "Just remember that I am but a whisper away."

Chapter Thirty-Three

John left the headquarters at the FSB. As of late, his work left a bad taste in his mouth, which only partly lessened by cutting ties with Black. He shuddered inwardly as he considered the vile creature encased in human flesh.

Having sex and spending time with her had been as distasteful as spending time in a rotting swamp. He should've never agreed to 'watch over' the fetid snake. When he accepted the assignment, he had no idea he would risk his humanity. The woman was like a succubus draining every ounce of goodness a person possessed, then shucking the hull of human flesh off as waste.

The only saving grace was his lovely Cassie. He had fallen arse over tin cups for the second part of his assignment in Wheeling, West Virginia. If Black was the disease-infested swamp, Cassie was the hope and wonder of a new spring day.

He owed her his sanity and the rejuvenation of his soul. He knew he would lose her in a split second if she ever suspected he had used her.

The thought of losing Cassie ripped him apart. All his adult years he'd been searching for the perfect counterpart to his id. Who would have ever thought he would find it in the hills of West Virginia, in an old steel town on the banks of the Ohio River?

But, there she was. Her vitality struck a chord when he first laid eyes on her, and for once, he thought he just might enjoy an assignment.

Within a few weeks, he knew he'd met his match. The young lady with bouncy curls slowly stole his heart with her down-to-earth banter and zest for life. She was honest, open, and ready to give her heart.

The subterfuge of his actions ate away at his insides. He should have walked away as soon as he knew his emotional ties were compromised, but he couldn't. Her soft brown eyes called to him, holding him captive. He'd been completely lost from the second date.

Now, it would seem, the whole mess was coming to a head. Just as he spotted Ryeth as Magis' black-eyed demon, he was certain Ryeth recognized him as an agent. Why Ryeth hadn't blown his cover on the spot made no sense at all. To top it all off, the currently 'at large' 613 was hiding in full view on the Saffle's deck.

He should have gone running to his boss with the news, but he hadn't, which left the FSB wide open.

What possessed them to play the cat and mouse game for the remainder of the weekend? For that matter, why had he stayed and not made some flimsy excuse to get out of there and report his findings? What kind of agent was he anyway?

Would the Omnis take action against him and tell Cassie? Did she already know? Was Cassie a pawn or a full-fledged member of their cover-up? He hoped not; he preferred to think of her as completely innocent and unknowing of her best friend's secret.

Two days of walking on eggshells at the Saffle house had frayed his nerves; Sunday had arrived just in time.

He loved his job; well, he *used* to love his job. When things were black and white, the line was easy to draw, but the sex coupled with 'watching over' another agent, had developed into a gray area where his scruples were tossed out the window. He'd never compromised his integrity before, and now that he'd done so, he knew with certainty, he'd never do it again.

Growing up John only wanted to be one thing, an F.B.I agent. If he had to choose between Cassie and his job, Cassie would win, hands down. But would she ever forgive him? After the siege, could he live with the secret and never tell her?

Down deep where it counted, he was old school. You marry for better or worse, you love until the end of time, you trust one another, and you *don't* keep secrets.

Until recently, he'd learned nothing of value to report to the FSB. He could kick himself for planting the bugs at the Saffle's house. If Ryeth had appeared half an hour sooner, he wouldn't have planted them at all. Once they were discovered the snowball would start its descent downhill, picking up anything and everything in its path.

Going forward with his assignment was an effort made easier by Black's demotion. His boss, was close to making his move; he knew him well enough to know that the calm voice he'd heard on the phone was the same calm before the storm he'd witnessed on his last assignment. His boss was very good at his job; when he made a move, it was always swift and final.

To John that meant his time with Cassie was limited and would soon draw to a close. He could not expect Cassie to forgive him, let alone love him, if he carted her best friend off to the FSB detention area.

He picked up his phone and pressed the number for Cassie's speed dial. Pangs of regret filled his heart as he heard her voice.

* * * * *

"Well, well," said Ryeth as he withdrew from John's mind, "John Thaddeus Ryan has a heart."

If ever there was a man who wished to go back in time and reverse his actions, Ryeth supposed it would be John Ryan.

It was a shame. Alexandra's friend, Cassie, was a sweet girl, much like Alexandra. That she ended caught up in their Prophecy was unfortunate. That John had identified Ryeth as the one who tortured Magis was also unfortunate, but not unexpected.

Ryeth stroked his chin. Not many men had his presence, so he realized he would be easy to spot in a crowd, let alone at a small family gathering.

Another piece of the puzzle came into view. The day of reckoning would soon be at hand. For the first time in his life Ryeth had to rely on faith. With Alice Jane and his sweet mother at his side he could weather any gale force. His time of standing alone passed into the wind, replaced by a solidarity formed by the wisest and strongest Sensates.

Their future was written in the past, and now came full circle into the present. The ninth moon approached. Nine moons since Alexandra came into her powers; nine moons' time of preparation for their best outcome, as well as the worst, and nine moons for him to heal and become the Sensate to stand with Alexandra and ward off the danger threatening their people.

Checking in on John sated his curiosity of the man's character. At some point John would decide to plant his feet on one side or the other.

Ryeth left John Ryan's thoughts to his highly capable Alice and concentrated on the venomous Black.

Chapter Thirty-Four

Dave Edwards leaned back in his chair at the FSB headquarters and considered his options: flagrant disregard of his assignment, or total chaos of a civilization so far unknown by man. If it wasn't him to run the operation to seize the Omnis and their knowledge, it would be someone else. At least if he controlled the operation, he could reduce the loss of life.

He reached for his phone and dialed the number for his boss at the Department of Defense and cleared his throat. When he answered, he stated, "Edwards here, I'm going to need a B-2 Bomber equipped with one bunker buster."

"Blasted mother of a monkey, Edwards, we've never used that against our own people before. Are you sure?"

"Are they 'our own people'? I'm not so sure." He knew he was hedging a bit on that one, but blast it, he'd made his decision and there was no going back. "Just put the paperwork through. I'll let you know the time table once I coordinate the cover operation."

"You got it," said his boss. "The risks should be minimal considering our potential return. This strike of yours could assure our military strength for decades, if not centuries, to come. The President is very anxious for your success, especially since that last Howdy Doody made us the laughing stock of the globe."

Not eager for a political debate of the issue, Edwards ended the conversation. Only time would tell if his decisions were just or the cause of ruination.

He grabbed his coat jacket from the back of his chair and headed out of the office toward Anderson's hangout. As the cool air sucked the warmth from his core, he pushed his hands deep into his pants pockets, making giant strides to the unassuming building.

Closing the door behind him, he glanced up to see Anderson talking with a colleague. Edwards caught his eye and motioned for him to join him.

Anderson came to his side. He looked over the room before speaking.

"I set it in motion this morning by requisitioning the bunker buster. A few days of red tape and I should have a 'go.'"

Anderson shook his head. "Man, this is a big step. We don't know what these people are capable of…" He gave a small laugh. "For all we know, we could end up conquered instead of conquering."

"Don't you think I've thought of that too?" said Edwards. "I can't sleep. I'm chewing Tums like no tomorrow. Hah, get that, no tomorrow. This move could even assure that there *is* no tomorrow." He ran his fingers through his comb-over. "If I could do it all again, I'd pass up the chance to run this mission. I never thought far enough down the road to see this. Heck, part of me still doesn't believe these people really exist."

Anderson shuffled his feet and shifted his weight from one leg to another. "They haven't made one move against us," said Anderson. "I don't consider regaining one of their own, or freeing those who were marked for extermination by that hag Black, to be subversive. If you want to compare apples to apples, Black tipped the scales first. Who in Hades gave her the power to order exterminations anyway? What a flippin' mess."

Edwards rubbed the back of his neck. Every time he thought about his intended actions against the Omnis, his stomach rolled over. He popped a few Tums and chewed them. "That big, black-eyed guy took action against a non-Omni first when he tortured Magis. But, if I had the power to scare the living daylights out of a kidnapper without touching him, I might have done the same thing myself. As a matter of fact, after reading the reports of how Magis treated the girl, I might not have stopped when he did."

"Me neither," said Anderson. "She's a beautiful girl."

A huge breath escaped his lips. Edwards took his time speaking. "Route 882 winds against the base of the mountain for almost the whole length. There's an area where the internal cavity comes close to the outside, maybe a hundred feet or so. This will be our point of access. I want you to plan a cover-up to block Route 882 for the entirety of the operation. The only vehicles allowed will be ours. I want ambulances on hand for the extractions, and cots set up in the hanger until we can place the Omnis elsewhere."

Anderson nodded.

Edwards continued. "I'll take care of the guards and security, you plan for enough EMTs to keep them unconscious and continually observed, even if you have to place a guard and an EMT on each Omni. I don't want to lose even one."

"Understood," said Anderson.

"You're my first in command," said Edwards, if anything happens to me, you are in charge of the operation. I expect you to follow my plans verbatim. Are we clear?"

"Crystal," said Anderson. "You have my total support."

"As usual, everything is on a need-to-know basis, and we keep the needing to a minimum."

"Correct, Chief."

"To keep things circumspect, as soon as I have clearance on the B-2, we move," said Edwards.

"Agreed."

A chill ran down Edward's back as he turned and walked out of the building. Verbalizing the orders set them in stone. The five-minute walk back to his office was wracked with trying to shake impending doom off his shoulders. No matter how many times he mentally tried to dislodge the load, each step brought it down with more force.

Back in his office, Ruby brought him a fresh cup of coffee. He removed his jacket, slung it over the back of his chair, sat down, and took a hefty gulp.

He felt the burning liquid enter his mouth and scald the back of his throat. On it tumbled as the liquid fire entered his stomach. He felt the rise of the blister on the roof of his mouth and slumped over in pain and gripped his waist.

He straightened, drew in a breath, and then raised his eyes skyward. "Guess I deserved that one," he said. He shook his head. "I'm sorry, I'm in too deep."

Hours later Dave Edwards grabbed his jacket and left the building. As he stepped outside, he looked back. He wanted to remember what 'normal' looked like, for he thought he might never see it again.

He got into his car and drove to the airport. His Piper Cub was fueled and ready to go. He stepped aboard, closed the hatch, and pointed the nose toward Waynesburg, Pennsylvania. The die was cast.

Once in Waynesburg, he set his plan to capture the Omnis in motion. He planned the allocation of personnel, equipment, and facilities to the nth detail.

Because of the secrecy and potential leak, he chose not to utilize Black's FSB team from Dayton.

Edwards placed a call to his 411. The phone rang in his ear, and John picked up.

"Yeah," said John.

"Come to Waynesburg," he said, "I want you here."

"Will do."

"We've set up a field office at the Greene County Airport, behind the runway, in a technology center."

"I'll be there in a few hours; I'm winding things up here in Dayton. I'll hop the first plane available."

"Thanks, John. I know this operation has been tough on you. But if all goes well, you'll find yourself justly rewarded for your contributions."

Edwards heard no reply, just a grunt on the other end of the line.

He ended the call with a heavy heart. He should have never placed John in the same room with Black, let alone the same bed. He'd only suggested the liaison to John because he'd seen how Black's unashamed eyes devoured him. As it turned out, he was right. His assumptions regarding her lack of conscience and her power-hungry ways led her to sidestep humanity. When the operation was over, he'd make sure she never held a position of authority again.

His mind broke off with a tangent thought. After the operation, would they let him walk away to other assignments, or, due to the high level of security, would he be strapped with the heavy load of the Omnis for the rest of his career?

He didn't see his remaining years with the Bureau tied up with top secret confidentiality similar to that of Area 51. The men from that detail led miserable lives, unable to speak of the horrors of the experiments, or of the aliens themselves. Many ended up under psychiatric care, or they left the world by their own hand.

No, he wasn't up for a daily drain on his humanity. He had no desire to be the 'go-to' man if a leak occurred. The publicity, protestors, and downfall of the Nation's trust was something to be avoided.

He couldn't do it. He wouldn't do it. He would leave the bureau.

Chapter Thirty-Five

Alexandra awoke with a queasy feeling in her stomach. Instinct moved her hand to her mid-section. She swallowed, hoping to suppress the urge. Saliva filled her mouth as she flashed to the bathroom, her hand over her mouth.

As was his normal routine of late, Jediah had left earlier, allowing her the privacy she needed. If he were present, her secret would be revealed.

After dressing, she headed to the kitchen for some tea and dry toast. The nausea abated only the slightest as she walked onto the rear deck. The autumn chill cleared her thoughts and sent shivers down her arms. She rubbed them, but the goosebumps prevailed.

The whole world seemed topsy-turvy. She looked around at her beautiful home on top of the rolling-hill mountain. Early morning mist still hung in the valley below. Berries on the Winterberry tree glistened bright red against the green foliage. A woodpecker rat-a-tat-tatted some distance away on a hollow tree; the sound echoed slightly in the wind.

She cleared her mind by sucking in a deep breath of cool air and blowing it out through a tiny opening in her lips, and then focused on the task at hand.

Her course of action lay before her in a precise, intricate path. No longer did she question any detail; all was accepted as fact. If the Sensates were to survive unmolested, she could have no reservations.

She did, however, have regrets. What if her child didn't survive? Could she live with the knowledge that she had harmed the result of Jediah's and her love? Since the moment she knew it grew within, the love for her child had grown exponentially with each passing day.

A sacrifice on her part was inevitable. That she had to choose between her child and the welfare of their community was her hardest decision. It came down to the life her child would lead if she failed. The life they would all lead. A passage from *Star Trek* passed through her mind: '*The needs of the many far outweigh the needs of the few, or one.*' They were powerful words, and ones that decided the fate of her child.

What if her plan failed, and it cost her Jediah and the baby? As pressure built within her chest, tears filled her eyes. She brushed them away with the back of her hand. It would do no good to ponder a decision set in stone.

Enoch? She reached out to the one person who knew her plan. She read his thoughts.

Yes, Alexandra?

We need to do some trial runs. Are you up for it? she asked.

Come and get me, I'm ready.

Before she flashed to his off campus apartment, she said a small prayer of thanks that she'd been able to locate Enoch and that he was willing to assist.

Of course he had his own reasons for helping, which was enhanced knowledge of physics, but she also sensed his deep commitment to right and wrong. Heck, if he'd had the recessive gene, he would make an excellent Sensate candidate. As it was, his expanded creative mind was more than a match for her abilities.

She landed in his living room, and after pleasantries, wrapped her arm around his waist and whisked him off to Heartseed.

The day passed quickly. Enoch assumed his part in the plan with no reservations. He didn't question her or the plan, or the right or wrong of it.

After several hours of testing and refining her technique, Alexandra sensed Jediah's arrival, and made a hasty decision not to hide Enoch from him. Instead, she invited Enoch into their home and introduced him to Jediah.

"Jediah, this is Enoch Farmer, a graduate student at Albright Technical. He's been gracious enough to assist me with some physics questions and calculations."

"It's a pleasure to meet you, Enoch," said Jediah.

Alexandra continued, putting on a stalwart front. "I've asked him to stay here at the house with us for a little while."

Alexandra, what in Hades are you doing? How does he think I got here? he asked.

"There's no need for telepathy, Jediah," said Alexandra. "Enoch knows all about us."

She watched for the only reaction possible and sensed massive betrayal, disbelief, fear, and anger. She deserved everything he threw at her.

Jediah stopped breathing. His body went rigid as he hissed and said, *What have you done? You know how we guard our secret. You could be ostracized from the group. We trusted you. I trusted you.*

"I won't be ostracized because they will never know," she said with pursed lips.

When she committed this foul deed, she knew she would have to remain stalwart. She was just sorry Enoch had to witness her come-uppance.

Enoch looked sheepish, but spoke anyway. "Jediah, your secret is safe with me. Besides, if you wish, you can remove the knowledge of your existence from my mind once I have aided Alexandra."

Jediah's face turned to stone, so hardened were his beautiful features she barely recognized him.

To present an outward appearance of strength, she moved about the deck as if nothing changed and set out their lunch. As a shocked Jediah took his seat at the table, he asked, "How much have you told him?"

Alexandra shrugged and placed filled plates before them. "Just about everything," she said as she sat down.

"Balisier?"

"Yes," she said.

"Our numbers?" he asked.

"Yes."

Enoch responded with great excitement. "I'd love to meet William," he said, "just so I could believe my ears. It's uncanny that Sensates live as long as you do. Imagine the continuation of one's work. What if Einstein had that opportunity?"

Jediah looked at Alexandra with sadness in his eyes. She sensed his defeat and disappointment in her.

My love, she said, *I would not have compromised our safety had it not been absolutely imperative. You must trust me. You must have faith in my actions.*

Alexandra, you make it impossible for me and the others to trust you.

A great sadness washed over her. She sensed the magnitude of Jediah's regret. His faith in the actions of his new wife lessened with every breath.

She saw it in his eyes, she had lost his respect.

I don't even know you... he said, and then vanished.

Tears welled up in her eyes and fell down her cheeks.

A soft, caring voice entered her mind. *My beautiful granddaughter, do not punish yourself so. Remain strong and remember the lesson of the willow so that you will bend, but never break.*

She felt her strength return as Kayè's voice continued.

He does not know, nor can he know, but if he did, he would understand. My heart swells with pride for you. I am watching, memiki. All is as it should be...

Though Kayè's voice reassured her, it did not stop the pain from entering her heart.

She looked up to see Enoch watching her. He said, "I'm sorry, Alexandra. He doesn't understand."

"Thanks. I don't think I understand either, I just know my path forward and I pray it will work," she said, wiping her eyes with her napkin.

"Then let's finish lunch and get back at it," said Enoch. "There's just a few more refinements until I think it will be perfected. I know you have a specific purpose, Alexandra, but for me, it's a free look into the vast beyond."

She smiled at the charismatic face she had grown to trust. Without a second glance he had pledged his commitment to her and would remain by her side until the completion of their mission. She sensed his obligation was just as strong as hers.

Knowing they each benefitted from their association helped with the regret she felt for bringing him into their Prophecy. He'd found his inner peace through using his mind and gifts to help another.

She refused to think what would happen to him, to all of them, if they failed. Her resolve was firm; they would not fail.

Chapter Thirty-Six

Throughout the many decades of his life, Jediah had never felt so lost. The roar of the waterfall in the chasm did little to drown out the feeling of helplessness that engulfed his very being. He reviewed every facet of his relationship with Alexandra and could find no fault in the girl's virtues. All seven were perfectly intact and had been displayed repeated times since he'd entered her dreams at an early age.

Why then, did he question her actions now? Was it his male ego that felt slighted?

Just the other evening he'd sworn his loyalty to her decisions and vowed his unconditional support. But this new twist? She brought an outsider into their confidence, which was one of their fiercest taboos. Their group did not even tell their non-Sensate families of their abilities. Their pledge to the group was a necessary hardship placed on all who entered. Each dealt with it in their own way. Over the two thousand years of their existence *not one* had broken the vow of secrecy.

He considered that she could have withheld the information about Enoch from him, but she hadn't. Now, it placed the burden of honor on him as well. Does he support his wife, or tell the others of her flagrant disregard for their security?

He snuffed that thought as soon as it came to light. No way would he betray his wife. He believed in her goodness above all other things. She was marked with the hwihs. Centuries of trust

228

that one would come and save them all couldn't be squashed with the blink of an eye. Teater had even devoted his life to her coming.

Somehow, he knew that he'd failed her already. When she needed his support, he questioned her ability. When she crossed the line, instead of knowing she wouldn't have done it without good reason, he played the wounded spouse and left. He should have supported her and trusteed her.

He was not proud of his actions.

Besides, who was he to thwart her methods? Hadn't he been driven like a mad man to implement an additional safe haven *inside* Balisier?

After the FSB's blue gas that rendered Ryeth and Ari unconscious during her rescue, didn't he toil day and night to install ½ inch reflective black mirrored glass over all the walls of the tunnels to protect that particular area from Ground Penetrating Radar? Where had that idea come from?

At the time, he thought it was overkill, but he completed the installation like a drone bee following orders no matter the outcome. He was compelled to get the job done just like Alexandra.

He set his jaw and called a meeting of the High Counsel.

* * * * *

Everyone appeared on time and took a seat. Jediah remained standing to address the group.

"Thanks for coming, everyone. I just wanted to touch bases with you regarding preparations for the Prophecy.

He looked around the room to Teater, James, Val, Alice Jane, Ryeth, William, and into the adoring eyes of Alexandra. He sensed his wife's confidence, maturity, and bravery.

"I've noticed that a compulsion toward getting a particular something-or-other in place has been happening among our group. To others, these compulsions may seem odd, or even against things we believe in."

Glancing toward Alexandra, he said with full-commitment, "This is a time for leniency. It's a time for recognizing our strengths, and our willingness to trust each other more than ever."

Walking around the large oval table, he said solemnly, "Today, I found myself questioning one of our own who has given me no reason for distrust. Don't let the same misgivings plague you. We must all reach deep inside, and no matter the cost, be willing to support Alexandra and Ryeth. They were chosen long ago as the two who will ward off the Prophecy, which we now know to be the FSB. It is our support of each other that will see us to a successful end."

Jediah walked over to the empty seat next to Alexandra and sat down. She reached across his lap and took his hand in hers.

William, never silent and always alert said, "Can you tell us your plan, Alexandra?"

She straightened in her seat and raised her chin. "I'm afraid I can not. The success of the plan requires that none know what the plan entails. So, I ask that none try to find out, and that all support me without question."

Alexandra stood and looked to each member. "I am aware that compared to many I have very little experience both in life, and with my powers. It wasn't long ago that I transported myself by accident and was nearly discovered."

Jediah sensed some members were shocked at her revelation, but she smiled at them and said, "Regardless of my shortcomings, and I admit I have a few, I accept the responsibility that was foisted on me by my betters."

Jediah caught her quick peek at Teater, who had the decency to blush.

"I have great hope for our success," she said, "and when that happens, we will no longer fear the FSB."

It was apparent to Jediah that William wanted more of an answer, but he was willing to accept her words for now. He knew William would be watching his wife to make certain she didn't fail. Although if William was as lost as he was, he doubted William's dissatisfaction would get him anywhere.

A deep voice from across the table drew Jediah's eyes to Ryeth, whose expression gave nothing away as he spoke. "I just want you gentlemen, and ladies," he nodded to Alice Jane and Alexandra, "to know that I am as much in the dark as the rest of you. I have had compulsions to get certain tasks completed. One of which was to locate the 'one who could doom us all.' I was sorry to find out that John Ryan, Cassie's boyfriend, was our mole."

No eyes went to Alexandra. Jediah saw they all looked down at their laps instead.

Teater spoke next. "Alexandra, I've done something in support of your path that I am not proud of; it went against my grain. But I did it anyway, because like Jediah and Ryeth, I was compelled to do it. I apologize to those I offended without their knowledge, and I hope, that if I am found out, that they will forgive me."

Jediah watched William for a reaction and was not disappointed. He furrowed his brows, leaned sideways in his chair and pulled out the worn stone from his pants pocket. His thumb rubbed across the stone as Jediah sensed William struggling with his convictions.

Valentine Jellan, their doctor and heart of the group asked, "Alexandra and Ryeth, do you need anything from us?"

"I'm good," said Ryeth, then looked at Alexandra.

"I'm good so far," she said, "but I know I will need all of your support when the time comes. If I could count on that as a given, I wouldn't worry about it."

"Can we each give our word of unconditional support?" asked Jediah.

No one spoke, but all heads nodded their agreement.

"Thank you," she said. "I know that couldn't have been easy. It's hard to trust in the unknown, and to place that trust in me, the youngest Sensate, the one with the least experience. Believe me, I share in your doubts… at least I did until I realized that my actions can have no room for doubt. I must be fully engaged in my obligation to our group. I must trust in myself, and know that I have the ability and desire to help save us all."

Jediah read strength, patience, and humility in his wife. Pride swelled in his chest for the woman who sat next to him. He squeezed her hand, and when she looked into his eyes, he lowered his lips to hers.

Val stood to address the group. "I have some news that could affect us in the future. Like several others in the group, I was summoned forth to complete a task, but there was no stipulation that my part be kept secret. As a matter of fact, the only compulsion was to *complete* the task, which I did, a few days ago. I now wish to share the results of my labors."

One at a time, he looked from member to member. After he looked at the last member he said to all, "I have just given each of you the ability to filter any foreign substance from your mind as Ari did during her captivity. I added another aspect that Ari, with her limited knowledge of human physiology, could not obtain. That inability probably saved her life. The second part is to remain fully conscious and functional while the offending substance is filtered."

Jediah said, "Am I hearing you correctly? You mean that drugs and gasses will no longer knock us out?"

"That's exactly what I'm saying," said Val.

William's brows came together in a frown. "I don't sense the mechanism."

"I don't either," said Ryeth.

All the others shook their heads in agreement; he didn't feel the addition either.

"That's because it's sort of innate, like the ability to sense other Sensates," said Val. "The only way I could assure our protection if we were already unconscious was to make it something we don't have to trigger. That way, we are covered no matter what."

"Are you sure this works?" asked James.

"If you need secondary assurance, ask Ari and Jonathan. Those two have been subjected to the strongest of sedatives - IVs, oral, and gasses - with nary a blink of the eye."

233

Jediah shook his head in disbelief. "Val, I have to commend you. It's a stroke of genius only you could have completed."

"I couldn't have done it without Ari's meticulous instructions and Jonathan's fortitude as a guinea pig. Those kids made this possible."

"You've added another level of security to our group," said James, "well done."

"Kudos to you, Val," said Alexandra.

The others joined in congratulating Val, who handled the compliments with modesty and said, "Jonathan and I will be giving the mechanism to all the Sensates. Ari wanted to help, but she hasn't been admitted to the group formally yet."

"That will come soon enough," said William. "Our group is changing quickly. It's almost more than a body can stand."

Jediah noted the look on William's face and smiled. It was good somethings never changed.

Chapter Thirty-Seven

After the meeting with the High Counsel, Alexandra's fears regarding Enoch were partially abated. She checked the time. Cassie would just be getting home from work. The desire to speak to her best friend coursed through her veins.

Her fingers shook as she pressed the number on her cell phone and placed the call on speaker.

"Hello," said Cassie.

"Hi. It's just me."

"What's going on in Heaven?" Cassie asked.

Alexandra smiled at Cassie's description of her life. Cassie considered Jediah the perfect male and their home, 'a little slice of Heaven.'

"Not too much," she replied. "We're battening down the hatches in preparation for winter. I've never lived atop a mountain in the dead of winter before."

"You know what's going to be fun, don't you?" asked Cassie.

"No, what?"

"Sled riding, tobogganing, and cross-country skiing. Oh, my thighs are aching just thinking about it."

Alexandra easily pictured Cassie's fantasy in her head. "How is it that you came up with that idea instead of me? Hmm, let me see, that's going to require a bonfire, hot chocolate, warm rolls, and a huge pot of beef vegetable soup."

"Oh wow, I can hardly wait for the first snowfall. You really know how to live."

"What you really mean," said Alexandra, "is that I really know how to *eat*."

"Well, the food did catch my attention more than the snow…"

"So, how are you and John doing?" asked Alexandra. As the words formed in her mouth she felt like a traitor. She hated hiding anything from Cassie. She hid being a Sensate, she hid her abilities, and she hid the fact that John was using her.

"We're great," said Cassie. "I never would have guessed that I'd fall so easily, but he's just so perfect. He's a real part of the family. Mom and Dad love him as much as I do. Hey, hold on a minute, let me get out of these heels before my feet fall off."

"Ouch, I still can't believe you wear those things every day," said Alexandra, "it's all I can do to tolerate them for special occasions."

"Not all of us were gifted with your lofty view of life," said Cassie.

"I'm only six inches taller than you."

"No sir, it's seven if it's an inch," said Cassie.

"That's no reason to wreck your feet," said Alexandra.

"I'll wreck them until I snag John Boy, then I'll slip into some flats. And, by the way, I think the boy is snagged, hook, line and sinker."

Twinges of anguish squeezed Alexandra's stomach. "Cassie, that's great. Then I'll be hearing wedding bells soon?" The words felt like acid on her tongue.

"Na, nothing like that yet. I think he'll take it slow and easy, just like he does when he kisses me. Say, talking about kissing and what comes after, how are you feeling little mama?"

A bit of anger surfaced. Did everything have to be a lie? Drat this conversation, drat this stupid Prophecy, and drat the world. She took a deep breath and continued. "Just a bit of queasiness in the mornings, nothing to get excited over."

"When do you plan to tell big Jed?"

"Soon, I just want to wait and keep this to myself for a bit."

"You told me…"

"Not the same thing and you know it," said Alexandra. "We've been two peas for a long time. You *are* me."

"Well," said Cassie, "I'll bet the big guy will walk on cloud nine."

Alexandra smiled. Jediah would be thrilled. He even said about a month ago how happy he'd be to hear little feet running across the deck. "We might have to peel him off the ceiling," she said.

"I wonder what a baby between John and I would look like?" asked Cassie.

"For one thing, it would probably have your thick curly hair," said Alexandra.

"Don't curse the kid, Allie."

"I never understood the dislike for your hair," said Alexandra. "It's beautiful."

"It's been trying to spring off my head ever since I was born. It's bouncy, unruly, and under no circumstances my friend. It has never once given me a reprieve and just laid down. It's like it has energy all its own."

Alexandra heard the candor in Cassie's words and the frustration in her voice.

"I'm short and I have bouncy hair," said Cassie. "I'll be labeled a 'moppet' even when I'm old and gray."

Alexandra had to admit that was probably true. Some people look young and animated even though they are very old.

"Being a moppet is not a bad thing. I always envied your hair. I think it's one of your best attributes. I guess we are often at odds at what we are given in the looks category."

"Yeah, I suppose," said Cassie.

"Well, I just wanted to check in on you," said Alexandra. "Tell your Mom and Dad I said 'hi.'"

"I will; I have to be going anyway. John's stopping by for a last hurrah before winter barbecue, and I'm standing here in panties and bra."

"Get busy, girl. Tell John we said hello."

Alexandra hung up the phone with a sense that something was incomplete. She had yielded to the compulsion to call, but it hadn't sated something inside. There was more, she was sure of it.

Chapter Thirty-Eight

Ryeth couldn't fathom his part in the Prophecy. His contribution *had* to be more than ferreting out a mole. After a few days under his favorite pawcohiccora, and feeling he was forcing the issue, the notion that pounded at the far reaches of his mind came together at long last.

Canisters. His compulsion centered on canisters. The use was not clear, but he did know that they had to spray a talc aerosol upwards at least 2000 feet for half an hour.

The process required a hefty aerosol or gas mixture to propel the talc particles that high, and some decent sized canisters.

It didn't make sense. Talcum powder. Their plan was to ward off the FSB with talcum powder? He smiled and shook his head. The largest, meanest, and baddest Sensate was in charge of baby powder.

If that was what Alexandra needed, who was he to question it? He began by discussing the project with a gas/aerosol expert in Lancaster County, who determined the amount of talc and the chemicals to use for combustion.

"I'll need some canisters of a fine talc powder, that when sprayed, will shoot at least two thousand feet in the air," said Ryeth.

"What do you need it for?" asked the guy.

"I can't really say." He shrugged. "The person who needs them gave me the specs. I'm just the delivery guy." He smiled.

"That's some request," said the guy, "I supposed the one who wants them has all the permits for shooting this stuff in the air?"

Ryeth shrugged again. He hated playing the part of a ninny, but he didn't really have a choice.

"I honestly have no idea whether or not they got permits. That's not really my job."

Ryeth sensed the guy's exasperation with him and had to suppress a grin.

"How many do you need?" asked the guy.

"Ten. That will allow a few extra for testing," said Ryeth.

The expert performed the necessary calculations then said, "We're going to need an aerosol/combustion mixture that produces heat in order to get the particles that high, and we're going to need something that is environmentally friendly."

He looked questioningly at Ryeth and added, "That is assuming you intend to release these outside."

Acting the part of the ninny and being treated like a ninny chaffed Ryeth a bit more than he anticipated. He was just about ready to hang this man from his britches on the nearest peg, but instead, he nodded and said, "Yeah, I think it's for outside."

After that, it looked like the guy decided to keep the questions to himself, a fact that made Ryeth extremely grateful. Heck, the whole thing was unclear to him, so how could it make sense to the canister guy?

Bound by the Prophecy, and feigning ignorance, he continued his discussion with the expert until he was satisfied they would turn out perfect.

The manufacturing of the canisters would take place immediately, which was unexpected on Ryeth's part. Through the exchange of crisp bills, Ryeth placed the order.

Driving back home, Ryeth realized that the force that guided him was omnificent, for his mother seemed as confused as he was concerning all the compulsions and secret tasks. They all heeded the compulsions without question, and he was no different.

Within twenty-four hours, he took the first canister off the line. He teleported to the far reaches of the Gibson Desert in Australia, where he was certain the temperatures matched, set the canister on the sand, and released the stopper.

A white cloud pushed upward into the clear sky. He watched as the cloud billowed upward and created an opaque plume. Equipped with an altimeter, he checked the height of the plume. Perfect. It soared to twenty-two hundred feet and then mushroomed into a large blanket covering the area. It hung, suspended in mid-air until the wind displaced it from its origin.

He sensed from the ease in his mind that the first part of the compulsion was acceptable.

The following day, Alice Jane refused to let Ryeth make the trip to Lancaster alone. Never a man to leave a lady wanting, he smiled and bid her to come.

"Um, the truck has a bench seat," she said as she slid into the passenger's side and continued sliding to the left until her hip pressed next to his.

"You're not going to make this a comfortable trip, are you?" he asked his sultry wench.

"Of course not." She cooed into his ear.

Her warm breath sent chills down his spine. The woman was a witch who had captured his heart. When this Prophecy stuff was out of the way, he planned to make her his wife. He'd decided to give her no clue at all as to his intentions; to just let her stew until just before it bubbled over.

It was unbelievable how she fit perfectly into his life. Her soul had melded to his in an exquisite union. She had the look of his mother, the survival skills of a tigress, and the loyalty of an albatross. Comfortable in his skin for the first time in his life, Ryeth was pleased to spend the time with her.

In Lancaster, they retrieved the remainder of his canisters. After securing them, they made the four-hour trip back to Waynesburg.

As he drove, he pondered the next phase of his part, knowing it would be a bit trickier to implement, for he had to do it without anyone's knowledge.

Late that night, Ryeth placed six canisters on the ground in a circle formation where he was sure the final confrontation would take place.

Not one to use his back unless necessary, he surmised the size of the tank and then teleported the contents of the hole away to another part of the woods. Next, he set the tank inside and used a few tufts of grass to conceal the top, leaving only the nozzle visible.

Ryeth set the remainder of the canisters in place using the same technique. When he was finished, he blew leaves around the nozzles to cover them from view. He stood there for a few minutes to survey his work.

It seemed fitting somehow, that this place would be their O.K. Corral. A confrontation to decide their fates. He leaned against the cold stone and considered his path up to this point.

As one corner of his mouth drew up in a snicker; he realized he was guided throughout his life to be exactly who and what he was at this very instant. He was meant to assist those he'd considered adversaries for centuries.

His path had been a winding one, and not easy by any means, but he *had* arrived at the dark hour and he would fulfill the Prophecy.

An unfamiliar feeling settled over him, and at first, he didn't recognize it. It crept into every pore of his skin and passed through each cell of his body. Though the air chilled his exterior, he was warm within. The hairs on the back of his neck that raised in defiance a multitude of times over the centuries, were smooth and quiet. The tense stance he'd donned as a normal state, eased and left his body.

Ryeth was at peace.

Chapter Thirty-Nine

The fax Edwards held in his hand glared at him and soured his stomach. The approval for the air strike marked the beginning of the operation.

He called a meeting for the heads of his air and ground forces to convene at 1300.

"Gentlemen and ladies, I request your attention to every detail that I set before you today. It is imperative that my instructions be carried out swiftly and accurately if we hope to accomplish our goal."

Faces of honorable men and women looked back at him. Tomorrow's operation would affect each and every one of them for the rest of their lives. How the upper management handled the Omnis would affect the world.

"Due to the clandestine nature of this operation, any and all unauthorized outside communication by enlisted personnel will cease from this point forward." He paused to allow his words to sink in.

"I want you to keep a close watch over your personnel to insure this mandate is followed. I, and I alone, will be the only person to authorize outside communication. The outcome of this mission depends on this, so don't take my words lightly. The punishment for any infraction will be considered treason."

Edwards scanned the faces before him. None appeared shocked at the severity for disobedience, so he continued.

"The operation will commence precisely at 0600 tomorrow morning with the arrival of the road crew and two squads of troops. At 0800, six National Guard helicopters lift off from Greene County Airport, and two squads will ascend to the house. The helicopters are to be in position by 0807 with the multiphase diffusion lasers at full power."

He walked to the diagram on the wall and pointed to the six blue dots on the map. Large overlapping circles surrounded each dot, which completely covered the mountain.

"At 0810, the B-2 bomber will drop the guided bunker blaster to penetrate at this location."

He pointed to a place on Route 882 where the wall of the mountain was the thinnest. A red X marked the spot on the map for the location of the bomber strike.

"If the bunker blaster fails to break through to the inside, a secondary blast by Charlie Platoon," he nodded to the commander, "will complete the entry point. Once the muck is cleared from the blast, the Alpha Platoon will enter the interior of the mountain to secure the Omnis."

Edwards leaned over the table he used as a podium and rested his hands on the top.

"Now, we're not anticipating any resistance, but I want your soldiers to be prepared for anything. Although I don't believe our troops will be fired upon, I don't expect the people inside the mountain to be as docile as sheep either."

He stretched his back to relieve the stress build-up, stood, and placed his hands in his pants pockets. He looked down to the floor. "After the technicians dose them, we begin the extraction."

A sigh escaped his lips. He removed his hands, and looked at the group. With the plans laid out, a bit of relief eased his mind. Tied to his decision by setting plans in motion allowed him no time to back pedal.

"Please coordinate your operations so we aren't tripping over ourselves. That is all. If you have any questions, please contact me personally in Hanger One."

Edwards walked from the area to allow the individual section chiefs time to work out the details. He motioned for Anderson to follow him and decided on a leisurely walk around the whole area.

"I can't believe how this operation came together so easily," said Anderson.

"Yeah, it was more luck than sense that a nearby airport had a National Guard unit, ground troops, and equipment there as well. Seems a bit too good to be true."

That thought sent an omen of dread streaking through Edwards' mind. He ran through his plans one more time to pick out any holes where they might break through.

"The locals are used to the army trucks running the roads every now and then," said Anderson, "so their movements won't draw any undue attention."

"It all seems pretty darned concise," said Edwards as he scratched his neck. "Too clean, too smooth. Something's bound to go wrong, very wrong."

Anderson glanced sideways at him. "I don't think I'd worry about it too much. You're essentially breaking new ground here. We don't have any idea what we're really dealing with. For all we know, huge cannons could pop out of the side of the mountain and blow us to smithereens."

Edwards stopped dead in his tracks and turned to Anderson. "Are you supposed to be cheering me up? If you are, you are doing a lousy job of it."

Seemingly unaffected by his comment, Anderson continued. "They could also have the capability of lifting the lid off the mountain and flying away in their starship."

Edwards gave a snort. Anderson was not to be deterred, it would seem. His friend, and cohort since the eighties, was steadfast in pointing out the potential pitfalls of the operation.

Maybe he should lighten up on himself... those Tums were beginning to have no effect at all. If he didn't get a grip on his stress, he might just as well lay down and let a heart attack take him away for good.

"You're right," he said. "Thanks buddy, I needed that wake-up call. Come to think of it, maybe I should have a camera crew here for posterity's sake."

"That's the spirit," said Anderson. "If all else fails, you could write a book, sell the movie rights, and retire to your own island in the Caribbean. Now, *that's* something to look forward to."

He and Anderson continued their stroll toward the trailer he'd brought in so they could sleep on the premises.

"John will be joining us first thing tomorrow morning," he said. "I wanted him to watch the operation unfold, so he knows his sacrifice was worthwhile." He paused. "You know, I think he's taken quite a shine to that girl in Wheeling."

"Really?" said Anderson. "I thought Black would've turned him against all woman."

"Apparently not. I can hear the change in his voice when he talks about her." He looked at

247

Anderson and nodded. "Must be nice. Although, I'd hate to be him when she finds out he helped capture her best friend."

Edwards' thoughts soured. It had been years since he'd felt anything for a woman. Must be the job, he concluded. A bit of envy ran across the strings of his heart. He missed soft eyes looking into his... When did the change in him take place? How long had his heart been cold?

They reached the door of the trailer. He turned to Anderson. "How about an antipasto salad and a sausage and pepperoni pizza from that Pizza Villa down the road? They deliver."

"Sounds good to me," said Anderson. "I'd like to eat early tonight. A heavy meal late the night before a campaign is certain to cause nightmares."

Edwards closed his eyes and let breath expel from his nose. Did Anderson *have* to bring up nightmares? Couldn't he leave that one alone?

"I'll give them a call," said Edwards, resigned to a sleepless night.

"Sure," said Anderson, "I'll be with you in a minute. I want to touch bases with Diane before I commit to the communication lockdown."

"Hey, buddy, that never applies to you," said Edwards. "That wife of yours is like a member of the unit. She's been a real trooper all these years. Be sure to give her my best."

He waved Anderson off from the doorway of the trailer, and watched as he reached for his cell phone. He'd give his right arm to have someone like Diane in his life, but it hadn't been in the cards.

Yeah, he would carry off this last mission, and then turn away for good from the life. He'd given too much and gotten very little in return. The people he associated with who lived on the outside of polite society had transformed his façade from a pleasant grandpa to that of someone who expected the worst in everyone.

He'd never get the years he gave the Bureau back. If he left the service now, the chances were slim of finding the perfect someone to live out the remainder of his life with in peace and happiness.

As he gave it one last thought, he wondered if he'd recognize peace and happiness if it sat on his lap and kissed his cheek.

Chapter Forty

4:00 A.M.

Edwards turned in his sleep; excruciating pain from a stiff neck brought him straight up out of the chair. He cursed himself for moving to the recliner when sleep evaded him. He rubbed his neck and moved it carefully until it moved freely. So the day began.

Though the air was cool on his walk to the command center, beads of sweat appeared above his upper lip. He used the time to multi-task and rolled up his shirt sleeves, knowing they would bug him later.

Helicopters lined the tarmac, their blades a mishmash of giant pickup sticks. The cockpits mimicked giant all-seeing eyes that focused on him.

Life's burdens weighed heavily on his shoulders, which resulted in a noticeable slouch. The man who loved his job carried grave misgivings with him as he neared the threshold.

The command center was positioned between the hanger for the infirmary and the hanger for satellite communications for easy access. He stepped inside and glanced around the room, which was a bevy of activity.

Anderson was performing the final checks on the communications and the equipment; he looked up and nodded as he passed. For his plan to succeed, there could be no malfunctions. One tiny opening in the multiphase diffuse lasers would allow the Omnis to escape in the blink of an eye; they could teleport anywhere in the world and end up out of his grasp forever, which meant he would end up answering to his superiors with a multimillion-dollar price tag in his hand and nothing to show for it.

Edwards checked his watch; time passed too quickly.

5:00 A.M.

John Ryan arrived in Waynesburg with thoughts of losing Cassandra Hudson foremost in his mind. Instead of anticipating the addition of a major military coup to his resumè, his emotions were caught between the proverbial 'rock and a hard place.'

Last night's supper with Cassie compounded his guilt. For some unknown reason, Cassie bubbled over every time she spoke of her best friend, Alexandra. Her bubble and his impending action of popping it, made the food at Undo's stick in his throat.

In hindsight, he probably should have just stayed away, for it did nothing to help him with the dilemma at hand.

His affiliation with Black, who had the ability to eviscerate the soul from a saint, had soured his life. Each time he rode the Cassie and Black seesaw he eroded the relationship with Cassie.

Although Cassie was a strong Christian, he doubted her ability to forgive him for placing her best friend in harm's way, and his intimate surveillance of Black. Heck, he couldn't even forgive himself.

He blew out a deep sigh, put the gearshift in Park, and turned off the engine. Stepping out of the car and into the Green County Airport signaled a complete reversal in the direction of his life. He took that step with zero confidence, plodding along like a Lemming to total annihilation.

Resolved to his fate, John shoved his hands in his pants pockets and surveyed the area. The airport was a bustle of activity. Helicopters lined the right side of the throughway. Soldiers' barracks nestled close to the edge of the tree line at the far end of the field; their temporary housing set up in four long, neat rows.

He had to admit, that when Edwards took control of a mission, it reeked of military precision and order. Without a doubt, he also knew Edwards would have reviewed the entire personnel list himself.

Edwards was the only real father figure John had as he entered his adult life; he had him to thank for developing his moral character. Loyalty to this man was paramount.

John watched as Ron Anderson crawled out from under a helicopter and headed toward a building on the left.

"Anderson," he yelled.

Ron looked his way and halted. John jogged to his side.

"Quite the setup you've got here," he said.

Ron shook his head. "You have no idea… I'm short on time, but let me give you a quick go-round."

Ron showed him, in hasty detail, what the Omni's were going to face. With each passing electronic feature, John's horror grew. In the best outcome, he imagined all the Omnis gone for parts unknown with the FSB left looking at an empty mountain and a high price tag for their venture.

The worst outcome, that his mentor succeeded, was unimaginable.

After the FSB's plans were laid out before him, it was apparent that no best outcome existed for the Omnis. Edwards had them boxed in and tied up with a bow.

"You're not hungry for the kill?" said Ron, who apparently picked up on his lack of euphoria.

He shook his head. "Sorry, no. I keep thinking that they've done nothing wrong, and I wonder what their lives are going to be like after tomorrow."

"I've been where you are," said Ron, "but I had to pack it up and just do the job."

"It's a hard thing to do, isn't it?" he asked.

"Sure is. It's eating at Edwards too." Ron rubbed the back of his neck. "I wouldn't say anything to him about the number of Tums he's eating; he near knocked my head off."

"Thanks for the warning," he said.

Ron tipped his ball cap to John. "I got to run. Edwards is in the trailer," he said pointing.

"Thanks, Ron."

John turned and headed for the trailer. His steps were slow. The FSB's plan weighed heavily on his shoulders. He wanted to scream to the mountain, Get out! Run! They're coming for you! But loyalty held him tight in her rigid clutches.

5:00:30 A.M.

Onatah began her observation of the day's events when Ryeth awoke at 5AM. Each time she looked upon her son, her heart swelled with pride. Strong and enduring, he represented the years of separation from her physical form. Though she watched over her flock, and learned new and exciting things, the old ways and times was where she found peace.

The day she realized she was different than other Indian maidens, she saw this day unfold in her mind. Over two thousand years ago the details made no sense, but through the years all the pieces had fallen in place – the men with large flying bugs, the terrible-sounding noise that dug a hole in the side of her mountain, the people with metal needles who made her people sleep, and the capture of those who meant no harm.

Dreams that followed her through the years never came together with an ending and left her wondering why the future had been revealed to her at all. What was the purpose in knowing, for it surely distressed her more than not-knowing.

Did this happen because of man's fear of the unknown? If so, it was no different now than when she was a maiden, stoned, and forced to leave her tribe. Two millennia passed in which man failed to evolve. When would man feel comfortable in his own skin? Saddened by her thoughts, and no closer to any form of resolution, Onatah assumed the familiar position of overseer.

Watching her children over the years was Onatah's favorite pastime. Though she watched and listened, she allowed them to make mistakes and did not intrude in their lives. She could not help herself from easing Alexandra's suffering at the hands of the evil man, Magis. It pleased her that he was in prison and could no longer harm others.

Throughout her existence, Onatah never really questioned her role. She was Onatah, nothing more. Why her spirit continued after her death she did not know, yet she accepted her fate in death as she had accepted it during her life, with appreciation of a gift given, and honored that she was chosen.

5:10 A.M.

Ryeth tenderly lifted the covers just enough to allow his departure without waking the sleeping beauty at his side. Alice Jane's breathing was light and steady. What a glorious sight she was with her dark hair splayed across the cream linens, her cheek slightly blushed from sleep. Ryeth smiled. Alice Jane was his perfect match.

A frown crossed his brow as thoughts of Morgan Black, who called her activities for the day the 'climax of her vacation,' entered his mind. He could have enjoyed the splendor of a beautiful fall day in the arms of a tender woman. Instead, he had to protect Ari from Black, a woman who gave nothing in life and deserved nothing in return.

He hadn't shared Black's arrival in Waynesburg with the High Counsel; he wanted to handle her interference without involving the others. Knowing her plan ahead of time made it child's play, an annoyance, nothing more.

Ryeth sensed the Prophecy was near - days, maybe hours away. Once the face-off between them and the FSB took place, a new future awaited. He cocked his head. No Sensate ever spoke of what happened next. So focused were they on the battle for their continued independence, their 'after' existed only behind the curtain.

Chapter Forty-One

5:30 A.M.

Edwards reviewed every facet of his plan for potential errors. At 0530 he called together the mission leaders and gave them the go ahead to commence the operation as planned.

Although the area was a bevy of scurrying last minute preparations, Edwards' solitary walk to the command area marked him as Atlas, carrying the full weight on his shoulders.

Sweat dripped down his back and made his crisp white shirt stick to his skin. It would do no good to change into a new one. Sweat was his constant companion during tough missions. To replenish the water loss from his system, he grabbed a bottle of water, unscrewed the cap, and downed half of the contents before pulling up a chair and setting in front of the monitors.

The road crew, whose vehicles were equipped with front-facing cameras, pulled out of the airport and made their way to the base of the mountain. Edwards watched as they set the detour signs in place at the turnoff to the mountain road, and another at the opposite end. The Asplundh Tree Expert trucks pulled off the side of the road and set the truck levelers in place. To the normal passerby the scene was typical of crews preparing for winter by clearing away tree overhang. Edwards nodded; so far, so good.

Screen three displayed the platoon dressed in orange Asplundh jumpsuits who were assigned to the blast entrance. They set up a perimeter around the GPS coordinates for the bunker blaster. Edwards rubbed his chin with satisfaction and noted the platoon maintained a discrete distance from the intended target.

He checked his watch; the military ran a mission like a fine oiled machine, and followed orders precisely. That part of a mission, the known, was always easier.

The time to hold his breath was now, for if the Omnis knew of their intentions, they would surely flee the area before he had time to close in on them. If they were as powerful as he assumed, and had special abilities, wouldn't they have taken measures to ensure their safety?

The unknown of the mission was the really tough part. What if they came out blazing like Butch Cassidy and the Sundance Kid? What would the Omnis use against them?

Edwards unbuttoned his top button and wriggled his tie loose. His team was ready. Only time would tell.

6:00 A.M.

Alexandra was up before Jediah. The night was a rough one, where thoughts raced through her mind and whipped from one thing to another refusing to settle. In the wee hours she was still awake, jumpy, and on edge. She tip-toed through the bedroom and sat in the rocker next to the window to watch the dawning of a new day. Life dealt her a sizable blow at eighteen with the death of her parents, but had balanced out four years later by turning her into a Sensate. One event could not compare to the other, yet the two did form the hills and valleys that made up her life.

The Prophecy was so close she could almost touch it. The guiding force that pushed her along a singular path could not be denied. Qualms regarding the right or wrong of it swirled around her head and made her dizzy with confusion. The only way she could reconcile her involvement was to think of herself as an instrument, a tool, to be used for the greater good.

She had to let go of the responsibility for the outcome, for she existed merely as a puppet for another to command. All that was required of her was to trust; trust in the unknown and to trust that a greater power would set things right and protect the benevolent Sensates from a terrible fate.

A smile caught on her lips as her gaze caught the shape of her husband, fast asleep, his arm thrown over his head.

He rolled over and stretched. Jediah's hand reached for her and finding the space empty, he opened his eyes to scan the room and caught her watching him.

"I couldn't sleep," she said in a whisper.

The early morning sun flickered through the trees and danced across the bed where he lay. An unshaven chin plus the way his hair fell over his forehead gave him just enough of a rough appearance to wish she was closer. She sensed the lifeblood flowing within his chest, and the increased beating of his heart.

In one swift movement, he threw back the cover to allow her access. She ran from the rocker and slid in next to him. His body was warm, so she snuggled close.

Wrapped in his arms, the worries of the world ebbed as she fell into a deep sleep.

7:00 A.M.

An hour later, Alexandra watched as Jediah's well-formed bottom walked the path to the shower. Drowsy and sated, her nerves calmed, so she closed her eyes and pulled up the covers as sleep beckoned her from the conscious world.

7:30 A.M.

The hairs on the back of Ryeth's neck raised in anticipation of Black's arrival. Poised in his invisible orb, he waited just inside the foyer of the Saffle's farm house.

The doorbell rang. Ryeth entered Ari's mind as the sound woke her. She rolled to check the clock on the nightstand.

Ari, don't be frightened, he said.

Ryeth? He sensed her confusion as she grabbed her slippers and robe.

Yes. I'm in the foyer. I checked on the housekeeper, she won't arrive for another half hour.

What are you doing here? she asked, as she made her way down the stairs to the foyer.

Protection, he said.

Ryeth sensed Ari's fear building as she asked, *Whose at the door?*

The enemy, he said, *but don't worry, she can't hurt you. It's get even time.* Ryeth sent confidence to Ari, and immediately sensed a change in her.

Ryeth moved his orb close to the door and prepared to make himself invisible to Black so he could disperse the orb.

Ari sent the vision she saw from the peep hole to Ryeth. It was a beautiful, slim, dark-haired woman, dressed in a suit. The woman appeared to be in her late thirties and wore black glasses.

Ari opened the door. Just as she did, the woman held up a small canister and sprayed blue gas in her face.

In the split second it took for Ari to agree with Ryeth that the woman was no friend, Ryeth had popped his orb, made himself invisible to Black; twisted some specific nerves in Black's head and rendered her unconscious.

Ryeth caught Black before she hit the floor, and turned to Ari with a grandiose smile. "Good morning, Ari," he said.

The startled girl watched as Ryeth removed the brown wig and glasses from the woman.

"That foul human!" yelled Ari, recognizing her. "How did you know, Ryeth? Oh, never mind…" she stammered. "What's she doing here? How did she find me?"

Still holding the limp Black, Ryeth asked, "Mind if I place her on the couch?"

"I'm sorry," said Ari. "That will be fine. Should I get some rope?"

"That won't be necessary. She'll be out for quite a while," Ryeth said as he placed Black on the couch.

"I'll be right back," he said. He flashed, then came immediately right back. Could you put these on her while I move her car?" He handed her a packet of clothing.

Ari held up an orange jumpsuit with large numbers across the front and back. She nodded to Ryeth. "I'd be more than glad to."

He vanished from Ari's view, placed his hand on Black's car, and teleported it to the far corner of the FSB parking lot in Dayton.

Ryeth returned to Ari's side within a few minutes. He placed his hand on her shoulder and said, "You are completely safe. Go about your day as you normally would. Don't let this incident bother you. Alice Jane and I will stop over later tonight and tell you everything."

He walked to the couch and picked up Black's body. "Don't say anything about this to anyone. I want to have a little fun with Black." Ryeth winked at Ari. "I think she deserves a bit of fun, don't you?"

Ari's face lit up as she caught the devilish glint in Ryeth's smile. "Yes, you should give her all the 'fun' she can stand, and then, just for me, let her have a little more."

7:40 A.M.

Ryeth created his invisible orb and headed home. There, he donned his black knit pullover, black leather pants, and long, black Mackintosh. Next, he took Black just a few miles down the road from Waynesburg. He looked down at the creature and entered her diseased mind for the last time to temporarily disable her voice. Revulsion brought a sneer to his lips. The sooner the woman was out of his arms, the better.

He entered Greene County prison and went directly to Magis' cell. The maggot had his back to him, shaving.

Before he made himself known to Magis, he needed to set the scene. Ryeth floated his orb down the corridor until he came to the guard station for Magis' section.

261

Holding Black in a standing position in front of him, he permitted the guard to see them, but only for a second. Once the imprints were in the guard's mind, he quickly made the orb invisible again. Entering the guard's mind, he erased his image completely, but made Black's image invisible to him for the length of his shift, seven and a half hours.

The guard looked in his direction, squinted his eyes, rubbed them, and looked again. He scratched his head, looked behind him, checked both sides, shook his head, and continued with the documentation.

Satisfied the illusion would work, Ryeth took Black back down the corridor to Magis' cell. While Magis' back was to him, he made himself invisible to Magis, dispersed the orb, and laid Black on his cot. The action made the springs squeak.

Magis turned to see a striking blonde-haired woman dressed in prison garb, laying on his bed.

Panic reflected in his eyes. His legs faltered so he placed his hand on the sink to steady himself. Furtive glances flashed around the cell.

"I know you're here," said Magis. "What do you want from me?"

He reached for the towel hanging from a hook on the wall. As he wiped his face clean of shaving gel, his eyes rested on the hourglass form on his bed. He licked his lips.

As he stepped closer to the female he said, "What's she doing here?" His chest rose and fell as his breathing quickened.

"I know it's you," said Magis, "it has to be you. Who else could get a woman in here?"

Just when Ryeth sensed Magis start to relax, he made his move.

Magis heard a swishing noise and turned around to see the black-eyed demon from his past floating a foot off the ground, his coat flapping in the non-existent breeze. Magis stepped backward until he hit the wall and pressed his back against it.

"I didn't say anything!" he yelled. His face reddened in fear.

Magis took his eyes off Ryeth for a split second to glance at the woman in his cot. He looked quickly back to Ryeth.

The blood vessels in Magis' neck and temples were large and throbbing. His breaths were fast and short. "I didn't say a word about you to no cop," said Magis. "I didn't do anything wrong. You can't do anything because I'm innocent."

Ryeth loomed closer to Magis, who pressed himself further into the corner, raised his arms in front of his face, and cowered away from the menacing form.

"What cop?" asked Ryeth, his voice low and menacing.

"No cop. There was no cop," said Magis. "And even if there was, I didn't say anything to him."

Unable to stop himself, Magis yelled at the top of his lungs, "Guard! Guard! Help me!"

When he heard the guard's heavy footsteps rushing down the hallway, Ryeth used the earlier imprint and made himself invisible to the guard.

The guard stepped before Magis' cell, his night stick drawn, and found Magis plastered to the corner of his cell.

"What's all the yelling about, Magis?" asked the guard.

Ryeth crossed his arms in front of him, and tapped his foot in the air.

263

Magis' eyes grew wild and frantic. "D-Don't you see him? Don't you see the woman?" he asked the guard.

"See who?" asked the guard.

Magis stood and pointed at Ryeth. "The big guy floating in the air with black eyes. You have to see him, he's right there," yelled Magis, as he pointed to Ryeth. He shifted his feet back and forth, like he was walking on hot coals.

"No one's there," said the guard with a heavy sigh.

"I'll show you," said Magis filled with bravado because the guard was there. "Watch, I'll grab his coat." He started forward, but could not make his feet move; he was held in place. Magis looked up at Ryeth as he remembered being under his ruthless control once before. That episode nearly fried his brain.

Ryeth raised his eyebrows, grinned wickedly, and shook his head.

Magis' thoughts returned to the boat where the demon forced his heart to a fevered pitch. The force of blood in his head had felt like his head was going to explode.

He grabbed his head. The last time he nearly died. "Stop him, he's going to kill me," screamed Magis. "He'll pop my head like a pimple."

The guard shook his head. "You've just earned yourself 48 hours of lock down," he said, "and I'm putting you in for another round of Psych Evaluations."

"But he's right here," said Magis.

The guard turned to leave. Magis became frantic. "Don't leave me with him. Get me out of here! You don't know what he's like," he said.

Putting his hands on his hips, the guard took one last look and took a step to leave.

"Don't go," yelled Magis. "Please don't go."

The guard halted and let out a sigh.

"What about the woman?" asked Magis, pointing to his cot. "At least get her out of here."

The guard laughed. "Now, I know you're off your rocker. Pipe down or I'll have you sedated."

"She's right there, laying on the cot," screamed Magis pointing to the woman.

The guard shoved the nightstick back into the sleeve on his belt. He turned to Magis and said, "You certainly made a mess of your life. You played against my boy in Triple-A football. I thought you were going places."

Shaking his head, the guard turned around and left.

"Don't leave me here with him," Magis yelled.

Magis looked back up at Ryeth. Alone, he lost his bravado and shrunk back into the corner. "What are you going to do with me?" he asked.

Floating down to the floor, Ryeth dissolved his orb and walked over to Magis, who backed away. Ryeth towered over him. He was so close, Magis had to wrench his neck to look up at him.

Ryeth narrowed his eyes and said, "You and the woman were cut from the same cloth. Crawl on over there and lay down beside her."

Magis quickly did as he was told.

"Wrap your arms around her and hold her close," said Ryeth. "She won't be with you long, so make the most of it while you can. I'll be watching," he said.

Satisfied that Black would awaken to a nightmare, he released the hold on her consciousness so she would awaken. When he saw her eyes flutter, he said, "I'd like to stay and see how you two get along, but the stench of the place sickens me, as do you."

He nodded to Magis. "Until the next time," he said, and vanished. As he traveled to Balisier, he heard Magis' voice.

"Quit pushing me away," said Magis, "I have to hold you tight."

Ryeth smiled, things were progressing nicely…

He wished he had the time to watch Black's reaction to waking up in the arms of the woman-hating Magis, have no voice, and find herself in a prison where only the charming Magis could see her.

Chapter Forty-Two

7:45 A.M.

As the time neared for the air strike, Edwards' mouth went dry. Too jittery for coffee, he grabbed a bottle of water and resumed his watchful eye.

At 0745, he heard the whine of the helicopters starting their engines. His stomach grew tight as the wind caught the blades with a slow whir. The roar deepened as the full force of the blades cut through the air. The reverberation mimicked the beat of his heart, and increased in intensity as the helicopters lifted off.

Once they were air bound, the pilots switched on the thermal imaging, ground penetrating radar, particle tracker, and the multiphase diffuse lasers. One by one the video screens and instrument panels came online.

The technology before his eyes gave Edwards a sense of satisfaction. It was the best the U.S. military had to offer. Circular nets of invisible webbing stretched across the sky to cover the ground below.

Circling above, the high altitude surveillance plane was equipped with a scanner of the entire mountain. When it came online, Edwards verified each laser web overlapped another, which created an impenetrable blanket over the entire mountain.

7:57 A.M.

The mountain was secured. Edwards sucked in a gulp of air and let it out between pursed lips. The first phase had gone off without a hitch. He checked his watch, 0757. Three minutes until the airstrike. His mouth was dry and pasty. He grabbed a water bottle and chugged the contents, then reached into his pocket for the container of Tums.

7:58 A.M.

While enjoying her morning coffee, Alice Jane slipped into John Ryan's mind. It wasn't long before she discovered he'd spent a late night with Cassie, gotten up early and was currently on his way to Waynesburg.

Her heart pounded as she frantically searched his mind to discover his intentions. She followed his activities from the previous night and nearly dropped to her knees when she discovered the answer.

Ryeth! Meet me at Balisier now!

Ryeth landed first in the High Counsel meeting room, closely followed by Alice Jane.

She ran to him. "Ryeth, they're coming for us!"

"What do you mean?" he asked.

"I just listened to John Ryan. It's awful. The whole FSB team is here in Waynesburg and they have all sorts of electronic devices and radar. They intend to use it today, right now, to trap and capture us."

Visions of Ari's life on a gurney flashed in his mind. That would not happen to Alice Jane.

268

"We have to get out of here," he said, reaching for her hand.

She pulled away, defiance in her eyes as she said, "Not before we tell the others; they're all here, working on our defense. We have to get them out."

He refused to listen to her demands. Once she was safe, he would come back and help the others.

Quicker than lightning, he grabbed her around the waist and teleported. It failed, they bounced back.

Jediah! he yelled. *The FSB is coming for us. I can't teleport out of here. We're trapped.*

"Let's go!" He pulled Alice Jane behind him as he headed for the tunnels.

7:59 A.M.

When Alexandra rolled over at seven, it was amid a wonderful dream, so she relaxed and let sleep take her back to a time long ago with Onatah. The men of the tribe were off hunting, while the women tanned hides, tended their babes, and enjoyed a life of teaching the young the ways of their people.

Onatah in human form mesmerized her; she was the epitome of grace and beauty as she instructed women and children in the smoke dance. They circled the fire in the longhouse, and by fanning their arms long and wide, they cleared the smoke. Onatah played with the air as she forced it one way and then the other until the smoke wafted upward and out the top opening of the longhouse.

The women's shuffle dance was next. Onatah led the group outside to the formal fire where they formed a ring. She explained the importance of keeping their feet connected to the earth while swaying back and forth to symbolize the massaging of Mother Earth.

Alexandra could feel the dry earth beneath her feet, and when she looked down, her toes, with painted red nails and beaded toe rings, were covered in brown dust. Connected to Mother Earth in this manner, she learned to absorb power from hurricanes, tornados, and tsunamis in order to protect her people.

As she drifted in sleep, they danced around the fire until the drums took on an unfamiliar beat. The confused Iroquois ceased the gentle sway and looked up into the sky as the drums grew louder still.

Alexandra awoke to a roaring sound so loud it hurt her ears. She grabbed her robe and ran to the center of the house. Enoch was already there, holding his ears, and going from window to window. He caught her eye, and made a circling motion with his finger pointing upward, then pointed outside.

She read his mind.

Helicopters have surrounded the house! He yelled.

Vibrations reverberated in her chest. The deafening roar was a combination of Niagara Falls and several locomotives. Her first thought was that the National Guard was practicing a new maneuver, but never had she heard anything so violent.

She ran to the window and looked out. It wasn't one helicopter, it was several. In the opposite window, she could see more. From outside on the deck, she saw them buzzing around the mountain like bees.

Jediah, a bunch of helicopters are flying all around the house. No response.

She called to the High Counsel.

Hey, what's going on? Helicopters are all over the mountain.

No answer. She grabbed Enoch's hand and pulled him inside the house.

Gooseflesh covered her body. She placed her hand on Enoch's shoulder and teleported to Balisier only to blink and remain in the same spot. She tried again. Blood pulsed through her veins as she looked around the house trying to figure out what was going on.

Jediah, I can't get into Balisier.

Her voice echoed in her head; it went no further. She was unable to contact anyone. The beating in her chest pounded in her ears. Instinct told her to hide or flee.

Can anyone hear me?

The beacon she left open to alert her of Jediah's arrival was empty. It didn't make sense. Except for Enoch, she was alone. No Jediah, no Ryeth, no Onatah.

She glanced at Enoch, who looked strong and ready for action. No communication, no teleportation, just Enoch as a resource. An overpowering sense of doom entered her being. The Prophecy was at hand.

"Enoch, this is it," she said, gritting her teeth.

"It's soon, but you have everything you need," he said. His voice was calm; it helped to steady her nerves.

She took hold of his hand and closed her eyes. Slowly, the complete plan formed in her mind. She relaxed as all parts became whole and she realized everyone's contribution. It was an intricate plan that required precise actions.

"Enoch, I'm going to share the plan with you."

"I'm ready," he said.

Alexandra watched as the details of the plan filtered into Enoch's mind. His face displayed awe, excitement, concentration, and finally, jubilation.

"It has great potential," he said, squeezing her hand tightly.

"The Prophecy is clear," she said. "If I accomplish my part, it will all work out."

"I'm your tether. Hold tight to me and we'll be fine," said Enoch.

Alexandra paused to re-affirm her confidence. Their tests had work perfectly. Reproducing them on a larger scale should work, in theory.

If she failed... no she refused to even go down that road. She could not fail. Her birth was orchestrated for this very moment in time. She was their one hope. Failure wasn't on her radar.

Trying to remain composed, she walked slowly through the house and out the back door. Enoch followed. Her flimsy robe blew in the wind, held together only by a thin ribbon tied at the neck.

She stepped off the sidewalk and shuffled her feet through the grass, connecting with the earth to extract as much power as she could. Fear made her movements stiff and awkward. Her breath escaped in a huge gasp. She cautioned herself to remain calm, and that meant to breathe.

"Breathe in, breathe out," she said to herself. She shook her arms like spaghetti trying to loosen her nerves. Shuffling slowly one foot in front of the other, she continued down to the arbor.

She looked up to see helicopters in all directions. They were surrounded. Her eyes fell on Enoch, who smiled and nodded his reassurance.

As she crossed the threshold of the arbor, she felt its connection to all Sensates and to their mountain.

Tingling began in the tips of her fingers. She held her hands before her half expecting fire to shoot out of the tips. Instead, she cringed as the fire traveled through her body to the hwihs on her shoulder. There it burned as hot as a branding iron.

The pain was so great her knees buckled.

Enoch caught her as she faltered. As quickly as the pain came, it left. Breathing hard, she pulled down her nightgown to see the mark on her shoulder glowing bright red.

Enoch's eyes widened. "Are you alright?" he asked.

She took a deep breath and straightened her shoulders. "I'll be alright now," she said, "I hope that was a gift."

Enoch stood at her left side. It was time. Alexandra reached to the first stone pillar and touched it. It glowed a beautiful shade of light blue. She looked to Enoch and smiled. He nodded.

Chapter Forty-Three

8:00 A.M.

A tingling began in Ryeth's fingertips. It progressed across his hand and up his arm. The hwihs on his shoulder burned like it was singed with a hot iron. His hand went to hold his shoulder against the pain.

Jediah, he said from the middle of Balisier, *something is happening. The hwihs is burning a hole in my shoulder.*

Jediah left his mind open as he contacted Alexandra.

Alexandra, are you okay?

There was no reply. He shook his head.

They both teleported to Alexandra. The mechanism failed as they flashed and returned.

Ryeth created an orb and attempted to orb through the mountain to Alexandra, but the orb would not break through to the outside.

He concentrated all his power to get to the outside, but still failed.

Jediah, we can't teleport or orb. We can only communicate with those on the inside of Balisier.

I know. I tried too, said Jediah.

Ryeth verified which Sensates were at Balisier. Anyone who had the power to help Alexandra was inside the mountain, including Alice Jane and all of the Ultras. He spun on his heels and headed toward the far reaches of the tunnels.

I'm heading above ground, Jediah, he said.

Before Alexandra's construction was completed on the house, Jediah ordered a tunnel cut to the outside by way of Alexandra's cistern. The outside entrance was concealed by six feet of water and a windmill, and by using the sealed doorways of the tunnel system, an egress from Balisier was added.

As he ran down the tunnels, he came to the first of eight gates. Each gate required a specific animal rune to be pressed in order to pass to the next gate. If the incorrect rune was pressed, the system locked out all other options and could only be reset from within the High Council Meeting room. Only last week Jediah had shown him the secondary exit from Balisier. He pressed the correct animal rune. The stone gate slid open. Not taking the time to appreciate the technology, he ran onward to the second gate.

As he ran, voices of scared Sensates filled his head. Over two hundred were in a frenzied state, each one seeking Jediah for comfort and safety.

Jediah's concern for his wife transferred to Ryeth. *Take care of my wife, Ryeth. I leave her in your care.*

I'll do my best, Jediah.

Ryeth sensed Jediah's anguish as he placed Alexandra in his hands. Jediah's responsibility for the Sensates safety fought with the safety of his wife. He understood why Jediah had passed Alexandra's safety over to him. Jediah's position was not an enviable one. Although Ryeth admired Jediah's commitment to the Sensates, he realized the grit required to hold such a position was not in his own makeup. It would take Jediah's air of serenity to calm them and get them to safety.

He came to the second gate and opened it by pressing another of the eight runes. As it opened, he said to Alice Jane, *Help Jediah with the Sensates. I have to go to Alexandra.*

He sensed her concern. *Already there. Be careful,* came her reply.

After running a few hundred yards, the third gate came into view. As he pressed the rune, he sent all the love he had in his heart to Alice Jane's senses. Once through the gate he lunged for the next.

Eight gates. And each gate opened up as one of eight possibilities. He had to keep his mind on the task at hand. Only by using the correct passcode for the runes could he ever make it to the outside.

If he missed one gate and got lost, all would be lost. He could not fail; he would not fail. His Alice Jane, his way of life, the Sensates, sweet Alexandra... all would be gone.

The stone rune stuck on the sixth gate. He pushed it again, and again. It failed to open the gate. His heart beat loudly in his chest. He hit the rune with his fist; it didn't budge. Ryeth rechecked his passcode. It was correct.

The veins stood out on his arms; his eyes focused on the blasted rune as his lip curled.

"No," he yelled, "I won't be stopped by a stone or by anything else."

"Get thee the hell out of my way!" he screamed as he swung his arm in front of him.

The stone gate crumbled before him. Jediah would be none too pleased at his destructive nature, he was sure. Ryeth stepped over the rubble and ran forward to the next gate.

He glared at the gate with his hands fisted as he dared it to refuse his command. Ryeth pressed the seventh rune, his blood close to boiling. The gate slid meekly out of the way.

The next passage had steps, which he took two at a time, and a long inclined walkway that seemed to go on forever. The last obstacle stood before him. He pressed the rabbit rune on the ninth gate and stepped through into a long corridor that ended with a water-tight door.

The door resembled the hatch on a ship with a large wheel to tighten or loosen the compression lock. He grabbed the wheel and spun it to his left, the door creaked and opened. He stepped through and closed the door, spinning the wheel to secure it.

A six by four-foot room greeted a man with a six-foot six frame. He scrunched down and cursed Jediah for making it so short, but then remembered Jediah would have to duck too, so he took back the curse.

The space was small on purpose. The person escaping the confines of Balisier would have to hold their breath until it filled with water since the opening was six feet below the water level in the cistern.

Ryeth walked over to the last door and spun the wheel. Water spewed in quickly. When it was up to his chest, he sucked in a huge breath, ducked below the surface until the pressure reached equilibrium and swam out.

He glided up until he broke the surface. Just as the tunnels had been lit, so was the cistern. He looked for the missing bricks that Jediah said were hand holds. Once he found them, he pulled himself up to the top, slid open the cover, and landed on the floor of the windmill.

Without a second thought, he concentrated on the water molecules of water saturating his body, hair, and clothes and flung them aside.

The noise of the helicopters blasted his ears. At a glance he noted they were spaced evenly over the mountain. He sensed they were blanketing the whole area with something that prevented teleportation.

He attempted to disrupt the electrical system in one of them, but it seemed his own electrical system was unable to function. That meant he probably could not make the retinas of the helicopter pilots refuse to see him as well.

With invisibility out of the question, Ryeth stepped out of the windmill. A quick glance assured him that the plume from his canisters would shoot higher than the helicopters. For some reason he didn't understand, that thought gave him satisfaction.

He ran the short distance to the arbor, where he was shocked to see that Alexandra had someone with her. He was tall and medium built, with red hair mostly covered with a ball cap.

Enoch smiled at him and said, "I'll bet you're Ryeth."

Alexandra smiled at the exuberance of her companion.

Ryeth nodded to Enoch as confusion filled his mind. Helicopters surrounded the place, every Sensate in Balisier was worried sick, no one could teleport to get the heck out of there, and these two stood there in the arbor smiling.

Alexandra, are you okay? asked Ryeth.

"It's alright, Ryeth, you can speak freely in front of Enoch. He knows everything about us."

What? The ultimate Sensate broke their cardinal rule? Forget that, didn't she realize the Prophecy was at hand?

"I agree," she said. "The end of the Prophecy has arrived. It's time for us to do our part. We need to remain calm and concentrate."

Her words hit home. He needed to do the same.

Ryeth reached to his side for his sheath and pulled out a knife. He held it by the blade and handed it to Alexandra.

"I was told, 'When all is threatened, give this knife to one whose heart is pure'," he said, "I believe it is you and the time is now."

8:01:15 A.M.

Jediah and Alice Jane ushered the Sensates into the tunnels behind the secret door in the travel center. Once they knew their leader had a plan, they calmed immeasurably.

He gathered them together in a large open cavern.

"What's going on, Jediah?" said a voice from the back.

"Yeah, why can't we teleport?" said another.

Murmuring of questions and accusations spread through the group.

Jediah pushed his serenity into the group and their fears were lessened.

When he spoke, his voice was loud, clear, and confident. "The Prophecy is upon us. We are under siege from the FSB, a government agency that has discovered our group. Please remain calm; there is nothing to be gained from acting rashly.

"Our High Counsel has taken steps to insure our safety. The tunnel you are in right now has a secret door, so that even if we are infiltrated, they can not gain access. Black mirrored glass lines this area to protect us from ground-penetrating radar so we won't be detected. As we wait for others to complete their part in our plan, we must remain calm, and no matter what happens, we must trust that all is happening according to plan."

William, James, Val, Alice Jane, Teater and the Ultras stood by Jediah's side and began answering questions for the group.

Jonathan made his way to Teater. "Ari's at the retreat."

"I know, son," he said as his eyes saddened. "We're going to have to assume that's where she is meant to be. For all we know, she may be the one that gets away."

Jonathan took Teater's words as those from a father, meant to console and give hope, but as time went by, his hope waned.

An explosion shook the mountain. Screams, cries, and looks of terror were directed at Jediah. He pushed serenity to them.

"Are we prepared for bombs?" screamed a woman.

William stepped forward. "We are in the most secure place on this earth for people of our kind. Solid stone walls one hundred feet thick protect us from the outside."

"But they got to us with their teleportation blocker," said a gruff voice from the crowd.

"How did they find us anyway?" yelled another.

Teater spoke. "We believe it started in 1938 with the kidnapping of one of our babies. We thought the baby was dead and buried, but in actuality, it was alive and being reared by the midwife who stole it. As the child aged, she exhibited powers to her mother who then became fearful and turned in the child to the government."

Audible gasps filled the cavern.

Teater continued. "The government learned of teleportation when the child tried to escape, but since the child didn't really know how to use her powers, she was recaptured, and placed under sedation until just recently. All these years, the government has been searching for others like her and trying to obtain every bit of information from her to capture us."

The air of the group was solemn. No one spoke as the information settled in their minds. Even after his years of separation it was easy to see that Teater still had their respect.

Jediah patted Teater on the back. It couldn't have been easy for Teater to share the story.

Teater looked at him and nodded.

Looking over the crowd, Jediah knew the remainder of the tale must be told. "When we found out she was in danger of torture to ascertain her powers, we arranged a rescue mission."

Gasps came from the crowd, but he continued. "We were able to grab her without being detected, all thanks to the efforts of our Ultras, The High Counsel, and Ryeth."

Many of the Sensates cheered or clapped upon hearing this news. Jediah sensed they had renewed confidence in the High Counsel as he finished the story.

"We've been reacquainting her with her family and updating her with modern knowledge in preparation for inclusion in our group."

Val cleared his throat and stepped to the front of the group. "Since it looks like we are telling the whole story, let me share a bit of information I just put together yesterday."

All eyes turned to face the animated physician they all knew and loved. "There's a little-known test that has been approved by the government to be done on all babies delivered in the United States as part of a newborn panel. Mothers and parents accept this test blindly. This test started in 1963 and continues today because it is a very important test. It detects the presence of a severe ailment that begins the process of mental retardation. If not discovered in the early stages, it is permanent and irreversible, so you can understand why it is mandatory on every infant born."

He looked over the group and, by the eyes upon him, knew he had their attention. "It is my supposition that once the test is performed, the dot of blood on a card is forwarded a government laboratory where they have been cataloging each newborn's DNA since the test for DNA began in 1984."

Val waited for the murmurings from the group to subside before continuing. "Through no fault of her own, our dear Alexandra's DNA matched with the abducted baby's DNA in a family genealogy that included all of the Saffles. The baby was Teater's and Nancy Jane's."

A hush fell over the group as they finished connecting the dots. Teater and Jediah's eyes met; they turned to Alice Jane, who already had her head in her hands.

Chapter Forty-Four

8:01:30 A.M.

Alexandra took the knife from Ryeth. The moment her fingers touched it she knew its purpose.

She walked to the last pillar and pressed the blade to the stone. The pillar glowed like the other five. Alexandra returned the knife to Ryeth and said, "Thank you, Ryeth. That knife has undergone a very long journey, as have you, to get here."

She held out one hand to Ryeth, and the other to Enoch. They stretched in a single line across the center of the arbor. They were ready to begin.

Enoch shuddered as he glanced at the helicopters overhead. "I guess they mean business," he said.

Ryeth spoke, his words slow and forceful. "So do we."

She reviewed the procedure in her mind once more. Enoch had insisted she share her mind with him so he could oversee the time constraints. If she went beyond the time allowed for each task, the chance the mission would fail increased exponentially.

They agreed on warning squeezes with a one-minute variance as the control, allowing for a three-minute threshold for the mission.

The second safeguard was Ryeth. If, at any time, Enoch felt she was close to an energy failure, he was to tell Ryeth to send all the power he could spare to Alexandra, and hopefully, it would be enough for her to complete the mission.

A powerful explosion rang through the air. Alexandra felt the pressure in her chest.

8:01:45 A.M.

"A perfect hit," yelled Anderson as he watched the air strike on the mountain from his animated screen.

Edwards frowned. "Let's wait until we hear confirmation before we go jumping out of our seats," he said as he threw four Tums into his mouth and chewed.

He grabbed a bottle of water and washed the chalk from his throat with a few gulps, and then picked up the container of Tums and looked at the label. Multi fruit flavored. Bah, they all tasted like chalk.

He pulled out one of each color and tasted them individually. Green, it was the green one that left a terrible taste in his mouth.

While taking another swig of water, the phone rang.

"Edwards," he answered.

"A direct hit," said the commander, "but it failed to break through to the inside. They're clearing away the debris, but we'll probably have to set some charges to finish the remaining ten feet or so."

08:02 A.M.

Alexandra looked up to see a bomber pass overhead. An air strike; her cue to begin.

"We can *not* fail," she said, "It's time to begin."

Ryeth sent strength and confidence to Alexandra which reinforced her resolve. She set her mind to the task and cleared away any stray thoughts. Three tasks to complete...

Alexandra reinforced her connection to Ryeth and Enoch, and reached for the first stone pillar of the arbor.

The power surge began with the contents of the first pillar and surged through her veins like a hundred-fold caffeine high. Her hands shook as she clenched her teeth to keep them from chattering. The power jumped around inside her body looking for a place to land. It divided itself into millions of molecules and then they settled within the nucleus of every cell in her body. The shaking subsided. She understood the power; it was energy; the energy she would need to handle all the forthcoming steps in order to complete her goal.

The second pillar's power entered and made its way to areas of her brain that were previously untapped. Her thoughts magnified as new synapse connections formed to heighten her senses and expand her knowledge base. New thought patterns emerged filling her head with unprecedented connections between time and space, and the world and beyond.

Alexandra forced these thoughts to the back of her mind to enable the concentration required to complete her tasks. She placed a flexible wall around the newly created knowledge base to keep it contained and yet allow expansion.

She smiled inwardly as the power from the third pillar opened more synapse connections and stimulated a greater portion of her brain into usage. Mathematical equations and processes emerged and began to calculate every one of her bodily functions from heart beats to breathing. Some functions were shut down to conserve energy, like growth of her hair and nails, and others prepared and stored adrenalin, if it was needed.

With the flexible wall in place, she allowed that part of her brain to continue without distracting her from continuing onward. The knowledge and resources would be there for her to tap into when she needed it.

The forth surge of power didn't seem to have a purpose at first, until she followed it as it circulated through her body. Like the first power, it went into the nucleus of every cell. It was then she sensed its purpose: to secure her physical form from harm; to prevent burn out of used cells and to strengthen the cell walls.

Alexandra couldn't help the feeling of awe that over took her when she thought of their plan Designer. Who or what controlled their actions? Why were they compelled to blindly follow the force that had their very existence in the palm of its hands? Why were they so confident that this was the answer?

If a greater power existed, it had chosen this path for them, and if, due to their high moral code, they were selected to champion the mission, she was all for it.

Alexandra no longer sensed Ryeth's hand in hers, but she sensed that everything would work out, so she continued.

She reached for the fifth pillar, and as her fingers touched the stone, her mind whooshed like a rocket taking off. The speed at which her mind worked doubled, tripled, then sped on to Mach levels where instantaneous calculations were possible, then multi-calculations.

She quickly reined in the power and sectioned off that part of her brain to handle calculations without interfering with the operation of other tasks. It took a few seconds for her to slow her thoughts to a reasonable level.

Alexandra took a deep breath and extracted the last and final power from the sixth pillar. The surge rendered her weightless, or so she thought, so light was her mind and body. The power induced a state of consciousness that encompassed all aspects of time and place. Her mind reached out further and further, expanding to grasp anything and everything it needed to accomplish its goal.

Never before had she felt so in tune with the universe. As the expansion took place, she was able to organize her thoughts into compartments based on the severity of the issue.

Her senses filled with something unfamiliar. It wasn't taste, touch, sight, sound or hearing, yet it was. It seemed to be all and more, much more. It came from the mountains, the water, the trees, the air, and the earth. Slowly, it edged its way into every pore of her being until it engulfed her core.

Alexandra became a vessel for the Designer's powers to do the Designer's bidding. Realizing that, she wasn't fearful, she was at peace, for part of her wondered what she would become if the plan succeeded? She knew that answer; she would be Alexandra, just Alexandra, and she was more than comfortable with that.

Six canisters planted around the arbor by Ryeth erupted with a loud whooshing noise as plumes of talc rushed skyward and topped out at slightly over two thousand feet. A mushroom cloud formed overhead as the talc disabled the multiphase lasers and cleared the teleportation blockage within the eye.

Alexandra looked skyward, through the eye of the plume. She took a deep breath and wished with all her might that the process worked.

"Don't move!" she yelled before creating her astral self and vanishing upward.

8:05 A.M.

Jediah sensed fears were abated as the crowd of Sensates quieted. When he pushed more serenity over the group, he saw William and James offering their comfort to Teater.

His thoughts went to his lovely Alexandra. Did she have the confidence, strength, and knowledge to save them?

The crowd moaned. He spun to see that Teater fell to the ground. Val pushed his way to be by his side.

Alice Jane sat on the ground and placed Teater's head in her lap. Jonathan sat by her side.

"He's unconscious," Val said.

An intake of breaths filled his ears.

"He's had too many things happen to him all at once," explained Val. "It's no wonder his body needed a break."

Val caught Jediah's eye. Jediah noted the very slight shrug of Val's shoulders.

Alice Jane and Jonathan fell over, unconscious as well. Val quickly checked them over.

A Sensate yelled, "What's happening? Are they sick?"

"Gas!" yelled another.

Sensates began pushing and shoving each other. Their voices became so loud, his ears hummed.

Val stood and yelled into the crowd, "Stop it! Don't let panic grip you. It's not gas. Remember, gas can not harm us."

"What is it then? Jediah, tell us."

Jediah turned to face the Sensates.

"Plain and simple, it is the Prophecy. None of us knows what will happen," he said. "We have to trust that our plan works. Don't let fear tear us apart. Grab the hand of the one standing next to you. We are strong as long as we stand together."

A scream came from in front of him. The female eyes were round as she pointed behind him.

Reslyn and MacAila had fallen unconscious and dropped to the floor.

Val said, "They are not harmed, only unconscious. Try not to be afraid of the unknown. We have all put ourselves in the hands of Ryeth and Alexandra to do what is necessary to save us. Jediah created this area in case Balisier was compromised. Unless they dig up the whole mountain, they will never find us."

Jediah pushed the largest amount of serenity he could muster into the group. They calmed.

Whatever was going on had something to do with the Sensates with the strongest powers. His time was near, he was certain. He looked to the High Counsel.

"Val, James, William…" he said, "watch over our flock." He glanced back to the group as his knees buckled and everything went black.

Chapter Forty-Five

8:05:30 A.M.

Once above the mushroom cloud, Alexandra heard Onatah's voice. *I am with you, granddaughter. I will calm the wind to keep your cloud safe. You must hurry. All is as it should be.*

Alexandra continued by zooming her orb westward. She started her reverse orbit of the earth by circling to the memorized landing spots Ryeth had given her. Each counter-clockwise orbit went by faster and faster until she sensed the travel merely in her head and it happened by itself.

Scenes of her life flashed in her mind, days, years and decades, as time became a blur. Though she could physically see time passing, she seemed disconnected from time itself. In the space she occupied, time didn't really exist. Perhaps she was removed from the reality plane and existed now in an alternate plane, an alternate universe. That part wasn't clear, only the tasks before her remained foremost in her mind.

1938

When she felt the squeeze of Enoch's hand she slowed down her orbital speed in 1939 in order to reach the end the year 1938. The days of December counted backwards to the first week, and then the first day. She continued her orbit and moved back slowly as she viewed the events of the previous day in reverse. November 30, 1938 unfolded before her eyes as she came to rest at precisely 4:34 in the afternoon at Larkspur.

Alexandra floated around the old Victorian, entered, and located Nancy Jane in the parlor, knitting a baby blanket of the most beautiful shade of pastels.

Nancy hadn't aged beyond her thirty-five years yet. It pleased Alexandra to see the vibrant young woman who so loved Teater, that she put up with his antics. Alexandra cringed when she realized Nancy Jane wouldn't be able to reach her husband to tell him the baby was coming. Her power and the combined powers of the Sensates limited the length of her trip, and it saddened her knowing she could not undo Teater's departure. Perhaps the Designer knew the distance to retrieve him was too great...

Alexandra screamed, *Teater, get back here right now! The baby is coming!* and waited for him to appear, but even with her advanced powers she could not reach her wayward great-great-grandfather.

As she watched, Nancy Jane grabbed her stomach and hunched over with the first contraction. Nancy Jane straightened, and continued knitting.

Alexandra had to admire her mentor's fortitude; Nancy looked calm and at peace.

It was time for Plan B. Alexandra searched for the mental signature she knew as well as her own and located Jediah at Balisier.

Safely ensconced in her orb, she went to the desk where he was working over a stack of papers.

Over the last few weeks she'd worked out many scenarios to alert Jediah to go to Nancy Jane. Most of them ended up being down right spooky. It *had* to be something he could not brush off. She looked over at the phone. Clearly displayed on the front was 'ORchard 6708'.

She orbed back to Larkspur and up to the library. Alexandra picked up the phone and dialed OR-6708.

It rang and Jediah answered.

"Hello?" he said.

"Hi, Mr. Saffle, this is the midwife. I'm calling to tell you that Mrs. Saffle has gone into labor."

"Thank you for calling," said Jediah. "Tell Mother I'll be right there."

Not wishing to tempt fate, Alexandra hung up the phone.

She moved her invisible orb back to the parlor. Nancy Jane experienced another contraction. After this one, she put the knitting aside, stood, and made her way to the upstairs bedroom.

Nancy Jane stopped in the library and made a call to the midwife. From Nancy's side of the conversation, it sounded like Roberta Riggs would be right over. Alexandra frowned at the mere thought of the woman, but knew the day would continue as before, but, since her phone call to Jediah, it would have a different outcome.

Nancy changed into a sheath and placed a birthing pad on the bed. Then she lay down to await the babe.

Alexandra entered Nancy Jane's mind, using the very same mechanism Nancy taught her. Nancy was calming herself over Teater's absence, stating over and over again that she knew him long before she married him. *Teater, you're a rascal, but I love you more than life anyway. If you are somewhere and you can hear me but you can not respond, I want you to know that we are going to have a baby today. I promise to love it enough for both of us until you come home.*

She winced with another contraction and pulled her legs up to ease the pain in her back.

Alexandra wished she could help, but knew interference from her in a physical capacity could never be explained. All she could do was wait for Jediah to arrive.

She heard movement downstairs; so did Nancy Jane.

"Roberta, is that you?" Nancy Jane yelled.

"Yes, Ma'am." Came the reply.

"I'm up here in the first bedroom off the library," said Nancy Jane, "and I have freshly laundered towels and linens up here on the dresser."

Steps sounded on the staircase and then came down the hallway.

Roberta Riggs appeared in the doorway. "How're those contractions coming?" she asked.

"They're pretty close, but you have time to wash up," said Nancy Jane. There's an ewer with clean water, a wash basin, and some good lye soap on the stand next to the chifferobe."

"Thank you kindly, Mrs. Saffle," said Roberta. "I knew'd you'd be ready."

Nancy Jane looked questioningly at Roberta and saw the sadness in her eyes. "Honey, you were a few weeks behind me. Did you lose your baby?"

Roberta broke down as tears filled her eyes. "Yes, Ma'am," she said, "I lost the baby two weeks ago. And there's no more chance for another because my husband got kicked in the head by a mule and died."

"I remember that, Roberta," said Nancy Jane. "I'm so sorry for the losses you have suffered. You should have said something, I could have gotten another midwife, or even called my doctor. This is too close for you to be doing this."

Roberta quickly wiped her eyes and finished washing up. "I'm alright, Mrs. Saffle," said Roberta. "Besides, I need the money. After Jimmy died, the real money quit comin' in."

Roberta made her way to Nancy's bedside. "Now don't you worry none. I'm here to take care of you."

Roberta reached under the covers and felt Nancy Jane's stomach. "The babe's in the right position, so it shouldn't be long now."

Just then, Alexandra sensed Jediah on the premises.

Jediah yelled up the stairs, "Nancy Jane, are you up there?"

"Yes, Jediah," said Nancy Jane, "I'm here with the midwife."

Alexandra waited for Jediah to enter the room. He looked exactly as he did in the present, but he was dressed in clothes from the 1930's. Her heart filled with love so that she nearly burst. She loved that man in any century in any clothes.

He looked from midwife to mother, and when Roberta wasn't looking, he scowled at his mother.

Nancy Jane poo-poohed him with a hand gesture and looked away, well aware of Jediah's feelings for bypassing their very professional doctor.

It wasn't long before Roberta ushered Jediah from the room and checked Nancy Jane thoroughly.

"The babe is ready to come," Roberta told Nancy Jane. "You're handling those contractions like a champ."

"I've had two before, I think the path is fairly well worn by now," said Nancy.

"And here I was, thinking it'd be your first," said Roberta. "Where's your kids now?"

"They're gone," said Nancy Jane.

It was clear to Alexandra that Nancy Jane intended to let Roberta think the worst.

Roberta took the bait. "I'm sorry, Mrs., I guess you know what it feels like."

Her voice changed to excited. "Here it comes. Now push!" she said.

Alexandra watched as sweat beads dripped from Nancy's forehead, and the strain of pushing made the veins in her temples show.

"There's the head, let me wipe the babe's mouth out. Here comes the next one, push with all yer might!"

The baby wriggled out of its cocoon and fell right into Roberta's arms. The practiced midwife cut and tied the cord, held it by the ankles, smacked its bare bottom, and when it cried, cleaned out its nose and mouth. After she swaddled the babe, Roberta held it close and cooed to it.

Aware that Nancy Jane's eyes were on her, she turned and placed the babe on Nancy Jane's chest.

Roberta massaged Nancy's soft belly and squeezed. She massaged and squeezed again, until Nancy had the final contraction which freed her from the afterbirth.

Alexandra focused on Roberta. The young woman cleaned Nancy Jane, who could not take her eyes off the tiny, red-haired babe. After she replaced the bed linens and tied the soiled ones up in a ball, she used the remaining water in the ewer to wash up.

Toweling her hands, she said, "All done, Ma'am. You can call your kin back, if you want."

"Thank you, Roberta, for a wonderful job," said Nancy Jane. She raised her voice slightly and said to Jediah, who kept a vigil in the hallway, "Jediah, come and see our new girl."

The door opened and Jediah peeked in, and then opened the door fully. His face was haggard, but it changed when he saw the smile on Nancy Jane's face and he witnessed the wee babe on his mother's chest.

"If everything's alright, I'll be leavin'," said Roberta.

Jediah reached in his pocket and handed the midwife five ten-dollar bills.

Her eyes lit up at the more-than-customary amount.

"Thank you, Mister," said Roberta, "you're a generous man, to be sure."

"Thank you for attending Mrs. Saffle," Jediah said stiffly.

Roberta nodded, stuffed the bills in her apron pocket and turned to leave.

Once Roberta was out of earshot, Jediah said, "I'm calling Val to come over and check both you and the baby."

"Why did you come?" asked Nancy Jane.

Alexandra broke from the scene when she felt Enoch's hand squeezing hers. The baby was safe; little Arizona Higgins' life was assured; she would not spend decades in the hands of the government.

As Alexandra moved to her second stop, she watched Ari to make sure she wasn't abducted by Roberta Riggs, or by anyone else.

Chapter Forty-Six

4 Years Ago

Her trip back home to the present time started
by reversing her orbits and spinning them
clockwise. As the earth spun with her, already at
one thousand miles an hour, Alexandra boosted her
speed to compensate.

She could feel her cells drain from the energy
required to speed more than before, and also the
cells rejuvenating themselves. The calculator in the
mathematical area indicated she was operating
within chosen parameters, so she sped onward.

The blur of days flying by made her a bit
queasy, so she closed her eyes and concentrated,
knowing that Enoch would signal her as she neared
her target date.

She was aware of her own birth as the last two
decades whirred by, and Alexandra sensed her own
consciousness joining her on their path. It was
unlike anything she'd ever felt before; as if two
minds shared the same space. Two sets of
emotions; two hearts.

The warning squeeze of Enoch's hand alerted
her that she was close, so she zeroed in on the date
of her parents' deaths.

She knew the exact time the sink hole collapsed
and buried her parents alive. How could she not?
The date was etched forever in her heart. It was the
day her whole world changed; the day her only
family on the earth left the world, and left her alone.

Sure, she was eighteen, and by law, an adult, but in no way was she prepared to lose parents and home in one fell swoop. As she remembered the heartache that followed, her commitment to the Prophecy strengthened.

The mental calculations within the flexible boundary signaled her arrival at the appointed time.

Her consciousness flickered in and out of focus until she became fully aware as her real self, four years ago. She felt her arms. She had solid form.

The calendar on the wall of her dorm room at Bryn Mawr showed the correct year, and the clock on the wall indicated it was 7 AM. Perfect!

The dorm room brought back memories and she smiled. She sat at the desk. Her anthropology course work was spread out and a partially completed essay displayed her intended corrections in red.

She reached for the phone and dialed home.

"Hello?" said her mother.

Alexandra wasn't prepared for the sound of her mother's voice, one she thought never to hear again. With all her heart she wanted to orb to her and wrap her arms around her and never let go.

Her heart raced and her mouth went dry.

"Hello, is anyone there?" said her mother.

Alexandra forced the words, "Mom, it's me." Her voice cracked.

"What's wrong, honey? You sound awful. Are you sick?"

"No, I'm not sick," she said. "I just miss you and Daddy something terrible," which was as truthful as she had ever been. Her eyes filled with tears. What she wouldn't give to see them once more.

"Oh, darling, don't cry."

She could not hold back the flood of tears as she sobbed hopelessly into the phone.

Her mother's voice spoke once more. "Please don't cry, sweetie. I know you thought you were all grown up and ready for college, but sometimes it hurts your heart when you miss your family."

Alexandra tried to stop the blubbering long enough to speak. "I – can't come – home right now. I have – too many classes." Her sobs resumed.

"I know just what to do," said her mom, with a hint of finality in her voice. "We'll jump in the car and come see you. Would that make you feel better?" her mother asked.

"Oh, Mom, I'd hate for you and Daddy to have to do that…" she said sniffing.

"Don't you fret none. You know how much your father likes to drive. I'll stop by and get you some pepperoni rolls and we'll start right away. Your father was just saying last night how he needed a road trip. Honey, this will work out just fine."

"Are you sure you don't mind?" asked Alexandra.

"You are our only daughter, and above all, we want you to be happy. And don't you go thinking that this would be all for you. We miss you just as much. If we get on the road within the hour, we can be there for supper tonight. Does that sound okay?"

"Oh, Mom," said Alexandra with all the smiles she could muster, "that sounds just perfect!"

"I can't wait to see you," said her mother.

"Mom, you have no idea what this means to me. Knowing I get to see you tonight, makes me feel like I can take on the world," said Alexandra.

"I'll get going then so we can get on the road. See you then, Honey. I love you. Bye."

"I love you too, Mom. Bye."

She hung up the phone. Her chest still quivered from sobbing so hard. Grabbing a tissue from the nightstand she dried her eyes and blew her nose.

Her heart lighter than it had been in years, she breathed a sigh of relief that she talked her mother into leaving the house with her dad.

The qualms of lying to her parents only bothered her a tiny bit. When she compared the lie to their deaths, she knew she had made the right decision. She just hoped that her messing with history didn't screw up too much for anyone else.

As Alexandra separated from her younger self's consciousness, pangs of regret assaulted her senses. If her mission failed, the anguish of losing her parents would repeat itself. On the other hand, if she completed her tasks and reset history, life, which was already great, would be complete.

Enoch squeezed her hand to let her know it was time to move forward. She found it hard to leave a place and time where her parents were still alive. It was hard speaking to her mother on the phone, she couldn't imagine what it would be like to see them in the flesh for a few seconds knowing it might be for the last time.

A power greater than she had made the decision to keep it to a phone call, and for that, she was thankful. Before she thought too much on the subject, she forced her mind to the task at hand.

The day of her parents' deaths eked forward; Alexandra watched until the actual time of their deaths passed and she was confident they were nowhere near their home.

The jubilation that filled her heart knowing she might see them again was hard to contain. If a mirror were handy, she was certain it would reflect a grin from ear to ear. There was a small chance it was plastered there to stay. As she traveled forward in time, the smile never left her face.

She considered, things just might work out, until… another blast shook the mountain.

8:06:30 A.M.

Alexandra sensed the earth shaking beneath her feet. That blast was smaller than the first. Focusing on the trip home she concentrated on the last stop.

Shaking the world up worried her greatly. Countless movies and books always talked of a paradox. But hadn't she already shared consciousness with herself at another age? She hoped with all her might that the force that compelled her to complete this mission knew what it was doing.

Even Enoch had cautioned her regarding the paradox. Time loops. String Theory. That was the problem - no one really knew what would happen. In all her research, the only passage that made her feel like she could go on was one from Corey S. Powell:

'Whether you regard yourself as a pile of atoms, a DNA sequence, a series of sensory inputs or an elaborate computer file, in all of these interpretations you are nothing but a stack of data. According to the principle of unitarity, quantum information is never lost. Put them together, and those two statements lead to a staggering corollary: At the most fundamental level, the laws of physics say you are immortal.'

Couldn't she apply that same reasoning to Onatah?

Enoch shook her hand. Good heavens, she was lost in thought and her concentration had wandered.

Her orbit took her almost to the present day, but a few months in the past.

Enoch signaled it was time to slow down. It was the day of her wedding. The wedding was in the past and she was now Mrs. Jediah Saffle. She watched as the past Alexandra made her way up to Nancy Jane's rooms to check on her.

Nancy Jane shared an amazing ability with her.

After Nancy Jane completed the task, Alexandra stood before her in total awe; that this tiny woman had such immense power would never have entered her mind. Nancy Jane had given her an astounding power coupled with massive responsibility. The gravity did not escape Alexandra, who now felt weighted down by the sheer liability of owning such crushing might.

Alexandra stepped into the conscience of her past self and assumed her role. Knowing what happened in the past helped to prepare her for what lie ahead.

She heard Jediah and Alice Jane's footsteps on the stairs, and knew she must remain strong and not give Nancy Jane the key, even though she would be pressured to do otherwise.

They entered the room and stood at the foot of her bed.

"It is done, Alexandra. Release me from this life," said Nancy Jane.

She looked from Nancy Jane to her husband, and then to Alice Jane. She lowered her eyes.

"No, I can not do as you ask."

Jediah looked pleadingly at her as he said, "Alexandra?"

"You might not understand my reasoning today, Nancy Jane, but I believe I am making the right choice," she said.

Alice Jane said, "She's prepared, so are we. I don't understand.

"I'm sorry," she said as she took Nancy Jane's hand. "It is not your time just yet. I promise you, with all the love that I have in my heart, that I can not release you from this world."

She looked into Nancy Jane's eyes as tears slid down her cheeks. Alexandra offered as much as she could. "I can not accept your powers and release you, nor will I begin the transfer by giving you the key."

In a voice soft as a whisper, Nancy Jane said, "I don't know why you ask this of me, but I believe in you. I will wait."

Nancy Jane closed her eyes.

The three left the room to leave her in peace.

Before she got into a conversation with Jediah and Alice Jane, Alexandra separated from her past self, but not before giving herself a tiny memory to ensure she stuck to her guns.

Chapter Forty-Seven

8:07 A.M.

Edwards grumbled. He hated failure. "Get on it, then. Those helicopters don't run on air," he said and hung up the phone.

"The Bunker Blaster didn't make it all the way through," he yelled to Anderson, "we're going to have to blast it."

Pouring the contents of the Tums container on the top of the desk, Edwards picked out the green ones and threw them in the trash. He looked up to see Anderson watching him. "You got nothing better to do than watch me?" he asked.

"Well," said Anderson, "I was going to point out the huge mushroom cloud that appeared on top of the mountain, but it looked like you were busy."

His eyes flashed to the helicopter's video cams. Every one of them showed a distinct white mushroom cloud above the mountain. It looked like an atom bomb had exploded.

"There was no boom," he said. "Run tape 6 backward so we can see how that started."

Anderson did as he was instructed. Six dots of white surrounded a gazebo on the property. As the video moved forward, they shot skyward to form the mushroom cloud. At no time was there an initial blast. Something else made the cloud.

"The cloud extends above our multiphase diffusion layer of lasers, doesn't it?" said Edwards as he slammed his fist on the table.

304

He jumped up and turned his eyes in horror as he glanced at the radar. "Blast it, Anderson," he yelled, "look at the ground penetrating radar screen, there's no one left inside. They've all escaped!"

Frantic, Edwards ran his fingers through what was left of his hair. He spun his head to see a glowing red dot at the farm.

He picked up the direct phone line to the commandos who surrounded the Saffle's farm. "Close in now," he screamed into the receiver, "one is still there."

Slamming the phone onto its receiver he paced back and forth, his nerves frayed. Edwards rued the day he quit smoking for something, anything needed to be happening now with his fingers. Wringing them, holding them behind his back as he paced, and finally shoving them into his pants pockets did nothing to alleviate his jitters.

8:08 A.M.

The first thing Ryeth noticed was a shoe in his face. He drew in a deep breath as his thoughts cleared. As he pushed himself up on his elbows, his mind snapped to the present.

The Prophecy!

All is as it should be, Ryeth, said the soft voice of his mother.

Ma? What happened? he said, getting to his feet.

One look around told him a lot had happened since he bit the dust. Enoch still stood by Alexandra's side, holding her hand with his eyes closed, but Alexandra had a blank look on her face, and seemed to be staring off into space.

The canisters were hissing and pumping talc high in the air. When he looked up, he could see the clear blue sky high above through a hole in the center of the column of talc.

Explanations will come later. You are needed elsewhere.

He paused and listened. He couldn't hear the Sensates in Balisier, but he could hear one heck of a lot more. Sensing the use of the clear column, he created his invisible orb and shot straight up through it.

Helicopters were everywhere. Soldiers crept up the mountainside to encircle Heartseed. On the western side, armored trucks lined the road bordering the side of the mountain. Debris blocked the road from the blast. Several platoons stood at the ready.

Lines of ambulances, their lights flashing, were nearby.

Hey, can anyone hear me?

Ryeth heard Ari's voice. *I do, Ari. It's Ryeth.*

He sensed her state of panic.

I'll be right there, Ari, he said.

I've been calling and calling; no one answered until you.

He followed Ari's imprint to the Saffle's farm and landed the orb at her side. He made it visible, so not to scare her, and then dissolved it.

"What's wrong?" he asked.

"I'm what's wrong," came a familiar voice from behind him.

Ryeth turned to seen none other than the lovable John Ryan, the fence sitter, complete in an expensive suit and holding a pistol.

"Made up your mind yet?" said Ryeth, between clenched teeth. Glancing at the gun, he quickly added, "Do you really think that thing will help you?"

"Look out the window," said John.

Ryeth expanded his senses to include the surrounding area, and noted a group had surrounded the house.

"I guess you needed help to accost one female," said Ryeth as he glared at John.

"He knocked on the door," said Ari. "I thought he was a friend."

"I am a friend," said John. "How did *you* escape the net?" he gave a nod at Ryeth.

Ryeth shifted his weight; he sensed that move made John a bit nervous. "I have a bag full of tricks; I thought you knew that."

"Yeah, I caught the orb on your entrance," said John.

Continually monitoring the outside reinforcements, Ryeth sensed he had a few seconds before they burst through the doors and windows.

"You said you were a friend," said Ari to John. "I'm not going back to the FSB."

Ryeth saw John recoil slightly from the reminder.

"I am a friend," said John. "Ryeth, get her out of here, and knock me out. I came ahead of the others to ensure her safety."

Ryeth needed no further assurances that John was on their side. He smiled at John an instant before he rendered him unconscious, grabbed Ari's hand, encased her in his orb, and left the farm. As he orbed through the outside wall, he heard glass shattering.

8:08:30 A.M.

The phone rang from the ground forces at the Saffle farm.

Edwards sighed and picked it up. "Edwards," he said.

"We've checked the entire house and outbuildings, sir. Ryan's on the floor unconscious and we scared the beejesus out of the housekeeper," said the commando, "there's no one else here."

"Stand down. Apologize. Make up something about a training mission gone wrong. Pick up Ryan and get the heck out of there."

"Roger, sir."

He replaced the receiver and picked up his cell phone. He dialed the commander in charge of the blasting.

"Hold off on that second blast," he said.

The explosion came over the phone and rung in his ear.

"Never mind," he said and hung up the phone.

Edward's life inched forward toward impending doom. How could a maneuver go so wrong? The Director of the FSB had reviewed his plan just the night before and said what a perfect piece of ingenuity it was. He had gone on to say that the results of Edwards' efforts would go down in the annals of history as being the perfect coup.

His stomach soured all over again.

8:09 A.M.

"Where in Hades did they go? How did they overcome the teleportation? Blast it, Anderson, answer me," Edwards yelled.

Many years of working with Ron told him that Ron would never stick his head out just to let him chop it off. Anderson remained silent.

He pushed the folding chair out of his way with such force it fell over and made a loud clattering sound as the metal hit the concrete floor.

Edwards looked at the chair until it came to rest and clattered no more.

He let out a puff of breath, his mind beginning to take over. He picked up the direct line to the National Guard Commander. "Take the two helicopters from the far end and have them blanket that blasted cloud. It may be too late, but let's do it as quickly as possible."

"Roger that," said the Commander.

From the helicopters' video camera feeds, he saw his instructions enforced. The two helicopters from the far end of the mountain approached the cloud, which grew wider with every passing minute. Whatever fueled the plume continued to force the cloud to maintain its mushroom shape at the base.

As the helicopters approached, they stopped about two hundred feet away.

The National Guard phone rang. Edwards picked it up.

"What's the hold-up?" he asked the Commander.

"The pilots state their helicopters can't get any closer. They tried, but they can't advance," said the Commander. "What are your instructions?"

Edwards rubbed his chin and made a wry expression. "Tell them to try from all angles, and if they can't get closer, to back off to their original position."

"Roger that."

Edwards replaced the receiver. This was beyond his comprehension. This job didn't require the FSB, it required a group of highly skilled people with a metaphysical background. He did not fit the bill, and at that moment, he was glad he didn't.

8:09:10 A.M.

Ryeth dropped a bewildered Ari off at his home in the Poconos. He took a split second to share the events regarding Heartseed and Balisier with a quick mind transfer, assured her she would be safe there, and then sped back to Enoch and Alexandra's side.

What he found on top of the mountain was utter confusion. He scanned the minds of the FSB forces and located the one calling the shots.

A contented smile crept across his lips as he learned the full attack scenario. To his relief, he sensed the lead man, Edwards, was nearing the end of his rope. Each and every facet of his operation against the Sensates had fallen by the wayside.

Due to the implementation of Jediah's black glass lining the hidden tunnels and chambers, Edwards assumed his 'Omnis' had escaped. Word also reached Edwards that the assault on the Saffle farm came up empty; Ryeth couldn't be more pleased.

He took Alexandra's hand in his and resumed his original stance in the arbor.

Chapter Forty-Eight

Alexandra, the twenty-two year old girl, breathed a sigh of relief. All she had to do now, was go home. What awaited her there was anyone's guess. Three outcomes were possible: The Sensates were captured by the FSB; the Sensates were still trapped in Balisier and the war raged on; or, her plan worked and a new timeline had been created, which meant the Prophecy came to an end.

She received an energy alert from beyond the flexible wall in her mind. The available energy to complete the mission was almost gone. The calculation for home indicated she had a mere twenty- eight seconds to spare.

Enoch, I need power.

"Ryeth, send power to Alexandra, she's running low," said Enoch.

Alexandra felt a surge of power to her senses and rushed her orbits forward, back to the present day. Enoch signaled her final stopping point by releasing her hand.

Her orb came to rest atop the large plume of the mushroom cloud. She dropped down through the eye to the arbor and noted the canisters were spent.

Standing in front of her invisible orb were Enoch, her astral self, and Ryeth, just as she had left them.

The orb vanished as she took her place between the two men and dissipated the astral-projection.

311

She received a second energy alert from behind the flexible wall. No! She had misinterpreted the message. She needed *energy*, not *power* to her senses… her body was critically low on fuel. She had made a grievous error. Only nine seconds of energy were left to complete the cycle!

With a feeling of trepidation, Alexandra began the final phase. As she gathered the molecules from the talc in the mushroom cloud, she started to sway. Her eyes fluttered and rolled back in her head. Her knees buckled and everything went black.

8:11 A.M.

Ryeth, sensing Alexandra's loss of consciousness, reached for her and lowered her to the ground.

"Alexandra," said Enoch. He yelled, "Alexandra!"

He turned to Ryeth. She was out cold.

Ryeth's glaring eyes met Enoch's.

"Don't look at me," said Enoch, visibly flustered. "She didn't tell me what to do if she passed out. You've got to hurry. The last step needs to be completed within," he looked at his watch, "ninety-three seconds, or the cloud collapses."

Ninety-three seconds and he hadn't the faintest idea what to do. Ryeth tried to connect to Alexandra, even though he knew it was hopeless. No go.

He sent out a call to all Sensates, no response.

Blast it, he *knew* Alexandra, inside and out. She wouldn't have compromised the Prophecy without a fail-safe in place.

Pushing Alexandra into Enoch's arms he said, "Hold her."

Enoch sat on the floor of the arbor and rested Alexandra's head in his lap.

Ryeth stepped to the first pillar and touched it. Nothing happened. One by one, he tried the others. Nothing.

"Try to revive her," he said to Enoch as the seconds ticked away.

Ryeth ran his hands through his hair and rubbed his temples. Think!

What he needed was a copy of Alexandra's plan so he could complete the last step for her.

"Do you know what the last part is?" he asked Enoch.

"Not really, I timed the three stops, the trip out and the trip home," said Enoch.

"What are you talking about?" he asked, "What trips?"

"Trips back in time," said Enoch. He shook his head. "Don't you people talk to each other?"

"Time travel? *THAT* was the plan?" yelled Ryeth.

Enoch looked at his watch. "Yes. You have forty-nine seconds to figure out how to complete the last part or the time loop will collapse. I have no idea what happens after that."

Enoch's eyes bore into him, pleading with him to *do* something.

Frantic, Ryeth looked around. The fail-safe would be close at hand. Nothing seemed out of place. The only abnormal thing in the arbor was Enoch.

Ryeth didn't wait for permission, he plunged into Enoch's mind with vengeance. Formulas, theories and abstracts were stuffed into every nook and cranny. Hordes of mathematical calculations were stacked in numerous layers everywhere he looked.

Rushing onward, he could hear his heartbeat pounding like a drum in his ears. Time was short. His breaths were rapid and savage.

He continued his wild search through the genius' mind until at last he found a pile of neat and orderly information that reminded him of Alexandra. This was it.

The amount of information was staggering. He located each individual task and quickly went to the end, which was - closing the blasted time portal.

Ryeth quickly transferred the information to his own mind and exited Enoch's.

There was no time to think, so he gathered the talc molecules from the mushroom cloud and started them spinning rapidly, creating a massive white vortex that reached upward over two thousand feet.

He placed the bottom tip of the vortex above the top of the arbor, and then added more force to spin the vortex faster and faster. When the spinning vortex reached its limit, he mentally pushed the bottom tip upward into the top of the cloud until it resembled a flat disc.

Summoning his remaining power, he pushed the cloud disc upward to six thousand feet, and then removed its constraints.

The rotating cloud exploded into tiny particles that spread across the horizon until they finally vanished from view.

Ryeth dropped to his knees, his energy spent. He felt his body sway, and as his own world darkened, he glanced at Enoch just before Enoch disappeared from view.

Epilogue

Part One

"Hey there, lazy bones," said Jediah. "What are you doing out here lounging in the sun?"

Jediah's voice grew from an imperceptible whisper in her mind to a loud sound that brought Alexandra full-force into the present. She felt the warm kiss of the sun on her arms and face as she realized she'd fallen asleep in the lounge chair on the deck.

She squeezed her eyes tight and tried to recapture the essence of the most realistic dream she ever had. Two separate yet connected worlds swirled through her mind in vivid detail as past and present rushed to lace together the fiber of her existence.

Suddenly, Alexandra felt lighter than air as euphoria spread throughout her being. It was hard to describe, but she felt this essence of life. It couldn't be, yet deep inside where no falsehoods were permitted, she knew it to be true.

Her eyes flew open wide. Everything looked the same - Jediah, the house. She sat up straight as the full consequences of her actions settled within. Was it too much to hope that her dream was reality? Did she and the Sensates actually achieve the blessed outcome?

As her eyes raised to Jediah's, she sensed his questioning gaze before she saw it on his face. His hair tussled in the wind as he tilted his head waiting for her to respond.

Her Adonis spoke yet again, shifting his stance in mock annoyance. "Your mom and dad are due here in less than an hour."

What did he say? Alexandra stretched her arms and legs slowly trying to figure out what he was talking about. Her mom and dad? But they were...

Jediah leaned down and kissed her on the cheek. "You scamp!" he said. "You fell asleep. You'd better get a move on if you still want to make that salad dressing."

He held up a small plastic bag, and wiggled it in front of her face. She looked at it, and then at him, completely at a loss for words.

Jediah sighed somewhat loudly. "You said you had too much to do and made me go to the store for shallots," he said as one delectable eyebrow raised and he looked at her sideways. "Yeah, right. You won't catch me falling twice with that one."

Her parents were coming? She pinched herself on the arm. It hurt. It worked? It *really* worked!

She jumped up from the lounge chair as if catapulted and flew into Jediah's arms, hugging him tightly.

"My parents are coming!" she yelled excitedly as she bounced up and down.

She jumped backwards and did a twirl on the deck. With her hands on her hips, she turned to face her beautiful husband.

"Hah!" she said, smiling. Satisfaction reeked from every pore of her body. She was grinning from ear to ear.

"What's gotten into you?" he asked.

"Into me?" She shook her head slowly. "You'd never believe me in a thousand years."

316

She looked around, everything looked the same. Oh! Her hand went to her stomach. Was she still pregnant?

She kissed Jediah on the cheek, gave a squeal of delight, ran into the house, and swung the bathroom door shut behind her.

Kneeling down, she opened the door to the vanity and looked behind the stack of toilet paper. Her fingers closed around the pregnancy test kit. Yes. She opened the small box. It was exactly as she left it – three tests were gone.

She wet the strip and waited.

All at once, her mind filled with the missing strands of her life. In the blink of an eye, she was up to date. Everything was there! Four years of missing her parents were gone, replaced by backyard barbecues, hugs and kisses, Christmases, phone calls…

Alexandra's heart leapt with unabashed joy as memories of her graduation at Bryn Mawr found a permanent place in her mind. Her parents took so many pictures she thought she'd have a 'say cheese' smile stuck on her face forever. She remembered tripping on the uneven sidewalk as they headed to the auditorium and skinning her knee. Her dad used his ever-present handkerchief to blot the blood.

After she threw her hat in the air with the graduating class, she hugged her mom, who didn't stop crying until they were seated at the seven course graduation dinner at Miklas' Restaurant. Her dad joked they would spare no expense because he was using the money from the coal mine.

They were there – all the memories of her parents. The four years she missed. Alexandra's eyes filled with grateful tears.

Looking down, even more tears fell as her heart filled to overflowing. Her baby was fine.

She burst through the door and yelled, "Je-di-ah," as she waved the strip in her hand.

Part Two

Ryeth stroked the stubble on his chin. The goodie-goodie Sensates let their guard down once too often and now, had played right into his hand.

They assumed their safety by concealing their existence from the outside world, but they hadn't counted on him as part of it. They didn't know he existed. Over the years they had forgotten about the young boy they ostracized from their precious group, while he laid in wait for nearly five hundred years for this very opportunity.

His lips drew up in a menacing smirk. At long last, his time had come. Reaching for the massive leather garment slung over the back of a chair, he whipped it over his shoulders as his muscle-laden arms slid into the sleeves of the Hugh Jackman-inspired mackintosh.

Hovering over the top of the mountain in his invisible orb, he spied Jediah, their leader, walking the pathway to the arbor. He could sense the extent of Jediah's powers, and they mimicked his own.

As he readied to descend and become visible, he stopped short as the leader's lovely new bride ran to the arbor from the back deck.

Curious, he moved the orb closer to catch every detail of their conversation.

"Jediah," said Alexandra.

"Stop right there," Jediah said forcefully, as he looked around. "There's someone here with us."

Jediah stepped close to his wife and put his arm around her. "Show yourself."

Ryeth considered it wasn't going down as he planned, but decided to show himself none-the-less.

As he lowered his orb to the ground, he made himself visible. The breeze he created furled the edges of his cloak as he glided into view.

"Ryeth!" said Alexandra. "Did you think to scare me again with that performance?"

Shock and dismay furrowed his brow into a most menacing scowl.

"Who in Hades are you?" asked Jediah. "I warn you, whoever you are, if you think you can come in here and invade our space, you have another think coming!"

The breeze increased around Ryeth's cloak. The air grew thick with anger and distaste. As much as he wanted to toss the Sensate leader out of his way, the shock of the female's words sunk in and caused him to concentrate his stare and anger toward her.

"Who are you to call me by name?" he said to Alexandra. He watched the young girl's expression go from one of amusement to one where the puzzle came together.

As she broke from Jediah's protective embrace, she walked to a stunned Ryeth and put her arms around him.

The emotions that caught him completely off guard crushed his chest and stole his breath. If it wasn't from the strength of the girl's embrace, he might have fallen to his knees from shock.

His eyes met Jediah's where his bewilderment was mirrored.

"Ryeth," said Alexandra softly, "I have so much to tell you."

Try as he might, he could not remove himself from her embrace; he didn't have the strength. He looked around for something recognizable, something that made sense. No way was this scenario going as planned.

His eyes came to rest on her face as she looked up at him. Her goodness, purity, and strength of character captivated him as if his feet were firmly planted in concrete.

Unable to withstand the assault on his senses and person, he teleported home.

Her voice entered his mind.

This was not our first interaction, Ryeth. You and I are as close as brother and sister. When you are ready to hear an amazing story, open your heart, and I'll be there.

Her voice and the connection dissolved, leaving him with more questions than answers. Never had a plan backfired so undeniably. His plan, to make himself known and have them fear him, was met with a devastating hug and nulled his plan on impact. *That* result never once entered his mind.

Stymied, he walked out of the house and onto a well-worn trail into the forest. A waif of a girl halted him mid-stride with a seemingly insignificant hug. Yet, there was more to it than that. She'd hinted of a comradery between them. Heck, she'd almost laughed at his entrance.

She cut through his bluster like a heated knife through butter, unafraid, and offered the gift of her friendship. As he smiled at the memory, he couldn't help but ponder Alexandra's parting words to open his heart…

Part 3

Standing in front of the mirror at Larkspur, Teater surveyed his reflection. Wisps of unruly, sandy, sun-bleached hair refused to be caught in the leather throng at the nape of his neck. When he looked in his eyes he recognized sadness and regret. How long the wayward emotions would remain companions was still undecided. The cool ice blue eyes of his past, usually filled with anticipation and hunger, now seemed dull and gray.

His father had warned him early in his years that he would get out of life what he put into it. Although he spent years of his life in servitude to others, first the Madisons then the Sensates, his one faux-pas far outweighed the good tallied in his favor.

Returning from the planet just in time to bid his lovely, yet aged, wife farewell brought so much anguish into his life that he found it hard to cope with daily activities when he had such a gaping hole in his heart.

If it hadn't been for the love of his daughter, Ari, he might have gone the way of a recluse. Not only had he missed the birth, life, and Sensate indoctrination of his great-great-granddaughter, Alexandra, he'd missed the years with Nancy Jane; years he'd longed for nearly all his adult life. The lost years would forever haunt him; it was his burden to bear.

He practiced his smile, which appeared lifeless, and boosted his wavering confidence by sucking in air until his lungs hurt, then released the deep breath. It was the best he could do. Teater straightened his collar and prepared to put forth his best at Alexandra and Jediah's Octoberfest gathering, where he would meet his great grandson, Alvas, for the first time.

Alvas, and his father before him, carried the non-active dominant Sensate gene and had passed the active recessive gene to Alexandra, all of which

Teater missed because he followed the obsession to venture into the stars.

Teater braced his arms on the sides of the sink and hung his head, no longer able to face his own image. He knew what the future held; he'd seen it unfold last night in a dream so vivid it refused to leave his mind. Not one instant faded when he entered the world of consciousness. That dream was as vivid as the compulsion to assure Alexandra arrived on queue.

The first marker of the dream, which set the beginning would be the birth of his great-great-great grandson. The Sensates had time to prepare as long as Alexandra remained barren.

The second marker of time would be his confession, but how could he tell the Sensates his trip to another world set off a chain reaction where the outcome was unknown? Like a ripple in a pond, the event created an event which could very well impact every man, woman, and child on planet Earth.

Numbness took over as he turned away from the sink to ponder his future and that of all mankind.

* * * * *

Peace, unlike anything ever known, washed over Onatah as she listened in on the lives of her Sensate tribe. Although her spirit could not smile, jubilation filled her heart.

She whispered to the wind and made it flow into the minds of all her children, *All is as it should be ...*

322

After the devastating loss of her parents in a freak accident, Alexandra obsesses over the mystery surrounding Teater Higgins, her great-great-grandfather. She searches a deserted farm for Teater's gravestone, but fate intervenes and she plunges into a deep cistern. Trapped, cold, and alone, she finds a warm stone that facilitates her escape and prompts dormant psychic abilities to emerge.

As her world shifts into one where many miraculous things are possible and moral boundaries are put to the test, three men impact the destiny of her birthright. Jediah waits two hundred-thirty years to claim her; another plans for nearly half a millennia to exact his revenge; and a third captures her to bend her will to his own.

LARKSPUR, the first book of the Sensate Nine Moon Saga is a full-length novel, which chronicles Alexandra's introduction into the benevolent world of Sensates.

Sensates have existed on earth for over two thousand years. They maintain a safe haven in the mountains of Pennsylvania where they hone their abilities away from the prying eyes of those who would use them to their advantage.

Ryeth is the story of a young Sensate's journey through a life of rage and revenge that lasts for nearly five hundred years. Condemned as a murderer for the deaths of his parents, Ryeth must flee and face the world alone. When his extrasensory powers begin to emerge and he is shunned as 'not worthy' by the group of Sensates, he is thrown into a realm of disbelief and awe, only to be found out and tied to a stake as a demon.

Travel with Ryeth, the second book of the Sensate Nine Moon Saga, as he lives through the pain of loss, learns to use his special gifts, and tastes the nectar of first love.